'Jack Ketch's Puppets'

By Phil Simpkin

(Revised first edition - June 2013)

To Kate.

With my very best wishes.
Wishing you every success
with the music!

Phil.

xxx

Table of Contents

Copyright Information

This novel is intended as a work of fiction.

Dedication

Thank-you to my long suffering wife, who has spent many evenings of late, either on her own whilst I pinned myself at the Computer, or pinned to the chair whilst I bounced ideas off her, and who has been a frank and constructive critic throughout.

JKS, I could not have done this without you!

Also, thanks to my special friends who have taken the time to read the drafts of this novel and provide me with additional valuable feedback, and for giving me the confidence to publish. You know who you are!

Thanks also to **Simon Marchini** for his wonderful cover artwork. See more of Simon's work;-

www.simonmarchini.co.uk

Special Dedication

This book is dedicated to the memory of

David Dunn 26.6.1948 – 27.10.2012

David's inspirational last few weeks of life motivated me to finish this first novel.

Foreword

As a young Police Officer in 1970's Leicester, I was to experience the delights of walking assorted beats of what was then, Leicester Central Division. These included old parts of the City Centre, those on the Highfields, and those on the Hinckley Road side of the town.

Each section opened up to me the beauty and intrigue of Victorian Leicester, from the architecture and small streets of the Friars and St Martin's areas, to the narrow terraced streets across the Highfields, and the most deprived areas of the city abutting the River Soar around Bath Lane, Great Central and Highcross Streets.

My imagination would run wild considering what it would have been like to have Policed Leicester in the early days of the Borough Force from 1836, with cobbles, gas lamps, and fogs, and crime fighting was in its infancy.

This, my first novel, incorporates an element of history with fiction, as in researching this book, I have discovered so much about Victorian Leicester, that I dare say many people were unaware. I have lived myself within a few miles of the Centre for most of my life, and was oblivious of so much of the history of the old Borough.

I want to convey some of that history and at the same time delve into Leicester's darkest depravities.

Some of the characters in this novel are real, and I hope I have portrayed them in the light of research available, and demonstrated their part in the development of Leicester, in context with the time period I cover.

I have tried hard not to go beyond the realms of what is known or can be reasonably established about those who are real, and apart from some license to imagine what they must have been like (where no records to that effect exist) but they are all (in the main) some of the good guys.

Most characters are totally fictitious, and are created to bring this novel to life.

Some are my villains, however, and reflect the sort of persons who were also wandering around the streets of the Borough, and who challenged and brought of age

'The Borough Boys'

Chapter One – Samson Shepherd

'God, that smells rank, Joe. Even worse than when I left the old mother-in-law laid out too long, last summer.'

'Charlie boy, if this is what you're going to get nowadays, living by this stinking sewage run, I'm going to see about a move to the countryside. They say it's more like the old town used to be.'

Charles Church, the Boatman and Joseph Hudson, the Wharfinger stood huddled over the red brick arch that spanned the new West Bridge, pipes aglow, debating the stench, and what beast had caught up in the wharf posts or timbers, somewhere near to the houses on the town side of the river.

On this day, Tuesday January 1st, 1850, New Year's Day, the stench had become worse than they had ever previously experienced from the river.

Down on the river, barely visible to the onlookers on West Bridge, and obscured completely to the residents along the waterside, Thomas Parrott, fourteen years of age, and well known to all in the area as one of the growing band of 'river finders' tried to scratch out an existence.

Uneducated, and compelled to scavenge for as long as he could recall, he had found the river and its new industry *cast-outs*, a welcome source of income.

From the occasional dead dog that had proven highly valuable to the tanners in the Borough, whose carcasses sped up the process and improved the quality of the tanning; to the off-cuts of remnants of beast thrown into the waters from nearby butchers and slaughterhouses, and which could be trimmed and the resulting 'meat' passed on for a few coins to unscrupulous victuallers or desperate paupers amongst the drab streets nearby, this had become Thomas' working domain.

He had become top dog in the growing pack of likeminded boys and girls who were all competing for what would prove salvageable along, or in the river, and who now had to fend for themselves.

Thomas steered the small rowing boat, which he had 'borrowed' and which was rotting and leaked and had to be bailed out every few minutes, along the edge of the wharf and the jetties running down Bath Lane. Who it belonged to he didn't care, as it would be back before they knew it to be missing, yet again, and as always.

As he peered at the surface, littered with its assorted forms of rubbish and turds, the light from his small oil lamp reflected off something paler, larger and more buoyant than the other usual debris surrounding the boat.

He steered the boat towards it, and leaned out over the side to examine the object, his grimey hands prematurely hard and tarnished, from the years of graft that should have been his childhood.

Instinctively, his hand recoiled in revulsion as the fingertips sank into cold, wet flesh, and he realised that the face of a young boy looked back at him, one eye open, the other missing, as flesh pulled from the face and clung to his broken, well chewed, fingernails.

The motion brought the rest of the body into view, gracelessly bobbing up alongside the boat, bloated and rotting and clearly the source of the extreme stench that annoyed the residents and that puzzled Charles Church and Joseph Hudson, back on the bridge.

Thomas' meagre meal, which he had consumed just before he had set out in the fog, projected onto the bottom of the boat, and down the front of his already filthy rags, that, through no choice, he wore day in and day out. He had no others.

The few lumps of bread, and some vegetable off-cuts that he had scavenged from around the High Cross, and that he had boiled earlier and gobbled up, his first food of any nourishment for days, now wasted.

The young, lifeless body in the water lay looking up at Thomas, its arms reaching out as if pleading to be helped, as Thomas struggled to find a voice to cry out for help.

*****

For three days and nights the fog had clung to the river and nearby dwellings, shrouding them in a thick, swirling, sulphurous blanket; a blinding mix of fog and dense, acrid smoke and soot from the chimneys of the expanding housing, railways and the heavy Industry that now rapidly emerged across the Borough.

Only the flicker of oil and gas lamps by night cut through the gloom.

The River Soar at West Bridge laboured along, slowing from its confluence inside the border from Nottinghamshire, through the countryside between Loughborough and Abbey Meadows, where it transformed into the thick, swirling, noxious beast it became as it met the developing Industry, beyond the Abbey ruins.

The few residents and tradesman in the twenty-two premises along the Bath Lane, between West Bridge Street and the new Iron and Brass Foundry opposite Bath Street, were becoming acclimatised to the constant stench of the river.

It pervaded their air; it was all that they got; it offered the best that they could currently expect. The clean air and green trees of just twenty years prior, was forever to be lost.

Prosperity came at a price.

*****

Samson Shepherd, just twenty-five years of age, the newest Constable of the Borough of Leicester Police, stood in the muster room of the Town Hall Police Station, a few hundred yards from the river, and towards the town centre, adjacent to St Martin's Church.

Now, on his first night shift, having joined only days before Christmas of 1849, stood together with the other Constables who were commencing duty, he anxiously awaited to be briefed by Sergeant Wright, one of the three duty night shift Sergeants.

This briefing would be part of the ritual for start of a shift, he had been advised, before being marched out with the other twenty one Constables of the night shift, as a column, and falling out onto his allocated beat.

Shepherd quickly went through his uniform pockets to make sure he had his 'appointments' – his truncheon and rattle - together with a small notebook, pencils, and a few coins in case he should require anything during the shift. A few sweets, that his aunt had slipped into his hand as he had set off, stuck to the lining of his pocket and were now fluff covered and sticky.

On each side of his collar he bore the rank insignia of Constable 3rd class, denoting his status as being at or near the bottom of the pile, and his collar number - 52.

The Public entrance door to the Station was both huge and heavy, measuring about five feet six inches square and about three inches deep, with a small step down onto the muster room floor.

The only public entrance to the station, even fourteen years on from the formation of the Force, it remained a rare event for public to wander in late at night, other than with a little coercion or 'reasonable force'.

Given the size and weight of the door, the Constables inside were clearly surprised, leaping to their feet, as it slammed open, and in ran a young urchin of about ten or twelve years.

Breathless and red faced he summoned their assistance, his small body travelling at such speed, that as he had landed on the flagstone floor, sparks spat from hobnails in his tatty boots.

'Quick; Tom's found a body in the river, at West Bridge; sent me to fetch the Crushers; get yer arses down there quick,' before beating a hasty exit back out into the fog which now rolled into the Muster room from the passageway outside, creating an eerie chill, even with Sergeant Sheffield's log fire burning in the corner, which crackled and popped with the sudden rush of damp, cold air.

Shepherd was no longer surprised that such a young boy could be out on his own. Even given the time and inclement weather, he now knew that the town would be full of such youngsters, some much younger, all looking for something to do to distract them from their abject poverty.

Sergeant James Sheffield, one of the 'originals' of 1836, looked over his twisted and battered pince-nez, from a small, high desk which separated the Muster Room from the Charge area, and upon which sat the large, leather bound Charge Book, where details of those arrested were recorded.

His large, voluminous moustache seemed to twitch, independently, like a small furry beast, curled over and hiding his mouth, stretching and yawning as he chewed on his pipe.

To his right, the large fire burned in the grate, keeping him warm at least.

The three cells within the station were already full with prisoners taken throughout the day, and yet to be charged or released.

Sheffield drew on his small grey clay pipe, and aromatic plumes of smoke drifted across the room, much to the annoyance of his colleagues, who were prohibited from being seen smoking on duty.

Being Station 'Charge' Sergeant meant he had nowhere to sneak off to for a 'crafty one' and so Head Constable Charters gave him special dispensation.

Gathered around him were an assortment of bleeding, bruised and bedraggled Constables, and their prisoners.

Many of these prisoners were drunks, having spent their evening roaming Leicester's numerous hostelries, or were Dollymops and Bunters, the girls of the night. Blood, vomit and other bodily waste were constant companions to the Charge Sergeant.

The respectable population would be safely secure in their homes by now, doors locked and curtains drawn, no later than a few minutes after the Theatre closed. They did not wish to expose themselves to the *seedy* 'other' Leicester.

Sheffield had not personally requested such a role, but a serious assault on him in 1846, and some degree of annoying and ongoing incapacity, had led to a decision to make him Leicester's first dedicated Charge Sergeant in 1847.

And so it had evolved; forty years of age and station bound. But, he had become the font of all knowledge, as he saw and knew more of Leicester's criminal fraternity than any other Constable, which held him in high regard with his colleagues.

Sergeant Wright, however, was more interested in the men of his shift. Younger and clean shaven compared with his experienced colleague, Sergeant Sheffield; with sharp features and narrow, dark eyes, he looked hard and intense, and came across as an authoritative man who would give in to little or nothing, and demanded the best. He did, however, have a wry humour – when it suited him – but one which he reserved for 'the job'. His Christian wife did not approve of humour, and it had no place at home, so Shepherd had been told.

'Beddows, it's probably a load of tosh, but I want you and Shepherd down to West Bridge, pronto, and see what's going on. Mind with this fog and the word of an urchin like that, I fear it may be a wasted journey. No stopping off for a wet on the way and then straight to your beat after!' *A little tongue in cheek, given that Beddows had a chequered past when it came to the local hostelries.*

Shepherd felt elated, as for the first time in a week, he had avoided making tea for everyone, which for some bizarre reason, also included any prisoners in the station cells. This 'privilege' he had been told, traditionally the unique responsibility of the newest member of a shift, marked a rite of passage.

Constable John Beddows, on the other hand was another of the originals. He had been promoted to Sergeant fairly quickly, but in 1842 had a propensity to excessive drinking, and had been reduced to the rank of Constable, 3rd class, by Head Constable Robert Charters, who would have much preferred to dismiss him.

However, a previous attempt to dismiss another Sergeant, for a similar offence, had led to a written complaint to the Watch Committee and the officer's reinstatement at a lower rank.

Bitter at the way he had been treated, Beddows had considered packing it all in, but had been keen that Police should become an honorable career, and as such gave up the drink and took what punishment had been offered. Charters still looked upon Beddows with some degree of contempt.

Beddows lived with his wife in Tower Street, at the back of the County Gaol, in housing that reflected the status of a Constable in the community. Of poor quality, damp and draughty, the house fell prone to all the ills of most of the local housing - and offered not much better than those in the Rookeries off Abbey Street. Policing remained a working class job.

Remaining as a Constable, however, offered a far better prospect than life back as a frame-knitter, his original trade.

It also paid more than the four shillings and sixpence which he had previously earned, and currently, still the average wage for frame knitters, all these years later.

As a third class Constable, his weekly wage now provided eighteen shillings - more than four times that of his previous occupation.

Beddows came across as a hard but fair man, and had been 'mentoring' Shepherd since he had joined in late December. Constables received two weeks in company with a senior colleague before patrolling alone.

Some of his advice and methods were seen as questionable by Shepherd, but generally Beddows had more experience than any other man in the Force. Shepherd recognised that this would not be a bad way to learn.

Beddows also knew that Shepherd was the nephew of another of the originals, Constable George Pearson, who had been badly assaulted during Chartist disturbances in the Borough some years earlier, and who had died of his injuries.

Pearson had been a great friend to Beddows during his punishment, and had never once judged him.

He had at times seemed the only man who had still offered any humanity and respect given Beddows' demise. *Pearson and his wife Sarah had been good friends indeed.*

For that reason alone, he had agreed to take Shepherd out for his two week mentoring.

Donning their tall hats, and dense serge capes, which would provide welcome extra warmth tonight, the two Constables set off at 'regulation pace' towards West Bridge.

*****

The two men presented an impressive sight, and would have even more so, had they been more visible, as they edged through the fog. Out of Town Hall Lane, onto Applegate Street, past the old 'High Cross' and down towards Thornton Lane, their ill-fitting hob-nailed boots striking the cobbles with the tempo of a slow walking horse, the noise alone now highlighting their presence.

Both took extra care as they had passed by High Cross, where the debris from Christmas markets had been ground into the dirt smeared, cobbled pavements, leaving them slippery, even without the damp from the fog, and with that smell of rotting vegetables that prevails at such sites.

The lights shone bright from 'The Nags Head' and 'Golden Lion', whose rooms now looked generally empty, when passing close by their ornate, saloon windows.

Beddows, by now approaching forty years, stood about 5 feet 10 inches tall in his boots, and considered tall for his generation. With his 'stove-pipe' issue Top Hat, he appeared much taller.

Strongly built, he had learned the art of street fighting first-hand, and looked hard in appearance, with a craggy, weathered face, full dark sideburns to match his greying but dark brown hair, and steel blue eyes. His truncheon felt comforting, loosely wrapped by its leather strap around his tunic belt.

This had been his saviour and given him the upper-hand in confrontations many a time, and he had no doubt that he had personally reinforced the use of the term 'Crusher' in the Borough.

Shepherd, presently twenty five years of age and of a similar height and build to Beddows, also had a strong physique, and although not yet tested as a street fighter, he had taken up boxing as a hobby and way of getting tougher and fit, back home in Sutton Bonington. This had resulted in his nose being broken twice before, and as he now thought, probably not for the last time.

A slight kink at the bridge gave it a distinguished look. His hands were extremely large and strong, and his knuckles hardened and scarred from his exertions.

However, with wavy, sandy hair, freckled face and hazel eyes, he looked younger than his age. Broad, but whispy, immature sideburns covered much of each cheek, as was the fashion. A whisp of moustache coated his upper lip, but had already been subject of much humour from his colleagues, and had been declared mere 'bum fluff'.

'Perhaps it should go?' he had thought to himself, more than once.

His Truncheon felt reassuring, yet alien, knocking against his right knee, its strap wrapped around his belt in a similar manner to Beddows', at Beddows' suggestion.

About two feet long and made of some exotic hard wood, Shepherd's was new and bore the Borough crest on the body. It looked pristine, and had not yet been christened. He did not relish using it, but knew there would be times ahead when it would be his best friend.

The ability to free it quickly and to loop the leather strap around his wrist, to deny any attacker a chance to free it for their own use against him, made enormous sense to Shepherd. The comfort of such thought gave him added confidence as he set out with his mentor.

Constable Samuel Simpkin had his truncheon taken off him by two drunken local men, not long after the Force was founded, and he had been severely beaten about the head with it; this had encouraged the technique of strapping tight around the wrist to be employed more generally, since.

They also carried their rattles, again tucked into their belts, to summons assistance should the need arise. At no time on a patrol should they be any more than two hundred yards or so from their nearest colleague on the next beat. The beats and patrols had been designed for such assurance.

Tonight, drunks and ladies of the night moved out of their way and into the doorways. Leicester appeared to be emptying, the cold and fog driving people indoors, and with the pubs, hotels and beer houses closing their doors shortly, unlikely to be a night that anyone would want to stop and fight them.

*****

Samson Shepherd had joined for such adventures as this.

To investigate and detect crime and to protect the community and other such youthful notions, just like his late uncle George must have once had.

The prospect of a dead body, a corpse, a cadaver, whatever people might call it, didn't hold any obvious fear to Shepherd. He knew the living posed far more of a threat to him in his new role.

His only fear now, how he would do his job, if in fact there really was a body?

Personally no stranger to death, death had become a fact of life in 1850, and Shepherd had seen relatives and friends laid out after they had passed, often some days after they had passed and starting to decompose. Thus, accustomed to it, and the smell of such death, as were most of the population, it held no mystery, so he thought.

He had also seen violent death, but only of animals, and had watched in fascination, after initial repugnance, as the local Butcher and slaughter man had dispatched their cattle, sheep and pigs.

Ironically, Shepherd had a love of fishing, and with the Trent at the bottom of his street in Sutton Bonington, he had become an expert with both the fly and spinner, and had regularly caught Salmon. The Trent in the 1840's ran clean and unpolluted, on either side of Nottingham, and had an annual run of about ten thousand Salmon, with ten caught by rod and line each day of the season.

Shepherd, however, still cringed every time he had to dispatch one, striking it hard with a wooden 'priest', administering 'last rights' quickly, or as quickly as the fish would die; it had nearly put him off fishing as a younger man.

He anticipated that the effect of striking someone with his truncheon would likely make the same dull, hollow sound, and worryingly, could have the same effect. He was wary of his own strength and what would be tested of his moral and physical courage.

As they walked from Thornton Lane, down onto West Bridge Street, the muted sound of people gathered and talking could be made out through the fog. Here, houses and small businesses sat side by side alongside and adjoining the bridge, where a few years previous they had also spanned the old bridge.

The two large gas lamps on the front of 'The Sailors' Return' Inn, indicated that they were close to the bridge and the voices seemed to be coming from the wooden staging along the wharf, on the town side of the river.

Walking into Bath Lane, they took the short flight of steps and narrow alley down onto the staging, and to a small group of river folk that had gathered at the bottom.

The Constables' hobnailed boots echoed off the wharf walls as they strode along the wooden boards, with the creaking of ropes along the waterside which secured the walkways in place, and the lapping of the obnoxious slurry on which they all were supported.

Audible cracking could be made out as the ice gave way, in the margins below the staging.

Beddows mumbled, 'Can you smell it, lad? That's *old death*, that is. This buggers been there some days, I'll hazard.'

Beddows thought he would wind Shepherd up and test his metal, as there would be nothing worse than your first suspicious death to make a man nervous.

Beddows had never used Sam's given name, even after duty. He was always to be Shepherd, and Beddows would be 'Sir' until he said otherwise - unless a Sergeant or Mr Charters was in earshot. Then it should return to plain 'Beddows', or else he'd be for it, Beddows had threatened.

Shepherd had only just become familiar with the normal and unpleasant smell of the Borough. Coming from the countryside, the smells that were commonplace in Leicester were alien to his nose.

He had been shocked, early in the previous year, when walking with his Aunt Sarah, from her home near The Infirmary, down along the riverbank, from Leicester Newarke Mill and along past the back of Leicester Castle, in order to view the new Locomotives at the West Bridge terminus.

The river had looked black and oily, or was it green and slimey? Boiling eddies stained with dyes and chemicals, and the foul detritus of modern living. He had doubted the prospect of ever catching a salmon from Leicester.

However, Shepherd could discern that this night the river smelt far worse than anything he had ever smelled previously, and he had no option other than to rely upon Beddows' experience as to why.

He started to feel uneasy at what was to come. He wished the fog to be so dense that he would not be able to see this corpse, but he knew his fear was now working overtime and both his sweating and his breathing had hastened.

'Imagination is far worse than the real thing,' or so Uncle George had told him. Now, Beddows had chosen to wind him up as well.

He had not seen a drowned man before, but had memory of dead sheep which, when bloated, bobbed up and down like empty barrels along the Trent, after floods had caught them unexpected. He anticipated something similar.

'No going back now, Sam,' he whispered silently to himself.

'With me, lad,' said Beddows, in an authoritative manner, climbing into the small, but stable, punt that would be manoeuvered by the Boatman, Church.

Gingerly, Shepherd climbed aboard, one hand carrying a small tarpaulin sheet, and in the, other a short-handled boathook that Beddows had sourced from the Boatman. Shepherd could only imagine what purpose each would serve, but dared not ask.

With both Constables aboard, Church moved the punt slowly out from the wharf, only by two or three feet, and in the direction of where the body had last been reported.

Silence had fallen, and apart from the movement of the oar, the lapping slurry, and the heavy breathing of the three men, nothing could be heard in the dense fog.

The light from two large oil lamps they had also acquired lit an obscure 'ghostly' path around the front of the punt.

'Here he is,' said Beddows. 'Grab that hook, and come to me,' anxious that the moment did not pass them by and thus require a second attempt.

Shepherd knelt alongside his colleague, now aware of the strange palid object bobbing in the surface just off to the side of the boat.

He did not try and comprehend the vision, merely thinking of it as some inanimate object and not dwelling on the fact it had once been a living thing.

'Got any gloves, Shepherd?' Beddows enquired; a deliberate hint of sarcasm in his tone, as he suspected that Shepherd would not yet have become so well equipped.

Shepherd reached into his cape and tunic, but he had left some at the station in his hurry to respond. In any event, they were a present from Aunt Sarah, and he did not wish to tarnish them. Constables had not yet been issued with warm or practical gloves as part of their uniform.

'Typical,' laughed Beddows, 'you'll have to hook the little bugger then, and we'll have to pull him on board. Just mind what you are doing, and expect the unexpected'.

Beddows sat back for a moment, recognising what a gruesome task this might turn out to be, but he chose to let Shepherd find out for himself, if necessary, the hard way.

Shepherd looked for something to hook, a piece of clothing or a belt, but it appeared that the body lay entirely naked.

He tentatively reached out with the rounded tip of the boathook, but slipped, and the hook sunk into the boys bloated guts, sending out a strange soft wail and the most obnoxious and putrid gas towards the occupants of the punt, before lodging in the poor child's ribs.

'Stupid bugger, I said be careful,' cursed Beddows. 'Now this is going to be grim. We'll have to pull him onboard as he is.'

He cursed silently to himself, wishing now he had intervened and shown Shepherd, instead of letting Shepherd try. He was himself, now, more than a tad anxious about what the body would do to get its own back, as they always did.

'You grab his arm and pull him towards me,' said Beddows, 'and I will have the tarpaulin ready. We need to get the tarpaulin under the body before we try and lift him, and mind that bleeding boathook,' desperately hoping Shepherd did not pull the boy's arm off in the process.

Shepherd, already retching, did his utmost not to throw up and disgrace himself.

He took hold of the nearest visible arm, shocked at how cold and loose the skin had become, and gently pulled the corpse towards Beddows and the waiting tarpaulin.

Shepherd had learned his first lesson, *be careful with decomposed bodies as they come apart a bit too easy.* He dared not apply any more force for fear of pulling the body apart, slimey and disgusting in his bare hands.

Beddows expertly pulled the tarpaulin under the head and along the body, passing behind Shepherd effortlessly.

'Got you first go!' cheered Beddows, glad that it hadn't got any worse and he hadn't disgraced himself, either.

It might have been alright talking the talk, but he grimaced at the thought of decomposing bodies and the havoc they created, and Shepherd had actually done alright.

Shepherd noticed Beddows wore a pair of large black leather gloves, which Beddows had persuaded one of the tanners at one of his 'tea spots' to knock up for him from trimmings.

'R.H.I.P.' said Beddows, smiling and shrugging his shoulders.

'R.H.I.P?' enquired Shepherd.

'Rank has its privileges, or in your case, PITFALLS!' chuckled Beddows.

Together they pulled the corpse onto the punt, tarpaulin, water, guts and all; laying it out on the floor of the punt, the handle of the boathook now sticking out over the side.

'You can take us back in now, Boatman,' said Beddows. 'You might want to get off before we take a closer look at the poor little bugger.'

Beddows wished that he did not have to go through the grim formalities, but now, being watched by Shepherd, he would have to show him the right way.

Charles Church needed no second invitation to get off the punt, tying it off at the main upright to the wharf, at a level where the corpse could be lifted straight onto the boards at hip height. He then left the boat and went off to join the waiting onlookers, at a safe distance, and out of view of any examination.

'Remember this,' said Beddows. 'This is the first crime scene. Forget the river for now as he could have gone in anywhere. Let's not miss anything. We'll have a look along the riverbank later.'

Shepherd thought how calm and composed Beddows appeared, and admired his seeming professionalism.

Beddows on the other hand, actually felt under extreme pressure to perform. Underneath the calm exterior, was a man working like mad, to keep up an impression.

'Send one of those little buggers back to the station Mr Church. Tell them we need a Sergeant down here, a Detective if they can find one - *if they're out of the pub yet,*' directed Beddows.

'We need some better lights, as well - someone bring me some more lamps,' he ordered brusquely, resulting in two or three sets of footsteps stomping off, and then stomping back, oil lamps in hand, cautiously set down a few feet from the punt, along the walkway.

'Keep your eyes open, lad, and have a pencil and paper to hand. Suppose you have got a pencil and paper? Let's see what we've got here,' said Beddows, in an almost ghoulish manner. 'By the way, I would prefer not to see *your* supper on the floor of the boat, understand?' he laughed quietly.

His own supper had thought twice about making another appearance, but he had managed to hold back, and the bravado now made him feel more confident; enough, at least, to tease Shepherd.

Beddows pulled back the tarpaulin, exposing the naked corpse. Shepherd gagged, felt the momentary bitterness at the back of his throat, and quickly swallowed again.

In the tarpaulin, lay a young boy, with dull sandy hair, now stained and matted with the filth from the river and riverbed, where he had probably rested for some days. The body had settled on its back, the face tilted up and away from the Constables, the arms splayed outwards.

Immediate observations showed the boy's right eye had gone; his face, partly eaten, by fish, or more likely, the rats that bred profusely and ran wild along the river, more densely so than anywhere else, currently, in the Borough.

The body had become bloated, prior to Shepherds little faux-pas, which had no doubt brought it back to the surface, given how cold the air temperature felt.

The boy, probably no more than five to eight years old and clearly emaciated - visible even in his current state. His fingers badly decomposed; bones showed where flesh once flourished.

'First things first,' said Beddows. 'Is he definitely dead?'

Beddows remembered back to his own, first, suspicious death, with a nervous, young Physician asking him the same question.

The Physician had been called to confirm death of a dried, mummified body in the cellar of a derelict house. Much to Beddows' amusement, he had nervously asked Beddows if he was sure the man was dead. The young Physician then had listened for a heartbeat and searched for a pulse.

At the time, it had seemed absurd, but it also sounded remarkably impressive - and he had recalled it and used it several times with new Constables at their first body.

Shepherd looked at Beddows' dead pan face, looking for some assurance that this had been said as a joke.

'I bloody well hope so, sir. If he's not, I doubt if he's feeling too well,' Shepherd responded - seeking a little light-hearted relief, looking for a reassuring smirk - which failed to materialise.

Beddows recognised the look, but denied him the relief.

'Don't get too smug, young fellow me lad; just remember, first rule of death is making sure they're dead. If they ain't it's a Physician's problem; if they are it's our problem, and then the Coroner's, and he won't be happy if you get it wrong.'

'*God, that sounded good,*' thought Beddows.

'Experience tells me you've made the right decision with this one, been dead for some time, like I said when I first smelled him,' Beddows smirked - at last.

'Somebody's son,' said Beddows, on a more serious note. 'But has he been missed? Will we have any missing boys reported? I doubt it - just another unnecessary mouth to feed, poor little sod.'

Shepherd looked at the boys face, or what remained of it, moving his eyes slowly down, until they reached the boy's throat.

'Sir,' Shepherd whispered, 'his throat's been cut' - shocked at the damage now evident before them.

Beddows noted the deep, vivid, crimson gash, which had become clogged with weed, dirt and insects, which wriggled about and squirmed in the shallow water in the tarpaulin beneath the corpse.

The corpse had been fly-blown at some stage, and had become meat for their table, probably in the first day, before it had settled in the mud at the bottom of the river. Some Physician would probably know roughly how long he would have been dead.

'Why remove all his clothes?' enquired Shepherd.

'Could be they were better than the ones on the person who killed him; or perhaps there has been a little 'jiggery pokery'. Some of our dear residents are fond of young flesh, don't you know?' Beddows replied, scratching his whiskers and pondering just the same thought himself.

'What next then, sir?' enquired Shepherd, eager to learn.

'Damn it,' cursed Beddows. 'We need to wait a while. This is going to be a long night. Never a Sergeant around when you need one!'

Nothing could be worse than sitting around with a dead body, especially on a night like this, considering the warm tea spots that Beddows would have preferred to be taking Shepherd.

Sergeants were never on time when you wanted them, but, heaven help you if you were late for your point, when they expected you.

'Here, young Thomas Parrott. Do you think you've seen this lad before? Looks like a scavenger to me,' Beddows called towards the boy, now waiting alongside Mr Church and the other bystanders.

Young Parrott was still in shock, and trying to get any help from him at the moment, probably totally out of the question. In any event, young Master Parrott had no desire to ever recall that face again.

At ten thirty, Beddows called to the Boatmen to send for a local Surgeon or Physician, as they formally needed to confirm that life was extinct.

'Should have thought of that earlier,' he muttered to himself, tutting out loud and shaking his head.

Word quickly spread from the small crowd of onlookers on the wharf, and soon a much larger crowd filled the parapets above West Bridge, spilling out from the local hostelries by the river, 'The Boat and Engine', or 'The Ship', or 'The Recruiting

Sergeant', seeking access to the alleyway and steps down to the wooden walkway.

A futile gesture really, considering the dense fog and the fact that now a section of rope had been tied across the walkway, denying entry to all but those required to be there.

Within a few minutes the small part of the Borough's population who were still awake, would hear through the grapevine, that something had occurred.

In this instance, it had been that grapevine that reached a Detective, one Sergeant William Roberts.

He had been nestled into the back room of 'The Ship' on Soar Lane, having a sociable pint - or three - with the Licensee, as expected of Detectives, and *officially* 'cultivating informants', or so he would profess.

Detectives in pubs, drinking, still proved a matter of divided opinion between the Watch Committee and Robert Charters, but the results achieved by the first Detectives, Francis 'Tanky' Smith, 'Black Tommy' Haynes, and Herbert Kettle, indicated that it could be a valid means to tackle the growing gangs and crime they were committing within the Borough and periphery.

It was not appreciated by the uniform Constables and Sergeants, many of whom had numerous reprimands for drinking on duty, who saw this as *victimisation*.

There remained a large degree of suspicion of Detectives by Uniformed Constables, and vice versa. Police regulations stated quite clearly it to be an offence for a Constable to be found, whilst on duty, in a Public House.

To the Constables *regulations* should have said 'get caught'- not 'be found' – because if you 'get caught' it's your own silly fault!

The *old* Beddows had been caught too often, and thereby nearly it became his undoing - as his reduced Constable rank regularly reminded him.

*****

Just after a nearby clock, probably on the tower of St Nicholas Church, had struck eleven, Roberts stumbled onto the walkway, grabbing out at one of the small group of onlookers from the original event, stopping himself from tumbling into the river.

At five feet eight tall, with brown wavy, tousled hair and large sideburns; dressed in a short-tailed suit of 3 piece tweed, much beyond the pocket of most Superintendants, and wearing the new fangled 'Derby Bowler Hat' that had only gone on sale that last Christmas, he not only looked over-weight and bright red faced, but he looked well over-dressed for his job.

How he merged into the population, like the other Detectives had done, beggared most Constables' belief.

Shiny brown shoes to match the suit looked much more comfortable than the ill fitting Police issue boots worn by Beddows and Shepherd. Roberts looked more the Toff than Copper - or more even, like a variety house artiste!

It must have been clear to the small group of river folk that he was *under the influence*, as he smelled somewhat like a small scale version of the new Everards, Son & Wheldon Brewery, which now turned out a range of good beers across from the river in Southgates.

This had recently moved from a small building at Narborough Wood, close to Enderby, and was recognised now as the largest Brewery in the Borough.

'Who's there?' called out Beddows.

'Sergeant Roberts, *who do you bleedin' think*? What you got that drags me away from my *other duties, Beddows*?' he sneered.

Beddows held Roberts in suspicion. He had proved a loner and couldn't be trusted, unlike the other three Detectives in the Borough, who had proved themselves good spies and thief takers and who were totally trustworthy.

Beddows saw everything that had been wrong in the originals of '36 in Roberts. He was never one to turn down free drink or coin to turn a blind eye, if it was to be in his benefit.

Beddows had waited his time, and had decided that Roberts would get his come uppance, one day, and avoided him like the plague, as best he could.

'Not to be the case, unfortunately, today,' thought a bemused Beddows.

'Who are you, lad?' slurred Roberts, looking towards Shepherd; a trickle of ale running from the corner of his mouth as he hiccupped.

'Constable Shepherd, sir,' replied Shepherd, disbelieving that this could be a Detective Sergeant, one of the Borough's finest.

'Are we taking on 'puppies' now then? He can't be more than eighteen! What the buggery we doing? Anyways, Beddows, who says it's a bleeding murder, which is what they were saying in the Ship?' grunted Roberts.

Shepherd held out his hand to assist Roberts into the punt, but aggressively, Roberts declined any help, pulling back from Shepherd, before slipping and falling onto his arse in the shallow and putrid swill on the floor of the vessel, soaking the posh brown tweed trousers and leather shoes at the first attempt, his new bowler, now floating upside down behind him.

'You'll pay for that you little bastard. You did that deliberately; cost a few weeks pay it will,' cursed Roberts.

Roberts felt rather more indignant and wished he'd had the sense to have taken the hand, and now regretted it. But he would make sure that Shepherd regretted it even more.

Shepherd looked across to Beddows, who shook his head briefly in response, whilst muttering, 'Twat', under his breath.

'I suppose the cause of death is that Boathook, is it?' Roberts smirked.

'Actually, sir, that was my fault, bringing him in to the punt,' mumbled an acutely embarrassed Shepherd.

'Look here,' said Beddows. 'Poor little bugger's had his throat cut,' pointing to the deep wound on display to the three men, but realising that he would likely get more interest from the wharf wall than from Roberts in his current state.

'Could have got caught up on wire; could have got cut by a boat hook or reed cutter, or you could have done it with your boathook, just like the other hole he's got now. So why is it murder?' said Roberts, looking for a feasible excuse for not investigating it as such.

'It looks just like a cut that would be used to kill an animal; clean and determined. A tear would be ragged and uneven; it's surely suspicious?' suggested Shepherd, cautiously.

'A fucking expert already, are we?' barked Roberts.

'The little bleeders obviously a scavenger and many of them don't wear clothes like civilized folk. We've got no missing kids; we never have these days. Who's going to miss him anyway? We don't need a murder do we, 'cos we'll have Charters climbing all over our backs and I don't need that, thank you very much!' Roberts continued.

Beddows responded, 'If it could be a murder, we treat at it as a murder. You're the Detective as I recall. The Coroner needs to know and that's what matters,' aware now that Roberts was looking to 'cuff' it.

'If you think I'm - *investigating* - around after this pile of filth, and by the rules, you're off your head. Let me speak to some of the boatmen, and they'll say the cut looks like a reed cutter, save a lot of bother. You sort out the Coroner; I'll sort out the rest of the witnesses. I'm off'.

Roberts lurched from the boat, onto the walkway and off towards the Town, no doubt to find another watering hole for the rest of the night, or sort out the shifty witnesses as he suggested, more likely.

Probably the both in the same watering hole - some den of thieves and dodgy dealers no doubt, thought Beddows.

Shepherd looked at Beddows, astonished at what had just been said.

'Is that what happens, if we don't want to deal with something? We just get our own witnesses and turn a blind eye to the truth?'

'I don't,' said Beddows, 'and don't ever let me see you treat any job like that. Roberts is bad. Watch out for him.'

'The Coroner's not as green as Roberts might think. Let's get a statement off the lad Thomas Parrott and then we'll get this corpse off to somewhere out of the public eye. Roberts we worry about later. Now where's that bleeding Physician?' said Beddows.

After a few minutes - that seemed like hours - Joseph Wilson, Physician, of The Newarkes, announced his arrival at the steps to the walkway, from where he made his way down to the Constables and the awaiting corpse.

'My god, that smells rancid - you know how to spoil a man's evening, Constables?' pausing for a name or names, in response.

'Beddows and Shepherd, sir,' responded Beddows. *'Why is it all the Physicians are stuck-up toffs around here?'* he thought to himself.

Physician Wilson looked a real, dashing Toff, turning out to a body, whilst dressed in a formal grey Top Hat and tails; with a crisp white shirt, and grey cravat, worn under a heavy woolen black overcoat. He obviously wore scent, which made Shepherd sneeze.

A slight man, of about 5 feet 8 inches tall, with a waxed moustache, and an upright gate, his voice surprisingly child-like and almost effeminate, suggested his age to be much less than that implied by his appearance.

'The body was found by a young lad, floating just off the bridge, near to the walkway. He appears to have been dead for some considerable number of days, in my experience,' stated Beddows, stating the obvious, from the condition of the body.

'I may be a better judge of that,' stated Wilson, who now came across as possibly younger even than Shepherd, and no doubt, fresh out of one of the medical schools in London or Edinburgh, much to Beddows annoyance.

'The boathook is my doing, sir, an accident, getting the body aboard the punt I'm afraid; but the rest of the damage had already been done,' explained Shepherd.

Wilson examined the body, and confirmed the boy dead, pronouncing life extinct at twenty minutes past eleven, much to everyone's relief.

Shepherd was relieved that he was *actually* dead, whereas Beddows was just relieved that he was *pronounced* dead, so now they could move on.

'He's been dead for probably five days or more. I can't suggest anything better due to the temperatures and the water damage. I would suggest that the wound is inflicted and probably not by accident. I saw a similar wound on a body in London during my dissection classes, and he had been held from behind and cut from left to right as you would with a beast. He would have died of blood loss.'

'Do you not wish to examine him further?' asked Beddows, uneasy at the thought of a riverside Post-mortem.

'I am afraid a Post-mortem is out of the question, as tonight I am in a hurry; but I am happy to give my expert advice to the coroner on what I have observed, in some detail,' said Wilson.

Post-mortem examinations were not yet a routine, nor always completed by the attending Physician, but Beddows was surprised at the response.

'I'll need a statement from you to that effect before you leave then, sir, if you wouldn't mind,' said Beddows, half expecting Wilson to tell him to call in the morning.

'So long as you are prompt then,' replied Wilson. 'I have a supper to finish.'

*****

The floor of the yard store, at the back of 'The Bakers Arms', further along the river and just inside Bath Street, offered about as cold as one could hope for storing bodies at this time of the year. It had also, satisfactorily, served as Coroner's Mortuary before.

Without a name or a family, and with no other option, the corpse of the young boy had been carried to the Inn, where just before midnight, the Licensee, Joseph Headley, acknowledged for the second time in recent months that the corpse could be stored there until the Inquest could be convened.

He knew this likely to be within the immediate twenty four hours, and hoped that as the body settled, it did not put off the customers or his family. Probably cold enough to get away with it this time of the year, he hoped.

He did not care to examine, or even, merely look at the body out of curiosity; a jury and Coroner who were to be paid to do just that.

The last one he had taken in, had lain in front of a fire for several days; one side cooked and the other side, gone off. It happened during warmer weather and the corpse had become putrid. He had helped his friend Jack Cooper, a nearby carpenter, who had made a cheap Parish coffin, together with the constable, place the body in the box, before the Inquest.

The guts had split and Headley had been covered from the knee down, in God knows what. His boots still tried to get up and walk on their own, to this day, he swore. Never again!

He would also prefer not to be seen as a suitable venue for inquests, but he could not legally object.

'The Bakers Arms' had a reputation as a well run and respectable Inn, and Joseph Headley a convivial Licensee. This made the perfect venue for the harrowing process of Coroners' Inquest. And Coroner Mitchell liked his wines.

But, corpses like that were bad for trade, and trade was already bad, for all Leicester's new found wealth.

Shepherd and Beddows again looked at the corpse. Definitely something deliberate about the wound to the throat. This could not be an accident. Shepherd and Beddows were sure of it.

Shepherd could see *something* but couldn't put his finger on it. It would come to him, it always did. He had an eye for detail and an astonishing memory, so he had been told by many.

The yard store gate was closed and padlocked, with the lifeless corpse, still wrapped in the tarpaulin, laid out cold on the ashes that covered the floor of the store. The area above the gates to the store remained open to the elements, so the cold and fog would blow in, and hopefully mitigate the smell of decay.

No Parish coffin for this boy yet, less he could be identified, and then someone else might pay for one themselves.

Joseph Headley warned his wife Mary not to go wandering into the yard, and promptly locked and bolted the inner door of the Inn, leading onto the yard. His dogs scratched and howled at the foot of the door.

'And whatever you do, don't let these out – there'll be nothing left for Mr. Mitchell, tomorrow,' he called to Mary.

Beddows and Shepherd began the slow walk back through the fog to Town Hall Lane, to seek orders for what to be done next, looking forward to the temporary warmth of Sergeant Sheffield's roaring fire.

*****

Shepherd felt the numbing cold around his fingers, ears and feet, and realised how little protection the basic uniform issued offered him.

The boots were hard and desperately uncomfortable. He slowly added to a mental list of 'extras' that he hoped his Aunt Sarah would knit for him, such as extra thick socks and some extra thick gloves!

The uniform itself, coarse and scratchy, itched like buggery with its high harsh collared tunic with broad sewn seams. The matching trousers were not at all comfortable or practical for modern Police work.

His tall hat felt hard, offering his head some protection from any blow, but the hardness made it uncomfortable and he always ended up with a tight red band around the skin on his forehead, and left his hair sticking upright.

In fact, at that moment, he regretted that he was not tucked up in his Aunt's house, in the modest but respectable 'end terrace' on Twizzle and Twine Passage, at the junction with Grange Lane, close to the Infirmary, Bridewell and Leicester Mill, where he sat and painted on summer afternoons and evenings.

*****

Shepherd had moved to Leicester determined to join the Borough Police, as had his uncle George back in 1836.

Uncle George had been Samson Shepherd's best friend and advisor, before George and his wife, Sarah - his mother's sister - moved to Leicester from Normanton on Soar, when life as a frame knitter in Normanton, as elsewhere at the time, had become too bleak a prospect to tolerate.

Leicester seemed to offer a brighter future for young families than Nottingham, which still relied *predominantly* on frame knitting and Lace at that time.

Shepherd's own Father, Samuel, had grown into a hard, brutal, Agricultural Labourer, too handy with his fists, and too fond of the ale.

Samuel's brother, also called Samson Shepherd, had been the Licensee of 'The Stockynges Arms' at Gotham, and Samuel would spend more time in Gotham than at the family home in Sutton Bonington, sometimes wandering off for days.

As a result of those beatings from his Father, Shepherd had learned to box - to defend himself and, too often, his mother and his siblings.

George had coached him, and had counselled him, and had shown more love and respect than his Father had ever done.

When George died, as a result of being assaulted by Chartists in Leicester, during fierce and bloody running battles on the night of 19th August 1842, Samson Shepherd made up his mind he would join The Borough of Leicester Police.

Nobody had ever been punished for that particular assault, let alone George's death. *'One day!'* Samson had vowed to find his killer, or killers.

On a night that Leicester would remember for years to come, large groups of Chartists, led, amongst others by Thomas Cooper, descended on Leicester after the 'Battle of Mowmacre Hill' and fought running battles with Police and officials along Churchgate and through the town to Welford Road, where the Chartists erected a large banner pronouncing their moral victory and plight.

Ironically the Chartist movement and key figures were to have a profound influence on improving the lives and welfare of the residents of Leicester over coming years, but in 1842 they were 'the enemy' and seen by many as anarchists.

When he told his parents what he wished to do, his Father rubbed had his hands in glee as it would mean one less mouth to feed; another blessing. His Mother, Charlotte, professed to be a tad heart-broken.

Samson worried about who would stick up for her and his siblings, but his younger brother Matthew assured him he would do so, and so, began his own boxing lessons.

Aunt Sarah agreed to take him in, during his attempt to join the Police, but had declared she remained a little apprehensive that he might meet a similar fate to her husband.

However, a lodger and a few pounds extra each week would make her own life easier, so it seemed all round to be a profitable and mutually agreeable arrangement, but she insisted that some of his pay should also be sent back to his mother.

No such thing as a Police Widow's pension existed in 1850; not for Sarah Pearson.

It was one o'clock in the morning, and by the time that Sergeant Wright had been given a thorough appraisal of events to date, and statement taken from the boy Thomas Parrott, news had reached Head Constable Robert Charters, who Shepherd had only spoken to once before, at his interview to join the Force.

Charters, a respected Leader and a proven investigator in his own right, with experience in Peel's Metropolitan Police before moving to Leicester to take over the Borough from his predecessor Frederick Goodyer. A family man, he and his wife, Mary, lived in the modest house, located in the rear of the quadrangle of buildings that formed the Town Hall, and from where he controlled the Force.

It had the appearance of a quaint Dolls' house, with a little tan door, porch and hanging baskets, and swathed in colourful climbing plants, which had spread across onto the Mayoral side of the courtyard, it looked surreal amid otherwise drab surroundings. It seemed at times like the only greenery still growing in the Borough and the last a small few might see, before they were 'necked'.

Mary, renowned for using copious quantities of rain-water from a butt in the yard for tending these plants, used more water in the process, than the rest of the occupants of the quadrangle buildings did, together, for drinking.

The butt dated back 1773 and stood in the rear corner between the Station and the rear entrance to the Great Hall, and currently provided safer drinking water, than the communal Conduit in Market Place.

Reported murders had been a rare event since the Borough Force had been created, with only one previous in 1846. Thus,

Charters wanted to know all, as he would be held responsible, no doubt, for the outcome.

Annoyed that there appeared a clear dispute between Beddows and Detective Sergeant Roberts, neither of whom he particularly liked, he was more inclined towards Beddows' experience, than to Roberts' integrity.

He was also keen to know Shepherd's view.

Charters was dressed in his full uniform, with its long tailed, braided coat and ornate, peaked, pill box hat, to enquire of events.

At 53 years of age, he stood as tall as both Beddows and Shepherd, but now balding, with dark, wispy hair, greying over his ears, and with long grey sideburns. A Geordie, with a strong but polished voice, he sometimes became hard to distinguish when he shifted back into his native accent.

He came across as a stern looking man, invoking not only respect from most of his men, but in some, fear. This was not a bad thing in 1850 Leicester.

'So why would Roberts think this not a murder? He is the Detective, after all,' enquired Charters.

'He seemed more inclined to returning to his *other duties*, or so he said, sir,' replied Beddows.

'He has something more pressing than a possible murder investigation?' suggested Charters.

'That's not of my knowledge, or else for me to comment on, sir,' said Beddows, with an obvious hint of sarcasm.

'God, he must know Roberts is bent by now?' Beddows thought to himself.

'Perhaps Sergeant Roberts would prefer not to investigate anything, other than in his own interest, is that what you are implying, Beddows?' said Charters, his eyes watching Beddows' face for some sign of confirmation.

'Some may well think so, sir,' said Beddows. 'I would have more confidence with Sergeant Smith or Sergeant Haynes,' came the straight and honest answer.

After a short pause, Beddows added 'what *does* worry me, sir, is whether Roberts does not want us to investigate *any murder*, or for some reason, *this particular murder*, tonight; and if so, why not? I have never seen him quite so determined to fob off something quite so serious.'

'Beddows; you have not always been of my favour. You were a Sergeant and a damn good one but let drink ruin that reputation. However, you were a Sergeant, and you are one of my most knowledgeable and experienced men, and seem to have put the drink behind you. For that I do respect your views, and will consider them in what I chose to do next,' said a pan faced Charters.

'So, Shepherd; what do you make of this sordid event?' enquired Charters, turning to his latest recruit, in a test of his self confidence and observation skills.

'There was definitely a distinctive clean wound on the boy's throat, sir, and all the clothes were missing from the body. I believe it is at least suspicious and justifies the Coroners involvement'.

'A succinct and honest appraisal, but how are your skills with the boathook?' said Charters mockingly, slipping back into his broad Geordie and displaying a subtle grin.

'I made a terrible error, sir, and I will never let it happen again,' Shepherd replied nervously, unsure as to how Charters knew that detail, as Beddows hadn't mentioned it.

'How can I be sure of your judgement, if it is as poor as your dexterity?' Charters smiled again.

'I have seen animals' throats cut at slaughter, and I have seen animals that have been caught on wire who have torn open their own throats in the throes of trying to free themselves. In my humble opinion, sir, this poor lad had been slaughtered'.

Shepherd confidently underlined the importance of the last six words of the sentence!

'I understand Mr Wilson, the Physician from The Newarkes who attended also, is of such an opinion?' said Charters.

'So it would appear,' agreed Beddows.

'Very well then – so it is to be a job for Mr Mitchell, in the morning. And by then I want enquiries initiated to establish if we have any missing souls matching the description; and have a report at my desk by morning, and a file to Mr Mitchell before you go off duty, too,' Charters directed.

*****

In the meantime Charters would send word for Detective Sergeants Francis 'Tanky' Smith, and Thomas 'Black Tommy' Haynes.

He suspected that by now Roberts would probably not be in a fit state to assist, if even he might be found, and he would deal with him when next opportunity arose.

Charters suspected that Sergeant Roberts had a propensity to become a problem he could ill afford.

*****

It was now getting on for three o'clock in the morning, and most of Leicester would be asleep, bar a small number of vagrants, rogues, and thieves, young and old, who dared to ply their trade under the noses of the Police.

Most of the Inns and Hotels were now closed, officially, but one or two imaginative licensees had invented the notion of 'friends of the licensee' who were permitted to drink provided no cash exchanged hands. Various means of ensuring this had been adopted, and cash up-front before closing time became a popular twist.

Every now and again, bursts of laughter could be heard coming from somewhere in the vicinity of the Market Place, where no doubt, 'mine host' would still be serving.

Also, there were some private beer houses, for which the Police had no powers, and they blatantly flaunted the licensing laws. Many of these were in rear, upper floors of larger factories and warehouses.

The most difficult area to Police presently, was the tiny streets and yards which accommodated the poorest and most cramped housing in the Borough.

This area started at the rear of Churchgate, bordered by Belgrave Gate, and Burleys Lane, and ran all the way down to the edge of the Town, close to Canal Street and Gas Street.

The area affectionately had become known as *'The Rookeries'*.

Green Street, Garden Street, Baker Street, Orchard Street, Abbey Street were all notorious areas of high criminality for the Police.

In these Rookeries, the Irish would be in fighting form no doubt; and excessively drunk, taking it out on each other - if nobody else ventured into their lairs that they might wish to set upon.

A day without a fight became a sad day for its male population and for a few Irish *ladies* too, who were probably bored out of their brains otherwise.

Shepherd had not yet seen much of this side of Leicester, as a Constable, as during his previous week's day shifts, life in the Borough had been different altogether.

Most of the population that had scurried about him fell into the category of shop workers and factory workers going to work with an early shift starting about at 5am; or market traders, or the posh, middle and upper classes, shopping, together with their array of servants and carriers.

The Borough seemed boisterous, lively and full of energy.

During the early evening it hosted the same posh, middle and upper classes, going off to the many Hotels and Inns, Variety Halls, such as 'The Old Cheese', or 'The Theatre'.

During the day the roads were filled with carriages of all shape and size, with fine horses pulling them; then the Carriers and Deliverymen, with their working horses, bedraggled and shabby in comparison, and the Farmers and Slaughterers who would be moving their stock to or from the frequent horse, cattle or other livestock markets held inside the old town walls.

Mixed in with each of these groups were a large and ever growing number of 'opportunistic' unemployed and paupers, with the same perpetual vagrants, rogues and vagabonds, each looking for something to steal, or somebody to deceive, or some fight to start.

They had nothing else to do. The only other choice, to be 'selected' for the Union Workhouse, a new, fearsome looking grey structure, recently built on the southern edge of the Borough, on the 'High Fields', at a point close to the railway station, where the town ended and the green fields extending out towards Oadby and Wigston Magna began.

It became renowned as an institution where they knew they would be broken with hard labour, for the benefit of a roof over their heads, and less food than the average frame worker.

Many consciously chose vagrancy; many sought refuge in the seedier side of Leicester, in the poorest areas, including the Rookeries.

Sex sold. Consequently Dollymops, Toffers, Bunters, Mollies and Mandrakes wandered abroad looking for trade, happy to wander into an alleyway or back to their 'Abbey 'or 'Cab,' with the highest bidder.

Many realised that imprisonment often gave them far more than they would have in the community, namely a bed, food, exercise, a dry roof over their heads, and less people to share with per cell than in any hovel across the Borough.

Thus, the risk of committing crime became a calculated, but often, favourable option for the poorer population.

It had become *more favourable* by 1850, because many of the offences that had naturally borne the Death penalty during previous years, had comparatively recently been reduced to terms of imprisonment, hard labour, an occasional whipping, or on a bad day for a more significant offence - transportation to the Colonies.

*****

Shepherd had been coldly surprised at the apparent imbalance or unfairness between sentences for offences against or including property, compared to offences against other persons.

The last day shift of his first week had seen him taken, by Beddows, to the criminal 'Epiphany sessions', held on Monday 31st December 1850, in front of John Hildyard Esquire, Recorder for The Borough, in the Great Hall of the Town Hall buildings.

Each of the prisoners was brought either from the Borough Gaol, or charged at the Police Station Charge Office, and immediately prior to 'sessions', lodged in a single, small, dark cell, located directly outside the yard entrance to the Great Hall.

The cell, no more than ten feet long by four feet wide and below ground level by about three feet, descended onto a sodden ash floor. Up to twenty prisoners for trial at each day of the sessions might be lodged in this confined area, with no separate privvie.

Each prisoner in turn was marched in and stood in front of the Recorder and close to the jury that would sit for such sessions, before hearing their sentence, or remanded.

The flagstones of the Great Hall showed heavy wear and tear between the yard door and the area before 'the bench', with the most wear at the point where the prisoners shuffled, nervously, awaiting their fate.

The Convictions of the day included;

- Henry Walter (16) Theft of meat - One month imprisonment and a severe whipping.
- James Smith aka (also known as) William Robinson (30) Theft of handkerchiefs - Three months imprisonment.
- Catherine Pratt (28) Theft of purse and coins - Seven years transportation.
- Jane Wood (45) Theft of six dozen yards of lace - One week hard labour.
- John Smith (12) Theft of purse, seven shillings and glove - Ten years transportation.
- William Geary (25) Theft of a spade - Ten years transportation.
- John Watchorn (18) Uttering counterfeit coins - Twelve months imprisonment.
- Charles Harris (19) Attempted felonious stabbing - Six months hard labour.

There appeared no obvious tariff for sentences, other than the death penalty, at the Assizes; and they were *subjective*, more often than not, based upon the identity and status of the owner of the property, or against whom the offence had been committed, or the prisoner's brazen gall in denying such offence, guilty or not.

Shepherd felt shocked at the plight of younger offenders, treated in the same way as the older criminals, or worse, as almost a moral lesson to the general public.

'Perhaps this is the right thing to do, to make a point and deter offenders?' Shepherd pondered.

*****

Beddows set off at 'regulation' pace from the Police Station, Shepherd at his side.

The pace had been practiced, day after day, shift after shift, to ensure that he could get round his given beat in regulatory time, and thus, not to miss a point.

Shepherd had not yet realised it, but he would sub-consciously pick up that pace himself, and would find it came instinctively in days to come.

'We'll have a wander through the town and see what low-life is wandering around. I have a few snitches who may be about and who might know of the murder by now, and throw some light on it,' suggested Beddows.

'The fog and darkness will mean there's no point in trying to see anything along the riverbank by night yet ; and, we don't know what we're looking for in any case, other than clothes or signs of violence , and that could have happened anywhere, anytime.'

Like an obedient puppy, Shepherd walked at heel, his right hand now tucked inside his cape, mainly for a little extra warmth, but also to nurse the strap of his new Truncheon, which he reflected, he may yet need to call upon.

Shepherd now felt more conspicuous and uncomfortable than on any shift previously - and strangely vulnerable. Soon he would do this alone.

A short walk down from the Police Station, and located at the entrance to St Martin's East, stood number 12, Town Hall Lane.

Gas lamps were still lit in both upper and lower floor rooms, and every now and again, women's ribald laughter could be heard from upstairs.

'That, believe it or not, my lad, is the local knocking shop, or as you might hear it called, 'The Cab' or 'The Abbey'; not to be confused with the religious kind, down along by the river. Know what I mean lad?' said Beddows.

Beddows had already made up his mind that young Mr Shepherd was not that kind of a person, but it had caught one or two others out over the years, and he had heard some strange confessions.

'I think so, sir, but I have never had cause to enter one, as yet,' Shepherd blushed.

No way did Shepherd intend to disclose that he still remained a *respectable* virgin; nor did he currently even 'walk out' with a girl, which he would put down to his lack of time in the Borough, if ever challenged.

'Good to hear it, lad,' said Beddows, to some degree relieved.

'The Abbess is a woman called 'Manky Lil' Ryan ; got a dose from a Sailor on home leave some years ago, and within weeks, half of Leicester's male population were itching and scratching like buggery.'

'Dirty whore she is - right under the noses of Mr Charters, the Judiciary, Mayor and hoi polloi of Leicester - her and her Dollymops. Mind you, half the Hoi Polloi are her Corinthians and I wouldn't be surprised if the old Recorder don't get so lonely every now and again he pops in himself. So if ever you see Mr Hildyard scratching his crown jewels - just have a think about why that might be!' laughed Beddows.

'What's a Corinthian?' enquired Shepherd, innocently.

'That's what they call the punters, the swells, the toffs, that pop in for a bit, if you know what I mean,' laughed Beddows, recognizing that he was probably talking a completely new language to the lad.

'She's got a couple of what we call 'Toffers'; good looking young girls; pretty, and a bit cleaner than most of the others she employs. They attract some important people. Come from miles around, they do. Also, keep a lookout for some of the posh growlers that park up around the front of St Martin's churchyard. Might look like they are in the big houses opposite, but more likely they're being exercised by their 'Toffers' - exclusive treatment they reckon. Pop in and out the back door off the lanes, so as not to be obvious, so they do; And don't forget to fling them one up and wish them a good evening when they pass by; let them know you know,' added Beddows.

Shepherd now sensed that Beddows liked to have an edge whilst out on his beat, and it sounded like it might be a bit of fun on such a dark winters evening.

He would also have to get used to the nicknames and street language, which were at present all new to him, but quite impressive or at least, coarsely imaginative.

On the opposite side, stood 'The King and Crown' Coaching Inn, run by Joseph Keetley and his good lady. This being another favourite Inquest location, Beddows Informed him; but also where you could get 'a wet' anytime of the day or night, as Mr Keetley had staff up all night for his guests' needs as they arose, having bedrooms for travellers over the coach house entrance in Coronation Yard.

Keetley's brother, a regular officer in the Indian Army brought home some quality tea - as Beddows reminded Shepherd, he had now reformed from 'the grog'.

At about half past three, as the Constables approached the bottom of Town Hall Lane, Beddows noticed some movement through the swirling fog, into an alleyway just inside Carts Lane, at the side of 'The Globe', now in complete darkness.

Pinching Shepherd on the arm, he gestured, putting one finger over his mouth, whilst reaching inside his cape for his trusty truncheon. Shepherd's adrenaline began to surge.

Gingerly, the pair moved across the junction and to the entrance to the alley, which Beddows knew led down behind the shops on the High Street.

Shepherd's hand strengthened its grip on his stick, and the pair entered the alley.

A short way down, almost obscured in the gloom, Beddows could make out two figures stood upright and close together.

Knowing this as a 'dead end' and with no other way out, Beddows challenged the shadowy figures 'Constables – who goes there?'

In these situations, Beddows felt at his most confident. Little physically frightened him and he had become 'street hard', especially when he had young fit arms and hands alongside him, as on this night.

Emerging slowly towards the Constables, two figures shuffled out into the diffused light of the street, their shadows cast short by the glow of three gas street lamps, set high on the walls above 'The Globe'.

Shepherd saw a man of short, wiry build; about five feet five inches tall and scruffily dressed, emerge first, apparently surprised at being disturbed, followed by a female of a similar height, in a dark bustled dress, cape and hat; her blouse undone and hanging loose over her skirt.

'And what do we think we are up to?' smirked Beddows, aware that they had disturbed what was most likely to be a 'Three penny upright' at this time of the night.

Beddows liked the 'we' concept, as he felt much more a part of the proceedings.

Beddows recognized the man as Edward Pawley, a carpenter and occasional undertaker, who had a small yard and workshop at the bottom of Churchgate, at the side of the new 'Star Foundry', backing onto Short Street, from where he could come and go, almost un-noticed.

'Well if it's not the inglorious, under-handed, undertaker of old Leicester town, Mr Edward Pawley, as I do recall?' Beddows mocked.

Pawley had come to notice before, as a suspected thief; the origins of his cheap timber at times allegedly unknown to him. 'It just turns up every now and again from kind Parish benefactors' he had once tried to persuade Beddows.

Beddows noticed that Pawley smelt like death and looked like death; pale and gaunt; skinny and dark eyed; like a living corpse. But definitely, the smell of death had established itself in his shabby attire. It smelt recent and almost familiar, but not unexpected, given the shabby nature of Pawley's business.

'And who are you, missus?' he asked, looking towards the sheepish looking, middle aged, woman, with round rimmed glasses and a pronounced hook nose, who attempted, inadequately, not to be too visible to the Constables.

Not one of the Dollymops Beddows had seen before.

Shepherd nudged Beddows. 'It's a bloke - in a dress!'

Beddows grabbed the 'female' by the upper part of her already disheveled garb and pushed her upright against the wall, causing the bonnet she had been wearing to fall off, and dislodging a curly blond wig, from beneath which, shone a balding pate, confirming Shepherd's observation.

'So, we've got ourselves a couple of Mollies, have we? Fancied a bit of rough did we?' Beddows baited them.

'Who is to be been Blind Cupid tonight then? Or is it just a quick blow job you had in mind?' *Sometimes being crude and direct achieved the reaction Beddows hoped for much quicker, whereas sometimes it just resulted in a confrontation.*

'You've got it all wrong, Constable,' uttered the man Pawley. 'We've done nothing wrong, and you can't talk to us like that.'

'And what do you say missus?' Beddows taunted the bald headed man. 'Hang about, I know you. You're Daniel Salt, from the Borough Planners office.'

'On what grounds do you feel you are entitled to manhandle me like that, Constable - Beddows? Yes I believe it is Constable Beddows, one of the Force Drunks, I do believe. You have just assaulted me Constable and that is an offence, don't you know, as is drinking on duty?' Salt composed himself.

'You stumble out of the back door of 'The Globe' and decide to assault two innocent people, who were, *actually*, doing nothing illegal as it happens, just to cover up your own little sins. I was merely coming back from a pleasant evening of fancy dress at

'The Stokers Arms'. How will that go down with Mr Charters and the Night Watch Committee?' Salt minced.

Salt was known to Beddows from a previous corruption scandal that had been exposed during the planning submissions and building of the new Union Workhouse, and for which numerous officials had been investigated and four of the Union Senior staff dismissed for their part in it.

Salt had been highly suspected of involvement and receiving 'back-handers' but nothing, *allegedly*, could ever be proven by the officers in the case.

'You slimey, perverse, obnoxious, devious, hook-nosed, effeminate, crooked little turd,' growled Beddows.

'Don't ever make threats to me like that again. You don't intimidate me. Let me make you aware, you disgust me. Whatever your little perversions are, and of two of your most depraved I am now aware, be warned, as the Law will catch up with you,' he added; nostrils flaring and cheek colour rising, now fighting mad!

Shepherd, now a little concerned about how confrontational this was becoming, promptly moved forward, standing between Beddows and Salt.

'I am Constable 52 Shepherd. I must warn you that you have been *officially* stopped as a suspected person, and, together with a reputed thief, you were acting in a suspicious manner, in an enclosed yard. We *actually* have every power under the Vagrancy Act of 1824, to stop, search and question you, and to use such force as is reasonable to detain you for such purposes. If you object to our rights as a Constables, we can also arrest you for that offence if you would prefer. I too, am sure that your arrest would not go down well within the Borough. So, what do you have in your pockets, *or is it a handbag tonight with your fancy dress?*' Shepherd warned the strangely attired Salt.

Beddows held back a smile. He saw fire in Shepherd's eyes.

'And I'm sure you would also *go down* well in the Bridewell, the House of Correction, or for that matter the Borough Gaol, Mr Salt, if you know what I mean. You would be very popular with some of the residents down there,' Beddows responded. 'Now, both of you turn out your pockets and handbag, like my colleague has just asked.'

Shepherd noticed a definite look of fear in Pawley's eyes, who sought assurance from Salt.

Shepherd saw some movement of Pawley's hands, which he had shielded behind his back, and something rolled onto the floor, which Pawley attempted to moved away with his heel.

'What have you just discarded, Mr Pawley?' said Shepherd, reaching down, cautiously, to the object on the floor behind the sweating man.

Shepherd gathered a small rolled up piece of paper. It weighed heavy in his hand, and upon opening the folds, inside Shepherd found four, bright, new, Guinea coins.

'That's a nice sum of money for a back-street carpenter and occasional undertaker. PC Beddows and I have to work hard, for fourteen hours a shift, to earn less than a quarter of that much money each week. Where has it come from?' said Shepherd.

'It's too much to pay for a knee-trembler, Mr Pawley, far too much; even from a *lady* like this,' said Beddows.

He wasn't overly bothered about Mollies as a whole, normally, but thieving, lying ones like Salt and Pawley, really wound him up.

'We won a Fancy dress prized down at 'The Stokers Arms'. Go and ask the landlord, or the organizer, they'll tell you,' snapped Salt.

'It's a well patronised event, and lots of money is paid in by people you will never have the pleasure of mixing with. Well to do people, who like to have a good night, and that is where the money comes from,' he continued.

'So why throw it away then, Mr Pawley?' said Shepherd. 'Do you have so much money you don't need it?' applying as much sarcasm as he thought he could muster.

'It was in my trousers; hidden so none could find it, and it fell out. You can't be too careful around this rotten place; full of robbers and cut-throats, not to mention corrupt Policemen,' croaked Pawley. He gulped and realised, he was probably getting a bit too brave.

Shepherd began to roughly 'rub down' the nervous Mr Pawley. From his neck, downwards, lingering under his armpits, and down through his jacket and trouser pockets, and the small of his back.

Apart from the stickiness of the clothing, and the smell of a practicing undertaker, which gave Shepherd a desire to wash his hands there and then, he found nothing else.

Beddows, who was now doing the same, cautiously, to Mr Salt, had not put his hands up a woman's skirt with such trepidation; not for a long time, and certainly not one being worn by a bloke.

'Mr Pawley, here is your coin back. I hope it has been worth its pain, or pleasure?' mocked Beddows.

'And, we will bid you both a good night,' said Beddows. 'But remember, your cards are now marked, and if I can find that you've been up to no good, then I'll see you before the Justices, God help me I will; so I would encourage you to sod off.'

The two figures, needing no second invitation, skittered quickly into the fog; furtively, onward to the safety of some sordid den.

'That's just how being a Constable is, lad,' said Beddows. 'You go out to do one thing, and come across something else that needs your attention, and you still have to get on and do what you were supposed to be doing in the first place.'

'So it appears, Mr Beddows, so it appears,' said Shepherd.

'You did well back there. I saw some fire; some initiative; and some moral courage; it was like having George alongside me again for a few moments. You'll make be a good Copper one day,' Beddows reassured his charge.

'Could we have arrested them?' said Shepherd, uncertain as to why they hadn't.

'For what?' said Beddows. 'They weren't actually doing anything just at that moment, but if they've been up to no good, we will know soon enough. That's when we'll arrest them lad.'

Shepherd felt definite inner warmth, content with Beddows' first, positive, comments.

'*George, not Pearson*!' he thought to himself.

*****

The pair walked onto High Street and down towards the 'Cole Hill' where High Street meets Churchgate, Gallowtree Gate, Humberstone Gate and Eastgates, and where the coal brought into the Borough would be weighed and sold; alongside the old Assembly Rooms, where the old stocks, delinquents' cage and pillory for the Borough once stood, and which many of the older population still called 'Bere Hill'.

En route they passed several of their colleagues who were doing the same old routine, shaking door handles and windows within their beat, and sourcing new, warm tea spots and bolt-holes for during the cold, wee hours.

This would probably include addresses of 'agreeable ladies', *probably of ill repute*; alehouses; or somewhere they could get their heads down if they could justify avoiding a 'point' with their Sergeant.

Beddows wanted to go and find *'someone in particular'* and he would most likely be around Cole Hill, looking for scraps of coal and cinder at this time of the day.

Beddows and Shepherd moved into a deep doorway to Elias Geary's Bakery shop, and watched and waited through the gloom, for the right shadow to walk past.

Beddows lit up a pinch of tobacco in his battered and well worn clay pipe, and took a long, eagerly overdue puff, then hid its glowing embers back under his cape.

'It's what capes were invented for, lad, can keep a pipe going for hours, and no-one's any the wiser,' smiled Beddows. 'Never thought of partaking yourself?'

Shepherd shook his head in disgust. Enough foul smoke polluted the Borough already, without adding to it further. And he didn't like the smell it left behind.

At about quarter past four, sure enough, a small shadowy figure scurried past from Eastgates, and started scouring the floor, just as Beddows had suggested.

The man; old; short; with a noticeable stoop from a crooked back, walked with a long stick, upon which he bore his weight whilst bending down, and wore a floppy cap and threadbare overcoat that had long since, seen better days.

Totally distracted by his quest, and clutching a small cloth bag, which he rapidly filled with the waste that nobody else had the audacity to scavenge, completely oblivious of Beddows, who took him by the collar and 'escorted him' back to the deep doorway, and out of view of passersby, few that there were at this time of morning.

'Good morning, Mr Issitt. How are we this fine morning?' said Beddows, 'apart from smelling like you've just shit your pants, that is,' turning his nose away and scowling.

Shepherd gagged at the smell.

'Well, well indeed, Mr Beddows, my dear. You scared the shit out of me - literally you did. And to what do I owe this pleasure?' he replied, completely unmoved by his 'little accident'.

'We're looking to identify a missing lad; a young boy, no more than eight, with bright sandy hair; possibly a scavenger. Any ideas?' enquired Beddows.

'If he's missing, how do you know what he looks like to identify him then, Mr Beddows?' Issitt quipped, wishing he hadn't as Beddows' right hand flicked across the side of his head and smacked hard against his left ear, knocking his cap loose.

'Don't try and be smart with me, Matthias Issitt. That coal belongs to the merchant, and I'm sure he wants every penny it's worth. Fancy a few weeks hard labour again?'

'Sorry, Mr Beddows; forgot myself for a moment; remiss of me; now then,' he said, scratching his goatee beard and picking out some dried morsel or more probably an old bogey, which he sucked off his fingers. 'A missing boy is it, or would you be more interested in missing *boys*?'

'What have you heard, Matthias? What's been going round the streets? Someone must have said if someone's gone missing. And when it comes to young boys, you're the man in the know, so to speak,' suggested Beddows.

'Not for me to say, Mr Beddows, not worth the risk. Some strange things going on round here at the moment, and as you know kids is kids, and kids is property, and it don't pay to show too much interest in other people's property - as you well know, my dear, as do I, much to my cost!' he said, looking nervously around.

'What you might do though is look at the papers. Look at the adverts. Seems to be a lot of ladies looking for people to look after their young children at present - or so it may seem. Not everything is as it appears. I'm going to say no more than that. Look at the adverts and then see who's put them in the paper and where they are now? You might be surprised,' Issitt grinned, feeling relieved that he had given Beddows a little something.

'That's got to be worth a coin or two at least, Mr Beddows?' said Issitt, his black teeth and stumps visible in what light made its way from the lamps dotted around the junction, holding out his grubby right hand, in expectation.

'That's only worth a bag of coal scrapings and a loss of hard labour at the moment,' said Beddows. 'Know what I mean? Now on yer way, yer little shit. If I like what I find out there might be a coin or two down the line - if my Governor sees fit. And by the way, get yerself cleaned up - you stink!'

'A few minutes and it'll be hard enough and dry enough to shake out, Mr Beddows; a bit more turd for the pavements. Letting it dry never fails. Tip of the day, Mr Beddows, let it dry before you shake it down your trouser leg, remember that, saves a whole lot of unpleasant mess.'

Matthias Issitt scurried off laughing away to himself, happy with his bit of business, and the thought of being back in Mr Beddows' good books again for a while.

'Who's he?' Shepherd asked.

'Our Mr Issitt used to be headmaster of 'The Poor School', down at St Mary's, until he took a shine to a little choirboy. Never been the same since. Nearly got lynched he did, and has never taught again. Like a pariah he is around schools and churches, but a clever man, and knowledgeable, particularly when it comes to kids,' Beddows replied.

*****

Beddows and Shepherd made their way back, into Cheapside, passing the dripping water conduit in the Market Place, where nature had created a large patch of ice across the freezing cold cobbles, before they walked onwards up towards Hotel Street.

The conduit still provided the main source for the Borough drinking water, and shortly, a queue would be forming, filling their containers to cart back to the nearby hovels, where the water was rank and more often than not, even more infected. This had become a daily ritual of Borough life, and would not improve for some years, so the papers recently suggested.

'How do you go about getting your snitches?' said Shepherd, eagerly wishing to soak up the skills he would need himself.

'Treat them hard, but treat them fair, and make them know you're fair. An odd coin here, or a blind eye there, provided it's nothing that can't be overlooked. Most of them have a likeable streak somewhere, like Matthias Issitt. He's now a poor man, eking out an existence every way he can, and because he's a well known character, most villains know him, and many will acknowledge him, and he can stand next to them in a pub or in the street without them getting nervous - then he becomes valuable,' explained Beddows.

'Mind you, looks are deceptive. Rumor has it, the old misers probably got more bleedin money than you and I put together. Wouldn't think so, would you?' Beddows laughed quietly, shaking his head in disbelief.

'The coal - I didn't think we could use discretion?' said Shepherd.

'Sorry, I didn't hear you, what did you say?' smiled Beddows.

'I said I didn't...' Shepherd ducked just in time to miss having his ear clipped too.

'I think I get the message, Mr Beddows,' he smiled.

'Good lad, you're learning!'

At about quarter to five, as they approached 'The Lion and Dolphin' tavern, Beddows grabbed Shepherd's arm, not for the first time this shift, and pulled him back into the nearest doorway.

Emerging from the tap room door appeared a short, squat figure, swaying from side to side, swearing incoherently at someone, who neither Beddows nor Shepherd could presently see, back inside the Tavern.

The figure wore a bowler hat; his voice well known to Beddows, and recognizable to Shepherd; none other than Sergeant Roberts.

Straight after, another figure came out from the same door, the dress and bonnet shape standing out in the fog, and bade goodnight to someone in the doorway in a squeaky, but without doubt, male voice.

'Night sweetie,' he called towards the disappearing Roberts.

'That's that little shit Salt again. What's he been doing with the dubious Sergeant Roberts?' said Beddows. 'Interesting; don't think Roberts is a poof, so I bet there's coins involved, and something underhand going on. Sweetie is it?'

Beddows and Shepherd continued on, back towards the Police Station. At the same time, from further down near to Carts Lane, two further figures came briefly into view.

This time Shepherd grabbed Beddows' arm.

'It's alright lad, it's only Tanky and Black Tommy. Not met them yet have you?'

'I thought I'd seen them both before, at the Sessions, but neither of them looked like that.'

'That's why they are good Detectives lad, not like that other bastard Roberts. Don't expect them ever to look the same - that's their specialty,' said Beddows. *'You wait to see their fancy dress box!'*

*****

'Had an interesting evening, I hear, Beddows?' Tanky Smith chuckled.

'Yes thanks, Tanky. I take it Mr Charters has spoken with you?'

'Don't let Mr Charters ever hear you call me Tanky, he'll have you for that. But as we know each other, I'll let you off. What about you, young Mr Shepherd? How long before you might get to call me Tanky?'

'I don't know, sir. I didn't know you knew me.'

'I'm not a sir, I'm a Sergeant. Beddows, you're a rotten bugger. Got another one calling you sir?' laughed Tanky, shaking his head.

'As if I'd stoop to something as horrible as that; he can call me Beddows as of tonight; done alright the lad has,' said Beddows, winking at Shepherd.

'Now then,' said Black Tommy. 'Now we've got the pleasantries over and done with, what about a bit of Police work? A little murder, to be more accurate, and the strange case of the missing corpse.'

'We've been down the Rookeries in the last couple of hours, and shaken a few branches, so to speak; pissed off a few of our Irish brethren and inclined a couple of others to tell us a tale or two,' explained Haynes.

'Do you know why they call me Black Tommy?' said Haynes, teasing Shepherd.

'No, sir,' said Shepherd. 'Sorry, Sergeant - could it be because your hair is black?'

'Could be; but tomorrow it could be blond or brown. Perhaps it's because yesterday, I looked like a coalman and my eyes were the only bit of white on show, or more likely, it's because I'm a hard and serious and miserable bastard like when I got woken up at three o'clock this morning, denying me a bit of snuggling up to my lawful blankets' rather large and comfortable milk jugs and warm derrière - and that puts me in a black mood. Take your pick.' Haynes looked deliberately menacing.

'Thank you, Sergeant, I'll remember that.' Shepherd went quiet and looked puzzled.

'And why do you think they call me Tanky?' Smith grinned, playing the same game as Haynes.

'I've no idea, Sergeant.'

'People say I have been known to *subdue* some of the more aggressive members of this community with my trusty night stick, and that it has sounded like a dull 'tank' - and so the ritual has been nicknamed 'tanking' by our criminal elements, or so I'm led to believe. Others say I spend so much time in those bleeding Rookeries that I can't say thank you anymore, and everyone gets the Irish version,' suggested Smith, in a passable Irish brogue.

'Neither Tommy nor I give a shit what people call us, so long as it's not too late for dinner,' Smith laughed. 'But what should matter to you is what we do, and how we do it, and where we do it, and that more often than not - *you and them won't even know we are there.*'

'Except tonight, when we shook the branches in the Rookeries, then they knew we were there,' laughed Haynes.

'We got away without as much as a bloody nose or a fat lip - but not for the want of trying. They're miserable bastards, those Irish. Just want you out of their little shit-holes, but can't understand they're in Leicester now, not Ireland,' explained Smith.

Smith had a well earned mistrust of the Rookeries. In the last few years, the number of Irish had gone up to nearly a thousand, and even though they made up only a quarter of the whole population, they ruled the place, and made life hell for other folk.

'Anyways, we found a couple of snitches. Didn't take too much persuading when we opened a bottle of stout or two, or three, with them down at 'The Fox and Grapes'. Still open it is, even now. It seems like we have a new industry, in buying and selling nippers. 'Child farming' they're calling it,' said Smith.

'There are so many nippers down the Rookeries at present, they just want rid of them. Old Fred Palmer in Willow Street has a new chimney boy from them every other week, and half of them have never been seen again, so they say. Don't suspect they're stuck up the chimney still, but you never know,' he continued.

'Then folks say that there are dozens going off to Nottingham to find work, while Leicester struggles. It's little wonder we don't get them reported - the parents are just glad to get rid of them,' explained Haynes.

'But this child farming sounds much more sinister. Sounds like there is some group of Toffs who are buying these young kids from adverts in the paper, and then some go off and are used as pleasure or entertainment for our local perverts,' surmised Smith. 'Parents get some coins for their pains, which I'm sure eases the sorrow of losing their loved one.'

'Eases their guilt, more like. That is, if they're capable of feelings,' suggested Haynes, who was even more of a realist than Smith.

'Strange thing,' said Haynes, 'the Micks are adamant that it's Black Annis who's taking them - and they'll turn up sucked dry and all skinned and boned - and they say it was the same in Ireland. When we told them Black Annis came from Dane Hills, they laughed and said we were wrong, unless she'd followed them over the water. They really believe it's her!'

'You been down the Rookeries yet, Shepherd?' enquired Smith.

'No Sergeant, not yet; don't know that much about them either,' Shepherd replied.

'Sounds like Beddows needs to get you educated and pretty quick,' laughed Smith, 'cos that's where you'll be spending a lot of your working life, and soon, by the sounds of it.'

'And by the way - for both of you - a bit of advice,' said Smith. 'If you want to be successful get rid of those bleeding hobnails from your boots. We could hear you for miles. Bet you never heard us, and we weren't more than a few yards from you several times tonight.'

'Good job too,' laughed Haynes. 'Would have trod in old Matthias Issitt's turd, if we hadn't heard what he proposed to do with it.'

*****

Leicester had a modest Irish population long before the famine of 1845, but 1845 brought Irish immigrants across to Leicester in such large numbers, with word of a growing town, and the prospect of lots of work in new factories, such as Corahs, that were springing up.

When they arrived, they drifted towards the Parish of St Margaret's, the largest in the Borough, and containing some of the poorest housing that merited pulling down back then, and to the Rookeries, where their relatives and associates already were.

Some of the housing had actually been created in converted pigsties, such as 'Hextalls Yard' off Mansfield Street, now affectionately known as 'Pork Shop Yard' and which had up to eleven people living in one converted sty. The eleven properties had over 60 occupants between them, and were owned by Abigail Hextall who still lived there and ran the large lodging house at the end of the yard, a dubious den of iniquity.

Most of the houses in Abbey Street, and Green Street, and down along Belgrave Gate to the Gas Works, were set in similar small yards, and these were filthy and over-crowded, full of drunken Irish and dubious, transient lodgers. All were escaping something, and the population seemed to grow daily, just like a Rookery in nature, and hence the nickname the area had earned.

Children were prolific and died at an alarming rate, even without criminal intervention, with the death rate in the Borough in 1854, being several times the national average, according to Dare and the reformers.

Yards were dark and narrow dead ends and houses may have had only one or two windows at most, to avoid the miserable 'window tax' and were built of cheap mud bricks or old fashioned wattle and daub, claustrophobically assembled around common 'privies'. It was in these confined areas that most of the population gathered and lived out their pitiful lives.

Everywhere smelled like shit; the people smelled like shit; the people behaved like animals!

So much shit had built up in most of the yards, the residents had now taken to shitting on the floor in their own houses, so they only had their own germs and smell to worry about - let alone the rubbish and the rats amidst the common privies and cesspits.

It was here that the Borough Police faced its most frequent problems. These yards and alleys were not places to be found alone as a Constable.

The local pubs were Irish pubs, such as 'The Fox and Grapes', 'The Horse Breakers' and 'King George III' - the haunt of the Irish Prize-fighters, 'The Fancy', as they were called, surrounded by 'Bruisers' - their minders; and the frequent fights at these localities were always bloody.

Anyone who didn't or wouldn't fight were called 'Dunghill Birds' and given a severe beating or 'done down' for their troubles.

It was not a community in which to live if you were a softy, English or Irish. It was a hard community, and it had its own hierarchy, and some Irish leaders were well feared for a good cause. Weak Police officers were sent packing and would be recognised as easy targets when the Irish wandered into the heart of the Borough.

Modern Coppers needed to be mentally and physically hard and determined, proper 'Crushers' like Beddows!

Chapter Three – Dark forces

At eight o'clock the following morning, in possession of the facts they had gathered from the boy Thomas Parrott, Physician Wilson, their own observations, and enquiries made by Detectives Smith and Haynes, Beddows and Shepherd were sent to the office of Oliver Mitchell, Coroner for the Borough, in New Street.

This would *hopefully* be the last task of the shift, but Beddows knew they would both be required back early to facilitate the inquest.

Since 1836 an inquest had to be held for any unexpected or unnatural death occurring within a Coroner's jurisdiction. It was an offence for any person to fail to notify him of such an event when it occurred.

An inquest would be held at a convenient time - within twenty four hours, preferably - of a reported death of such nature being reported. A suitable location had to be identified, with a jury of at least twelve men designated, and the inquest was to be completed only once the Coroner and jury had viewed the body in his presence.

Constables had now become the Coroner's Officers, and in the Borough, were Oliver Mitchell Esquire's eyes and ears. They prepared the evidence for him, sourced the jury, and they presented the evidence and witnesses at the inquest.

Coroner Mitchell had clearly had a rather enjoyable evening prior, and now demonstrating and feeling the effects of his excess. The last thing he really wanted today, the 2nd of January, was a smelly corpse or a smelly jury.

'Good morning, Constables, a long night I perceive?' Mitchell smirked, looking across at their tired and dark shadowed, bloodshot eyes, as he sat himself down at his polished desk, on the ground-floor of the opulent, New Street, premises.

New Street was the place to be if you were of the manner and status of Coroner, and the housing, much of which incorporated private offices, about the best you could get.

Number 10 was no exception, standing about half way along the street, with a large bayed frontage, and more windows than Beddows could recall in any building since the stealthy Window Tax had been introduced. Large polished brass plates adorned most of the front walls, announcing the names and occupations of the occupiers, Lawyers, Merchants, Architects, in the main.

The Offices of Mr Mitchell were spacious and spotless. They smelled clean, and wax polish could be detected above the usual smells of the Borough. Everywhere and everything appeared tidy, in difference to the office at the Police Station, where everything always cramped, dirty, smelly and untidy.

Mr Mitchell, however, lived in a rather more *modest*, but none the less *posh* house, in Cank Street, nearer to the Market Place, and merely had his 'official' offices, as Coroner for the Borough and South of the County, at New Street.

Beddows believed the Coroner to be a widower, and he lived with just a house-keeper to see to his every need; he had never seen or heard reference to a Mrs Mitchell.

Coroner Mitchell, a middle aged and well spoken gent, with a thirst for fine things, had a girth to reflect his thirst.

He also wore scent, and this matched his dapper and flamboyant dress style, with fine morning suits, with their frock coats and high collared shirt and neckerchiefs. He was also a fine and outspoken supporter of the Police, and relied on them to facilitate his role effectively.

The scent also gave a pleasant air; something neither of the officers was accustomed to.

Amusingly, as the Coroner grounded his ample bottom on his opulent leather seat, a large, loud and rasping fart rang out, releasing a ghastly fetid smell in the office.

'Whoops!' chuckled the Coroner. 'Sorry about that one, think it was me, or have you brought the corpse with you?' which he thought exceedingly funny.

'Thought I'd rid myself of the flatulence on my walk here this morning,' his guts bubbling audibly.

'The corpse, sir, is wrapped in a tarpaulin and awaiting yours and the Jury's observations at 'The Bakers Arms' in Bath Street, if that is agreeable to you, sir,' Beddows smiled in return.

'Ah Good; so, must have been me then. Too much port with my Stilton, I suspect. Or the Stilton was a bit too mature, perhaps?' Mitchell laughed.

'The body is secure, and from what we can establish from enquiries that have been made by Detective Sergeants Smith and Haynes, it is likely the boy is of Irish origin, and probably from the Rookeries, but unlikely that anyone will seek to admit ownership of him,' explained Beddows, by now struggling to keep his eyes open and desperate for his his warm bed.

'And it would appear we definitely have a murder?' said the Coroner, in a bright, cheerful tone which Shepherd considered hopeful and eager, rather than upset or disappointed.

'Yes, sir; dumped naked and with his throat cut. He's been dead for some days by the state of the corpse and the views of Physician Wilson. All rather unpleasant! That's why I thought the Jury may require some of 'The Bakers Arms' finest to get them through the viewing,' suggested Beddows.

'And Constable Shepherd, before I forget, I hear you're a dab hand with a boathook?'

Shepherd look amazed for the second time in the night, as nothing had been handed yet to the coroner in writing, neither he nor Beddows had mentioned the mishap.

'My boatmanship currently leaves room for improvement, sir,' Shepherd admitted, acutely embarrassed not just as a further reminder to him of his accident, but of the fact there clearly existed a grapevine which operated much quicker than Shepherd could currently comprehend.

'Never mind; we live and learn!' concluded the Coroner, ushering the men towards the door, as more flatulence could be heard rolling in his belly. 'See you both at six, with a fine Jury no doubt, and a drop of the Landlord's best?'

'Yes, sir,' nodded Beddows, thankfully, his mind now firmly fixed on getting home for those few short hours sleep, before the earlier than planned start, to their next shift.

As Beddows and Shepherd left via the large, glossy, black painted door, daylight had begun fighting a battle with the fog, and for the first time in days, visibility looked like it might lift.

It remained, however, bitterly cold; the heavy frost crunching beneath their feet, as the Constables made their ways home. Beddows looked forward to snuggling up to a warm wife. Shepherd just sought sleep.

*****

During the afternoon, Sergeant Tarrant, of the day shift, had identified and recorded the names and addresses of 12 good men of the Borough, and instructed them to make themselves present in good time for the Inquest at six o'clock at the given location.

At Five o'clock that afternoon, having reported to the Station after little sleep, and been reminded that they still had a night shift to patrol after the Inquest, Head Constable Charters sent both Beddows and Shepherd off to 'The Bakers Arms', to prepare for the Inquest.

In their possession were three files of paper.

In one, the written evidence of Thomas Parrott, Physician Wilson, together with the statements of themselves and Sergeants Smith and Haynes.

In the second, the names of those convened to form the jury, together with their addresses, for settlement of payment of one shilling, which each would receive for their ordeal.

In the third; blank official papers that The Coroner would require to endorse and sign at conclusion of the Inquest, and authorities to make payments to those listed in the jury file.

'How did Charters and the Coroner know about the boathook?' queried a tired and nervous Shepherd. His mind had been active throughout most of the day, and he had slept fitfully, nagging questions pounding away at him.

'Mr Charters knows everything, Shepherd, everything. His eyes and ears extend far beyond ours, and he has more sources in high places than we will ever know - and usually they are spot on. He and Mr Mitchell are thick as thieves, and dine together frequently, exchanging news and views. So I suspect they were conversing long before you and I visited Mr Mitchell this morning,' explained Beddows.

As a clock struck half past five, Beddows and Shepherd walked through the front door of 'The Bakers Arms' and were greeted by Joseph Headley, stood behind the bar with a fetching serving wench, busty and auburn haired, currently busily flirting with Physician Wilson, and one or two of the assembled jurors.

The cold and damp rolled in with them, causing the log fire to spit and splutter. The smell of damp wood smoke prevailed.

The Inn smelled welcoming, and Mrs Headley appeared to be baking, judging by the delicious aromas wafting through the rooms, mingling with the tobacco smoke and wood smoke from the fires. Beddows would give anything to sit and warm by the fire, but duty prevented such wishes.

'The room is ready, Mr Beddows, and I have a bottle of Mr Mitchell's favourite red on his desk,' announced Headley.

'I think I know which would be my favourite red,' said Beddows, eyeing up the barmaid. 'And his desk would be a fine place to consume her. Joking apart, I want to go and open up your store, and prepare the corpse. I take it you would not wish to assist us?' said Beddows, tongue in cheek, aware of Headley's previous funerary 'experience'.

'Once I have opened up the store for you, I wish nothing more than a quick inquest, a quick removal of the body, and to get back to my customers and normal business,' Headley replied.

Headley selected the keys to the yard store from the hook by the inner door to the yard, where he had left them earlier. The dogs had not even been allowed into the yard for fear of them removing more flesh. Both were unusually quiet.

The Licensee and two Constables walked to the store, the dogs securely locked in the entry.

'At least the smell has diminished,' said Shepherd, expecting to be met by the odour of old death which would remain indelibly etched in his memory forever, so George had once said.

He did not looking forward to viewing the body again, and for some strange reason, became apprehensive that it might sit up and hold out its arms to him, or he would turn his back, only to find the corpse had stood up behind him. He had not experienced such irrational fears for years.

As the padlock was removed and the gate opened, it became plain to all why there was no stench, as corpse, tarpaulin and all were nowhere to be seen.

'Mr Headley, we have a problem!' exclaimed Beddows, nervously. 'I thought you said nobody had been to the store and nobody had been into the yard?'

'They are the only keys, and only my wife and I have access to them. Mary would not wish to be anywhere near a corpse, so I cannot explain what has happened,' replied Headley, fearful of the consequences to his own reputation.

'Bollocks!' Beddows swore. 'Bollocks! Mr Mitchell will be here in minutes, and we have lost a corpse. Not just any corpse, just a murdered one. Jesus Christ, Shepherd, Head Constable Charters will have our Baubles off for this cock-up!'

'Who would want a decomposed, putrid, festering corpse?' said Shepherd. 'I thought body snatching and resurrectionists were a thing of the past?'

'These are not resurrectionists, Shepherd. This is dark arts at work; this is someone who doesn't want a body at all, who doesn't want a murder at all, get my drift?'

Beddows already pictured the good Sergeant Roberts and some of his miscreant associates, plotting the loss; saving Roberts a whole heap of work.

'What, Roberts?' offered Shepherd, partly in disbelief, partly in feint recognition of Beddows' assumptions.

'Roberts!' snapped Beddows, angrily. 'Smart lad, and thinking like a Copper now, aren't you? Look here, at the top of the gate. Something's been dragged across and it's all splintered and broke. The gates haven't been unlocked, they've took the corpse out over the top.'

*****

At precisely five minutes to six o'clock, Head Constable Charters, The Coroner, Mr. Mitchell and Mr. Mitchell's scribe, Edward McPherson, entered the designated room at 'The Bakers Arms'.

Mr Headley scurried out of view, head bowed down, until Beddows and Shepherd had taken the wrath that could be expected.

Beddows and Shepherd were already stood within the room, looking sheepish and clearly concerned.

'Are we ready then, Beddows?' Charters asked of the Constable, sensing that something was amiss.

'I am afraid, sir, that we have the gravest of problems - the corpse has been *stolen,*' said Beddows, waiting for Charters' wrath to descend upon him once again.

'What in the Devils name has happened, then?' Charters demanded, taken aback completely by the revelation.

'Sir, if we may have a word with you in private?' requested Beddows, realising the implications of what he was about to suggest, and concerned that it may get out if overheard.

'Gentlemen of the Jury, Physician Wilson, young master Parrott. Please could I ask you to leave the room for a few moments, and we will send for you shortly,' said Charters.

'Mr Mitchell, I am sure, will want to hear this,' suggested Charters.

'Sir, as we explained last night, I had concerns regarding the actions of Sergeant Roberts. He was adamant that as far as he was concerned, this was not a murder, and he was clear he would *sort it out,*' said Beddows.

'You are suggesting Roberts has arranged for the corpse to disappear?' said Charters.

'During the night, whilst on our enquiries, we came upon a man called Pawley, a backstreet carpenter and occasional undertaker, with premises off Churchgate. He was caught in a compromising situation with what appeared to be a Dollymop, but who turned out to be one Mr Daniel Salt, of the Borough Planning office, dressed in woman's clothing. We first thought they were a couple of Mollies having 'three penny worth'. Mr Pawley, in the course of being questioned, slyly discarded a small object which we found to contain four new, shiny Guinea coins, an *undertaker* of his poor means,' explained Beddows.

'And what does this have to do with Roberts?' said Charters.

'A while later, whilst in The Market Place, we came upon Sergeant Roberts leaving 'The Lion and Dolphin' tavern in an inebriate state, in my expert opinion,' offered Beddows, wryly, 'shortly to be followed out by none other than Mistress, apologies, Mister Salt - who we heard to call him *sweetie.*'

'And?' questioned Charters.

'What do Sergeant Roberts, an undertaker with four guineas, and a dubious Borough official have in common? Why would Pawley have four guineas? Why would Roberts and Salt be together? Sir, I smell a rat, as I feared originally,' stated Beddows, now even more sure that his assumptions had some substance.

'A most interesting hypothesis, Beddows,' replied Charters, also seeing the connections that Beddows had outlined, and suppressing some of the anger that he had considered directing at the Constable.

'Now, about the inquest,' interjected Mr Mitchell. 'It would be unusual, but I believe not unprecedented, to open an inquest without a corpse.'

'Do we have the evidence and all the witnesses, Beddows?' said Charters, with more than a hint of sarcasm, and still obviously embarrassed at the loss of a Coroner's Corpse.

'And a full jury, sir,' responded Shepherd, anxious that he and Beddows were still centre of Charters' attention and trying to divert his mind to other things.

'In that case, let us convene,' directed the Coroner.

Twelve good men took their places in the best room of the Inn, and were sworn in, as had originally been intended.

Mr Mitchell opened the Inquest and advised, 'Gentlemen, we have today, a remarkably unusual inquest. You will be, I am sure, delighted to learn that you will not be required to, or indeed be able to, view the corpse for which we have convened. Yet you will still receive your one shilling for your troubles.'

The witnesses were called, commencing with young Thomas Parrott, the river finder, who confirmed finding the body, and what a dreadful sight it was, he stated.

Constable Beddows gave evidence that he attended West Bridge, together with Constable Shepherd, where with the assistance of a local boatman, they recovered the naked body of a young white male. The body had wounds, one as a result of an accident with a boathook - which drew much laughter from the tense jurors, and a significant wound to the throat.

Constable Shepherd gave similar evidence, to the amusement of the jurors, and added that he had seen similar wounds as a result of a slaughter man's knife, not dwelling on his own mishap for longer than necessary.

Physician Wilson, gave evidence that he attended West Bridge, and examined the body of a young male and pronounced life extinct. He was of the opinion that the wound to the throat had been a deliberate and unlawful act, probably caused by the boy being held from behind and his throat cut from left to right causing the deep gash. The boy had been dead for anything up to one week.

The evidence of Detective Sergeants Smith and Haynes, accepted in statement form, indicated that early enquiries suggested that the boy was probably of Irish origin, and possible from the Abbey Street area. It was unlikely with current information that any parent or guardian would admit to knowledge of the boy.

Coroner Mitchell asked that the Jury consider their verdict, based entirely on the witness evidence they had heard or presented in written form.

In the time it took them to down a bottle of red, the Jury returned a verdict of *'Murder by person or persons unknown'*.

*****

Once the Inquest had ended, and the Jury dismissed, Head Constable Charters, Coroner Mitchell and the two Constables remained within the best room at 'The Bakers Arms', as Mr Mitchell began his assault on a second bottle of his favourite red, as was his norm.

'My dear Robert,' said Mitchell. 'You must really set about finding my missing body, as well as the person or persons responsible for his demise - and by the sound of it you have some promising leads.'

Mitchell appeared quite amused with the event, rather than irate, as Charters had expected, and had recognised that it had put Charters' in an awkward position - he had not seen him so concerned, previously.

However, he had heard what Beddows had said, and now optimistic that the 'dark forces' would be identified and the matter concluded, he would make nothing more of it.

'Yes, Coroner,' Charters responded sternly, his eyes upon Beddows and Shepherd, 'and find them we will,' angry still at the loss of a body, but seething at the thought of his corrupt Detective Sergeant's probable involvement.

'Back to my office, please, gentlemen,' Charters ordered.

*****

At about seven o'clock that same evening, Beddows and Shepherd stood to attention in front of Head Constable Charters at his desk, in the office beyond the Muster Room in the Police Station, the door firmly closed.

'What a shambles,' stressed Charters. 'Shambles,' he echoed. 'How can we justify losing a corpse?' his tone less angst than Beddows had anticipated.

'Sir,' said Beddows. 'For a long time now we have had the problem of where to keep bodies for The Coroner, and none of the present arrangements can offer us total security, other than sitting with them until an inquest.'

'Go on,' said Charters.

'Most of the Inns we use for Inquests have no secure storage. The Physicians won't help with dead bodies, and the Workhouse and Infirmary only have them when they've died there. I've been to bodies that have lain for days in the homes where they died, because there was nowhere to take them and nobody to bury them,' said Beddows.

'I know that,' responded Charters, sympathetically. 'But we can't afford to lose a body. Even if it means someone having to guard it until an inquest has been heard. But that won't resolve this current situation. I will speak with the Borough Watch Committee and see what the chance is of a secure Police Mortuary.'

'Thank you, sir,' said Beddows.

'Now then,' said Charters. 'Get hold of Sergeants Smith and Haynes. I want to speak with you all about how we are going to deal with this,' at which point came a knock at the door.

Standing outside were Smith and Haynes 'You wanted us, sir?' Smith smiled.

'We have several tasks that need to be undertaken. Does anybody know where Sergeant Roberts is at this moment?' enquired Charters, anxious to vent his wrath on the miserable man, who had now seemingly vanished off the face of the Borough.

'I've a pretty good idea' said Haynes. 'Do you want me to bring him in, sir?' hoping to settle a few old scores with the good Sergeant, and see him sorted once and for all.

'Not immediately, but I want to know where he goes and who he meets for the next day or so. He'll be up to something I fear,' said Charters. 'You and Smith have that task,' at which point they left the room and went off to their 'dressing up box'.

'And you two; you are off normal duties until I say otherwise, and I have two tasks for you. First I want this man Pawley bringing in. Use your initiative. Secondly, I then want Salt to know we have arrested Pawley, and then to see where he goes and who he meets up with - do you understand?'

'Yes, sir,' said Beddows.

'And I want the body back first, and we can deal with that now. Then we can deal with the Murder - as our suspects may have some light to throw on that,' said Charters.

'Yes, sir,' said Beddows. 'On it right away, sir,' at which point they saluted, then made off through the Muster Room, aware that things had turned out a lot brighter than Beddows had expected.

*****

Churchgate became increasingly shabby as you travelled down it, from the 'Five Ways' at Cole Hill, towards the start of the Rookeries, along Mansfield Street and Sandiacre Street.

Beddows had shaken the door handles to Pawley's workshop every night, and several times a night, when his beat had included the block between Churchgate and Abbey Street, and before it had spawned into the slums that now existed.

Only on rare occasions had he found Pawley there, later than seven o'clock at night, and he suspected only when he might be doing something more underhand than usual.

The front of Pawley's workshop could be accessed via a small wicket door to a yard alongside The Star Foundry, below Mansfield Street. The yard took you through to the small workshop which occupied the rear, and backed onto Short Street, running parallel with Churchgate.

Short Street had been built as one of those narrow, cobbled streets, where you could lean out of first floor windows and shake hands with the person in the opposite house.

At the rear gates to Pawley's workshop, the road widened slightly, to allow people to swing in and out with a small cart, which could be shackled inside the workshop. Pawley had occasional access to a mule from Delaney's builders in Mansfield Street, which occasionally he dressed with a black plume, and employed to pull his rickety, un-roadworthy, funeral cart.

The workshop itself looked dark, even when lit; it smelt of filth, much like the rest of the Borough, but on a scale where it clearly more a part of the Rookeries than other properties on Churchgate, and therefore the smell was more noxious. Death permeated the rickety structure and contents of the yard.

The yard to the workshop had its own privvie, a roughly dug earth closet in one corner, which smelt and looked like it had never been emptied before.

To call himself a carpenter could be considered questionable; and probably considered fraudulent by past customers. Pawley's 'handy-work' that could be found in the premises was poorly sourced cheap timber, warped and probably recycled, and tacked together with cheap horse-glue and even cheaper nails which he 'obtained' from over the wall at Star Foundry, Beddows suspected.

A 'Mackler' would have been a better description of his trade.

His undertaking business comprised of pieces of wood, as from old tea-chests, the cheapest you could imagine, which he 'mackled' together to make flimsy 'Parish' coffins.

These were sold by him at a comparative extortionate cost, to grieving families that wanted to send off a loved one with some degree of dignity, or to the Poor Law Union for those even less fortunate, who were to be buried in communal graves at the expense of the Parish, up at the newly opened Welford Road cemetery.

Many of them fell to pieces the minute they were lifted with a body weight inside them, or they warped when the juices of decomposition began to flow, as so often happened with poorer families' deceased, and then fell to bits.

Often, owing to the long and pitiful working week, the only day a family could bury their dead would be on a Sunday, if they were lucky enough to have any time given to them for attending church.

Actually making the arrangements meant not seeing an undertaker for days after the death, so it could be two weeks between death occurring, arranging and then carrying out a funeral.

The bodies sometimes were laid out by the 'woman who does' in the deceased's own home, and remained until the funeral or until the undertaker came for the body, by which time it had often become putrid. The rest of the family would frequently still be living in the same room as the corpse.

Joseph Dare, and John Buck, Health and Social reformers in the Borough had both, in recent years, commented on this most *grave* risk and pressed the Borough for some alternative means for families to prepare and temporarily store their dead.

In 1849 Welford Road cemetery had opened, and the Borough made provision of two 'Mortuary Houses' inside the gates of the cemetery, where corpses could be laid out or stored until such time as they could be buried.

This offered an alternative for families which could afford removal and transportation fees, but to most, it was still beyond their means, and so the corpses remained rotting in their homes until the funeral day.

*****

Beddows and Shepherd made their way through the easing fog, round into Short Street. This defined the start of the area where they would be prone to attacks, and chased from the Rookeries if they did not have the courage to stand firm.

A few scallywags and urchins wandered through the darkness and made rude gestures or a veiled threat to the Constables, but Beddows had no inclination to be put off.

One or two seemingly disabled beggars sat in the shadows on each street corner looking for some charitable 'mark' that would offer a coin from a full purse and that nearby thieves or pick-pockets could then target.

No doubt though, that word would already be going around the Rookeries that Constables were in their midst.

Beddows hammered on the flimsy gates to the rear yard. 'Open up - Constables Beddows and Shepherd,' thus, formally announcing their arrival.

Beddows could hear sawing noises from inside stop. *'Must be up to no good at this time of day,'* he thought to himself.

After a few moments, the sound of timber grating against timber could be heard, as Pawley lifted the latch and opened the well warped timber gate to the Constables.

'I was hoping that last night was the last I would see of you two,' Pawley said, sounding disappointed.

'You should be so lucky, Edward my old son, you should be so lucky! Why do you think we are here then?' quizzed Beddows, looking for signs of fear or guilt on Pawley's Face.

'I suppose you have come to taunt me for being found with that 'Three penny upright', as you suspected, but like we said last night, it weren't what you thought.'

'Oh, we know that now my dear, we know what you had really been up to and what you were doing with the sniveling little shit Salt. It seems we are missing a body, a corpse, and a stinky one at that - and you have that same smell upon you, even now - as you did in the early hours of this morning,' Beddows growled, angry that he had not made the connection there and then.

'I don't know what you are talking about. Corpse? I haven't seen a corpse for weeks,' came the timid response. Pawley had been caught unprepared and appeared to be struggling to come up with anything more plausible.

'Don't you know that hampering the Coroner is an offence, Edward? And not only that, this corpse is a bit more important than most, know what I mean?' said Beddows, leaning close to the man's face, before pulling back on account of his foul breath.

'I'm not saying anything; I don't know what you are on about,' Pawley squirmed, deciding that it was better to say nothing, than incriminate himself further. Beddows would have to prove what he had done.

'Well anyways, I am arresting you on suspicion of stealing one dead body, oh, and one tarpaulin belonging to Charles Church, just in case. That will do for starters. And we're going to have a look around your poxy, putrid, little workshop before we take you in, understand?' said Beddows.

'How many corpses have you got at the moment then Edward?' said Shepherd, anxious that he did not open or step in something he might regret.

'Haven't had one for weeks; had no call lately, like I said,' Pawley replied.

'Don't smell that way to me. Where's your cart dear?' said Beddows, noting an obvious item of Pawley's trade to be missing from the premises.

'Cart?' shrugged Pawley, trying to look oblivious to the Constable's observation.

'Yes, that tatty old four wheeler that you 'appropriated' from off of old man Ginns, the good and genuine undertaker across the road, when he threw it out.'

'I think you might be mistaken, Constable Beddows,' said Pawley.

'Do you really think I know nothing of these things? It's my business to know. Just the thing you use for your funeral activities as I recall. Chuck the coffin on the back; fleece the family or the Union; then chuck it in a shitty little pauper's grave and say you've done the family or the Parish a favour. I don't think so! You're a nasty little piece of work,' Beddows growled yet again - angry that the Parish even patronised him.

'Oh *that cart*,' Pawley replied. 'I think some rotten scoundrel must have stolen it, Constable Beddows. It seems to be missing. I must report it to a Constable when I see one that's interested.'

'Very amusing, Edward - but we'll see who laughs last. If I can connect you to the body, I might even see you swing for this last night's work!' Beddows laughed, standing on Pawley's right toes, and pushing his weight onto that side, grinding in his hobnails.

Pawley went decidedly pale and pissed his pants - and his eyes started to water.

'It looks like I've hit a nerve, Edward my dear - one way or another,' Beddows grinned, hiding his deeper revulsion and holding back the thoughts he had, to do the man much greater harm.

'You're making a habit of this, Beddows,' said Shepherd. 'How many more people will piss or shit themselves today?'

'Some nervous fellows around Leicester, lad,' Beddows replied. 'Quite rightly so, at the moment!'

Head Constable Robert Charters sat down for supper at 'The Pelican Hotel' in Gallowtree Gate, having extended the invitation to Thomas Thompson, the editor and proprietor of 'The Leicester Chronicle'.

The Hotel had a reputation as one of the better hostelries, when one wished to eat, and this evening, their meat pie had proven an excellent choice. A little on the tough side, but it tasted like beef - and accompanied by some well cooked root vegetables, no doubt acquired from the Market Place at little cost, but on the plate at a sizeable profit to the Victualler, Simeon James. All this washed down with a jug of his finest pale ale.

Thomas Thompson had been in charge of the newspaper since just after the Napoleonic Wars, and held a strong Liberal view, as reflected in the newspaper's content.

It had become the most extensively read newspaper in the Borough, and had a good trade in private adverts.

With three newspapers currently available within the Borough, excluding London papers that were delivered by coach to Humberstone Gate daily, news quickly spread around Leicester and its surrounding County towns and villages, distributed to the County via the regular local coachmen.

The reporters were still not quite sure what to make of the Police, but one or two were becoming quite 'pro', where others still tried to alienate the Police, portraying them as a needless expense to the Borough, as clearly thought some Magistrates.

Leicester had both a strong Liberal and Tory news, and they competed with each other for readership, sometimes elaborating on the real news, for the sake of more 'sensational *news'*, where real stories were created around imaginative plots and sub-plots. Thompson's rag had developed into one of the better ones for doing so, tastefully.

Both men were old acquaintances, and Thompson had already assumed a favour would be asked, and in return he would no doubt get a little more insight to current Police news than other journalists in the Borough - so it seemed mutually beneficial to meet.

'Thomas; I am going to ask for your help in one of our investigations. We have an informant who has suggested that there is currently a trade going on in this Borough that pertains to the sale and purchase of children - by means of advertisements placed in local journals,' explained Charters.

'And what can I do to help you? As I understand it there is no law that prevents such activity, and I hear tell of other towns where such means are used to offer shelter and hope to some of the poorest children in our communities?' enquired Thompson.

'You are quite right; but our suspicions are that this has a more unpleasant basis. It would be of great assistance to us, if we could have copies of any advertisements that are worded something to the effect of *'Good woman required to look after young child on full time basis'* , together with any information you might have as to whom placed the advertisement, and by what means they could be contacted. There must be some point of contact for negotiations to take place, and we do not know how long this has been going on for,' explained Charters.

'And what in return do you bring for me?' Thomson smiled inquisitively.

'Ah, what about a worrying little story about body snatchers?' teased Charters, slipping into his native Geordie accent.

'I thought the days of resurrectionists were over and done with, years ago?' said Thompson. 'And so, why might it be sensational?'

'What if it might also highlight serious deficiencies within the Borough, and place pressure on our politicians to improve conditions for our dead? You haven't rocked the boat for a few weeks!' whispered Charters, mindful of indiscrete ears nearby.

'Go on,' said Thompson with renewed interest.

*****

Beddows and Shepherd made a point of walking Pawley back slowly, and through the main streets of the town. Up Churchgate, right into Eastgates, on up High Street and St Nicholas Street, left onto Applegate Street, and left towards Town Hall Lane, stopping frequently under the brighter street lights or by illuminated public houses, to improve the likelihood of him being seen.

With the fog fractionally starting to ease, for this time of the evening the Town appeared busier than of late, and people stopped to view the sight of a prisoner being taken in, with a mix of cheers and jeers from observers - as usual when arrests were made, always attracting the attention of the nosier and noisier elements of the local population.

Several of the late shift were patrolling their beats, and would have noticed the goings on, and Beddows appreciated that one or two might be in Roberts' pocket, and that word would start to circulate that Edward Pawley had been arrested. That was his hope.

Upon entering the station, Beddows approached the desk of Sergeant Sheffield, who never *really* seemed in a good mood, and who looked like he was having a bugger of a day.

Shepherd held the prisoner close by.

'What have you got for me now then, Beddows?' asked the Charge Sergeant, avoiding eye contact, blowing his pipe smoke into the face of the prisoner, whilst at the same time opening the heavy bound 'Custody' register and dipping his pen into the adjacent ink-well.

'I have just arrested this man on suspicion of theft of one deceased body and one tarpaulin, from 'The Bakers Arms' yard, earlier today, and have brought him here for further questions to be asked,' Beddows explained, unsure whether Sergeant Sheffield wanted the official answer, in official jargon, or just some idea of what he should endorse in the book.

'Ah, the case of the missing corpse! Is that the one you two lost?' enquired a clearly amused Sheffield, causing himself to cough, hoarsely, whilst not biting hard enough to retain the pipe wedged between his teeth, which slipped, momentarily.

Embers from the pipe dropped onto the well used register, and Sheffield quickly brushed them aside, leaving small brown scorch marks, not for the first time, within its pages.

'The very same, Sarge,' smiled Beddows, nodding, aware what a dry old salt Sheffield could be when it suited him, and how different he had become since Beddows had lost his rank. More formal than he felt necessary at times, considering their history.

'Right then, let's get him locked up, and then Shepherd can make us all a nice cup of tea.' Sheffield directed his eyes towards the small mess area at the rear of the building.

'You are still the latest addition to the shift, even though you might have forgotten with recent events?' Sheffield reminded him.

Pawley looked pale and nervous, as the door to the smallest cell in the building, sited between the charge desk and the large fireplace, was opened up, especially for him.

It should have been the warmest cell, being so close to the fire grate, but in fact it always proved cold. And the only light came from a small viewing window opposite the entrance door to the Station, or via a hatch in the door, measuring about nine inches square, in the centre and at the officers' eye level.

The cell door was four inches of thick, solid wood, and secured with a bolt and padlock, the breadth of a man's wrist, the only keys to which were to be found on Sergeant Sheffield's belt.

Pawley lowered himself onto a cold, damp, narrow wooden bench, as the door slammed shut and bolted, and the key turned. He suddenly felt very much alone and frightened for his future.

Sergeant Sheffield peered through the hatch and enquired 'You're not in a hurry, Mr Pawley? We are just about to have a brew,' blowing him a little more smoke, just for the hell of it.

*****

Whilst Shepherd went about brewing the tea, Beddows stood by the window of the Station, looking out towards Town Hall Lane. The muster room felt strangely warm for a change and the high collar of his tunic rubbed against his neck, and he ran his finger round to ease the irritation, stretching the tight fabric, and eventually loosening the top button.

He expected to see one of two persons, either of whom would indicate that their walk back through the town with Pawley had been fruitful.

Although the problem with the fog remained, the bright gas lamps outside 'The King and Crown', opposite, gave good illumination of passers-by on both sides of the street. The large lamp over the station door also illuminated the entrance to St Martin's West.

As Beddows suspected, within minutes of making himself comfortable at the window, the figure of a *'female'* came into view. Beddows rubbed his tired eyes and focused hard, reminding him, that he probably would need spectacles soon.

The figure appeared dressed in an identical manner that Beddows had observed twice the previous night, and held an open parasol to shield it from unwelcome onlookers.

Turning into St. Martins West, and thus attempting to shield *his* face from view, Daniel Salt looked furtively inside, before walking onwards towards the adjacent churchyard.

'Cocky little shit!' thought Beddows - considering the possibility that Salt's peers may still be about the complex.

It probably also meant that Roberts must have been tipped off, and would be lurking somewhere nearby and keeping his head down.

To show out now would be his undoing, and, probably thinking, at the very least, that his days as a Detective were drawing to a close, he would need Pawley and Salt to say nothing, else his future was bleak.

Hopefully, Tanky would also be lurking somewhere in the shadows, Beddows reflected, keeping a watchful eye out for Roberts; and it would not be long before they could sort out Mr Salt once and for all.

As Beddows turned to settle down for his cuppa, he caught sight of a male walking into St. Martins, quite a few yards behind *Mistress* Salt. For one moment he thought it might be Black Tommy, but he couldn't be sure; he rarely was when Tommy and Tanky were 'under cover' and he rubbed his eyes yet again – but it didn't help.

* * * * *

Shepherd stood daydreaming, as he stirred the hot water and tea leaves, in a huge, brown, ceramic teapot, which showed the scars of what seemed like years of wear and tear. It had done well to survive in the hands of such clumsy and rough hands, he considered.

He contemplated what to do when he managed a few hours off.

 On a night shift it meant a few hours sleep less than preferred, followed by making every remaining hour of the day count, and that normally meant a walk to the river or canal and some watercolour painting or sketching, season and weather permitting.

He had been introduced to the renowned Leicester Artist and Art Teacher, John Flower, who lived and had a studio in a rather nice house on Oxford Street, near to the Bridewell.

This proved convenient with his Aunt's house being at the end of Twizzle and Twine passage, just around the corner.

He and Flowers had become friendly very quickly. Flowers considered Shepherd a fine young 'budding' artist.

Flowers himself was renowned for his local landscapes, particularly, and Shepherd had admired one which showed the town a few years earlier, looking across from the lush meadows towards the rear of Leicester Castle, which today he would have struggled to recognise. What a difference twenty years could make.

Flowers had taken him to the new Museum at the top of New Walk, not long after he had first arrived to stay as a lodger, and before he had joined the Police. Flowers had walked him around the great artworks on display, and gone to great lengths to point out such things as perspective, tone, hue, light, and detail.

Something he had said about the detail; the brushstrokes; that played on Shepherd's mind, and significant about the wound on the boy's throat, but at present it lay dormant.

Another reason for finding the time with Flowers pleasurable was his resident model, Sally Brown, with her long black hair and dark brown eyes.

Sally had grown into a natural beauty, breathtakingly stunning.

As a life model, she had been painted by Flowers and fellow students, and images of her adorned his studio walls. Her skin tones and sinewy elegance tested Shepherd's mastery with the brush to the limits, as he would hate to do her an injustice.

Life modeling classes when Sally sat for the group would cause Shepherd to fall into periods of dreamy arousal, especially when, after sitting, she would stroll amongst the students checking out their studies, and flirt outrageously, draped in just a flimsy gown.

Sally had a thing about Shepherd, and he hoped she would get to know him better. She filled his dreams most nights, and made life more tolerable.

On his time off after a day shift, he would try and keep fit. This had always been through boxing and sparring, which he wished to continue, but this created a new problem for him.

Some years ago, he had been in a legitimate boxing match, with a retired boxer from Leicester, of Irish origin, named Declan Kavanagh.

Declan Kavanagh had fought under Dick Cain, who had been one of the best pugilists within 'The Fancy' - the bare knuckle prize fighters that were idolized by the Irish - and had become infamous for a fifty-one round contest in 1841, which lasted for over two hours.

Police had tried to stop the contest but were scared off by the crowd, and the fight eventually continued until Cain had won.

Cain, his wife and family now ran 'The Castle Tavern' in Gallowtree Gate, and Declan, who now worked there as a barman, had invited Shepherd to go along and use the boxing facilities, which were run upstairs in the pub, if ever he found himself in Leicester. However, this would mean being on licensed premises and *potentially* associating with some particularly dubious people.

Shepherd had been wary of making contact with Kavanagh but he was also getting tense, and in need of a good workout.

He stood and shook his head, turning briefly at awareness that someone had entered the scullery, but unsure how long they had been there.

'Penny for them,' said Beddows. 'Guess who I've just seen?'

*****

Robert Charters had finished his supper, and now slowly walked back towards Town Hall Lane, taking the opportunity to check on his patrols and make sure he too would be seen, even through the gloom.

He anticipated he should see at least five Constables on the route between Market Place South and St Martin's West, which he was pleased to confirm he did. *And they saw him* and some would no doubt be passing his presence on to certain associates of theirs.

Charters considered he probably had a number of 'bad apples' and wanted to bring them to light. The Roberts issue could well expose one or two in the process.

On arrival at Town Hall Lane, Beddows and Shepherd gave him a comprehensive update on their progress.

With Pawley in the cells, and mistress Salt snooping around in his women's garb, it would only be a matter of time before they would find Roberts and try and *hopefully* locate the corpse. His day improved, minute by minute.

Charters showed his delight that things were going to plan. Not only that, he had Thompson sorting out the advertisements that Smith had alluded to, and he had given Thompson some ammunition about sourcing a Police Mortuary to prevent any further hindering of Coroners Inquests.

Social and welfare reform were huge issues in 1850 Leicester, and the reformists wanted every bit of ammunition they could get, to bring about the change that the people so desperately needed. Thompson became a useful foil in their armoury.

'For your information,' said Charters, 'Sergeants Smith and Haynes are currently attempting to locate Roberts and, I understand, Salt is under surveillance as we speak, ladies clothes and all - so we are making progress. I want you two to interview Pawley, as he is no doubt the weak link and will give us some indication of what we have on our hands'.

*****

The cell would be no place to 'question' Pawley. Dark, cramped and in view of people entering the Station, rare though they still might be, it lacked the privacy to conduct an interview, or some Liberals would say, interrogation, of this nature.

Thus, Sergeant Sheffield allowed them to use the main office, now that Mr Charters had retired temporarily for the night, St Martin's clock just chiming eleven.

The office, much smaller than the Muster Room and Charge area, lay behind the Muster Room along St Martin's West and to the rear of the building.

It appeared a plain office, compared to the opulent one they had sat in at 10 New Street, and considering it was used most of the time by the Head Constable of the Force. How the other half lived.

A few dusty law books sat on a high shelf, but they were about the only addition of note to the austere grey décor, which had likely not seen paint since first built. It had been designed to be practical, and practical it had to be; a utility room for all purposes.

Beddows and Shepherd fetched Pawley and sat him with his back to the outside wall, where they both had full view of him, beyond the large rectangular plain desk.

'So then, Edward - what you got to tell us?' said Beddows, hoping that Pawley would not drag things out and deny his involvement.

'I think you are picking on me because of what you think are my personal preferences and the friends I keep. You are just a bully Mr Beddows.'

'If I was a bully, we would not be doing this interview like this, or here in the Police Station, Edward - but we could always go somewhere a little quieter if you would prefer,' said Beddows, fighting the overwhelming urge to give Pawley a long overdue 'slap'.

'That won't be necessary Mr Beddows, here is fine,' realising he would be unwise to push Beddows to violence.

'Let's not beat about the bush, Edward. This is probably a lot more serious than you think. We are investigating a murder, not just the theft of a corpse, and like I said earlier, that implicates you in a capital offence,' Beddows explained, taking a more reasoned, but at the same time, menacing approach.

'And why would I want to murder anyone?' Pawley replied, unclear where Beddows headed, shifting uncomfortably on the hard wooden seat.

'You wouldn't actually have had to murder anyone, but by being involved you would be as guilty as the murderer himself. Many have hung for that; look outs, and people who have assisted the murderer, but not actually done the killing,' said Beddows, playing on Pawley's ignorance.

'Now you are just trying to frighten me,' gulped Pawley, his Adam's apple rising and falling noticeably.

'We are telling you the truth and trying to save your scrawny neck,' said Beddows, trying to give him a lifeline, but one that would hopefully lead to a bigger fish.

'So, where were you between three o'clock and six o'clock this morning gone?' said Beddows.

'You know very well, Mr Beddows, you saw me.'

'And where had you been before we saw you in Carts Lane?'

'The Stokers Arms, like Mr Salt said.'

'So what were you doing in your cart in Bath Street just after one o'clock in the morning?'

'I wasn't,' Pawley swallowed, fear starting to take hold.

'That's the answer that's going to get you hanged - because we have a little bird, who is well believed. A Detective; one that you really should be afraid of, and he will say he saw you.'

'You're lying - you're trying to make me admit something I didn't do.' Pawley breathed much faster; his eyes desperate to avoid contact with either Constable.

'Lock him back up, Shepherd. Looks like it'll be Jack Ketch for Mr Pawley, after all. He's had his chance,' growled Beddows, who had now had enough of trying to be nice and reasonable, patience expired.

'Wait a minute, wait a minute - I haven't killed anyone, and I had nothing to do with helping anyone kill anyone, you can't hang a man for that,' Pawley now openly starting to panic.

'Lock him back up, Shepherd, put him in the yard cell for Mr Hildyard tomorrow morning,' said Beddows, adding to the fear, now clearly building up.

'Alright, I'll tell you the truth, but hear me when I tell you I didn't kill no-one!' Pawley looked pale and sweated profusely; he had no more stomach for lying.

'Go on then, but don't piss us about any more,' Beddows threatened, aware that this seemed less likely.

'I didn't want to get involved, but Mr Salt called upon me for a return of a favour. He said that a friend of his had a small problem, a dead problem, that he needed collecting, else his friend was going to get into deep trouble.'

'And who was that friend?' said Beddows.

'I don't know, and he didn't say. But he said if I didn't return the favour he would close me down and make things very difficult for me, make sure I could never work in Leicester again.'

'So what did he tell you to do?' said Beddows.

'He told me that there was a boy who had been pulled out the river that was now in the back yard store of the Bakers Arms, and he wanted the body picking up and *losing*.'

'So what did you do?' said Beddows.

'I went and borrowed the mule from the usual place, and hitched up my wagon. Another bloke I occasionally employ came with me, but I won't grass him up, he was just a pair of hands, and he's a lot stronger than me; a big Irish bloke he is.'

'And?'

'We went up to Bath Lane and waited til the place was all dark, then I climbed into the store, and passed the body over to my mate. We could hear the dogs start barking so we pissed off quick. He knew a place where he could hide the cart til we could think of where to get rid of the boy, and I went back into town. That's when I went to meet Salt, as he said to fetch him when the job was done.'

'And where was Salt waiting for you?' Beddows asked.

'He had been in 'The Lion and Dolphin', with a load of his strange mates; all 'Mollies' they were. I didn't recognise him at first. We were walking back to Bath Street so he could make sure I'd done the job when you saw us, and he must have seen you first and pulled me into that yard,' said Pawley.

'So if he wasn't happy that you'd got rid of it, how come you had four guineas secreted about your person when you got stopped?' Beddows queried.

'Half up front, half after he was sure the body had gone,' replied Pawley.

'So you were going to get *eight guineas* for getting rid of a body?' Beddows almost choked as he asked. 'Eight guineas! Over five week's wages for one little job?'

'He said his friend was most anxious that the body disappeared, and he would make sure it was worth my while to make sure the body never got found again.'

'And where is the body, now?' said Beddows.

'I don't know,' said Pawley. 'I'd Been trying to find my Irish friend ever since, that's why I was at the yard when you called , as I thought that's where he would come for his coins – two guineas were for him. He's missing; my cart is missing; the bleeding Mule is missing; and my guts will be all over the rookeries if Mr Delaney and his boys haven't got it back by six o'clock this coming morning.'

'I don't think somehow that you'll have time to go looking for it. But I shouldn't worry about your guts, they'll be safely tucked up in the Borough Gaol before Delaney can get to you,' smiled Beddows.

'Promise me one thing, Mr Beddows – please,' said Pawley, pleading.

'What's that, my dear?' Beddows said insincerely, yawning.

'Please make sure nobody thinks I'm really a Molly, 'cos I'm not. That's Salt's preference, and it was his idea to make it look like it did. I'm as much a man as you are Mr Beddows. I've heard what goes on in the Gaol.'

'Don't you worry about that, Edward. You'll be there for so long, this time, that you might wish you were one.' Beddows smiled.

What would happen to Pawley inside the Borough Gaol did not feature amongst his current concerns. Pawley would have to learn the hard way, like everyone else who succumbed to the 'lure' of the Gaol.

*****

'That was a marvellous interview, Mr Beddows, is it always like that? I can't wait until I have those skills.'

'All in a day's work, lad. If I hadn't lost me Sergeant's rank, it might have been me out there with the Detectives, instead of that turd Roberts.' For a few moments, bitterness welled in his throat.

'So who was in Bath Street, Tanky or Black Tommy?' Shepherd asked, naively, keen to understand what had gone on.

'Nobody was, lad, not as I'm aware. But pound to a pinch that's what Pawley thought - so I threw it in just to see if he would roll over; and bless my soul he did!'

Making a villain think he was 'dead to rights' and that someone else could place him at a crime scene, was always a good ruse, and was one of Beddows' regular tactics, and it had worked with a more than a few villains in his time.

'So who do you think was paying Salt?' said Shepherd.

'Got to be Roberts, I would suggest. But I bet he's done it for someone else; 'cos if he's splashing eight guineas around, it won't be his own money. So, he wanted rid for someone else and at a high price, which makes me think that certain someone else knows even more about the murder.'

'What about this mate of Pawley - how do we find him?' said Shepherd.

'We've got more chance of finding the mule and cart lad. Trying to find a big strong Mick in the Borough won't be hard. There are nine hundred of the bleeders, and they're all in the Rookeries - probably one of Delaney's own - and they won't snitch or roll over like Pawley has just done.'

Beddows knew that trying to get a snitch in the Rookeries would never be an easy task, as snitches often just disappeared too. Tanky and Black Tommy had a few exceptions, but the two of them were cunning, ruthless and hard, and brought fear to as many Micks as did their own hierarchy.

'And the body?' said Shepherd.

103

'We need to find out who is taking bodies out of the Borough. They should all be up Welford Road these days. I bet this one's gone out of town though, if it was to be laid up somewhere. I have a mate who now works for the County Force; he might have an idea. Unless of course, like Tanky says, it's Black Annis, in which case it's probably up Dane Hills by now, skinned!' Beddows chuckled.

*****

Robert Charters rubbed his hands in glee, but made it look like he felt the cold, as Beddows and Shepherd updated him on Pawley's confession.

'So, now we have grounds to arrest Salt. That will go down well in the Watch Committee and Borough Finance office. They don't like him much after all that unpleasantness about the Union Workhouse. And he will, no doubt, implicate Roberts, to save his own neck too. Good work men,' proclaimed Charters.

'Heard anything from Sergeants Smith or Haynes, sir?' said Beddows, not expecting an answer, as Charters played his cards close to his chest, more often than not.

'They have been trying to accommodate Roberts, but there are two rumours at present. One is he is being hidden by our Irish friends somewhere in the Borough, and the other that they have already secreted him out to somewhere in the County. Apparently he has friends in high places, and Smith and Haynes are looking into the Borough end of things,' stated Charters.

'I have a friend in the County Force, sir, I could talk to him,' said Beddows.

'No, I want Pawley charged and locked up, but you need to speak with Coroner Mitchell first to see what offence he may have committed, if any, in addition to Burglary by stealing the Tarpaulin. I don't think we can charge for stealing a body anymore, but find out whether anything has changed.'

'Would Mr Goodyer help us out with his County Constables, sir?' said Beddows.

'I am meeting Mr Goodyer at a more respectable hour in the morning for that very purpose,' said Charters, looking at the hands reach 1 o'clock on his fob watch, which he tucked back into his waistcoat. 'It's been a good night, and it's past my bedtime unless anything new happens.'

*****

At eight o'clock, for the second day in succession, Beddows and Shepherd were sat in the office of Coroner Mitchell.

'I assume you have had some success in locating my missing Cadaver?' enquired Mitchell, optimistically.

'Some success, sir,' responded Beddows. 'We have arrested a man named Pawley, an incompetent undertaker, from off Churchgate, and he has admitted taking the body from 'The Bakers Arms', for quite a significant payment of eight guineas.'

'Ah, 'the weasel' or so I believe I have heard him called. A notably poor undertaker so I understand. Did a viewing at his yard once, and the damned corpse was the freshest smelling thing there, Jury included! So, someone appears to be somewhat desperate to have the body gone, you are thinking?'

'Yes, sir; we are currently still trying to locate Pawley's mule and cart, not to mention a large Irishman, who Pawley alleges was going to dispose of the body, probably outside of the Borough - but they are all still currently missing. Mr Charters is off to see Head Constable Goodyer of the County Force for some assistance in our endeavours,' explained Beddows.

'And what are you proposing to charge your Mr Pawley with?' said Mitchell, anticipating questions about Coroner's Law and bodies as property.

'At present, sir, we believe we can only charge him with Burglary, by entering the store at 'The Bakers Arms' and stealing the tarpaulin the body was wrapped in. Mr Charters wondered whether you had any other suggestions as he does not believe we can charge him with stealing a corpse?' enquired Beddows.

'An interesting one that, Beddows,' said Mitchell. 'After all the 'to do' with the Resurrectionists, and our friends Mr Burke and Mr Hare, the Government passed something called the Anatomy Act, in 1832. That made all *unclaimed* bodies the property of the Realm, by which the Government gave in to our Medical friends, donating such bodies for their Anatomy studies. So, strictly speaking, if your young boy is not identifiable at present, we could presume that he belongs to the Realm, and that your Mr Pawley had denied the Realm of that body, and as such, has stolen it. It would make an interesting challenge to the law as it stands.'

'That's a new one on me, Mr Coroner,' replied Beddows, 'but I will pass on your advice to Mr Charters, and he will no doubt decide what we should do. I would wish a very good day to you, sir.'

Chapter Five – A ruthless adversary

Thursday the 3rd of January 1850, at nine o'clock p.m, Beddows and Shepherd sat bleary eyed, in the Muster Room, awaiting Head Constable Charters visit.

Earlier in the day, Pawley had been charged with an offence of Burglary at 'The Bakers Arms', by entering a secure store and stealing one cadaver, the property of The Realm, and one grey tarpaulin, the property of Charles Church, Boatman.

Pawley now sat, shivering no doubt, in the holding cells for prisoners, located outside the courtyard entrance to the Great Hall, where tomorrow his case would be initially heard before Recorder Hildyard.

Likely he would be sent to the assizes, subject to the thoughts of the Grand Jury, and that Recorder Hildyard would remand him to the Borough Gaol pending his trial.

The remaining officers of the night shift looked at the two Constables, some with envy, that they had now been extracted from the normal rigors of 'nights'.

Others looked at them with suspicion, no doubt wondering whether their names had yet come to light turning stones over to locate Roberts.

Head Constable Charters entered the room, just as the shift paraded, and Beddows and Shepherd were ushered into the rear office, out of sight and hearing of their colleagues.

'Well, my good Constables; I see Mr Pawley is suitable tucked up in the yard, ready for Mr Hildyard tomorrow?' he said contentedly.

'And I am sure he is feeling very uncomfortable, sir. Seems he is fretting somewhat about how he will be received at Welford Road, after the little misunderstanding about his sexual tastes, so to speak. Probably regretting now that he appeared to us as a bit of a Molly,' grinned Beddows.

'I'm sure he will find out very quickly, Beddows, very quickly, I'm sure. I hear tell that the wardens don't take to kindly to that sort, and they are prone to make the other prisoners aware for their own safety,' said Charters. 'But we had best make the Governor aware, and keep Pawley safe until after trial - don't want him as a hostile witness if we can help it. Right then, what I want the two of you to do tonight is to try and locate the missing Mule and Cart, and no doubt somewhere nearby, we will find our large Irish friend. I suggest you start back down at Pawley's yard, as he may well be getting a visit from anxious parties,' suggested Charters.

'What did Mr Goodyer have to say about help from our County colleagues?' enquired Beddows 'If I might ask, sir?'

'Mr Goodyer has extended an invitation for Sergeants Smith and Haynes to spend some time in their company, and to broaden our search for Roberts. They are keen to assist in any way they can. I suspect that our canny Detectives are probably sitting in a hedge or barn by now, seeing what they can pick up,' replied Charters.

'If we find the missing mule and cart, and we can identify the Irishman, do you want him bringing in, or do we wait, sir?' said Beddows.

'Bring him in - we need to find that body,' said Charters. 'But tread warily; a big Irishman in the Rookeries is not going to come quietly.'

*****

108

The fog continued to ease, now more of a thick mist, as the two men set off towards Short Street. A cold one again though, and a sharp frost was again settling on the window frames and sills along the Lanes, as their breath condensed in front of the Constables' mouths and noses.

The chill wind caused Beddows to pull up his collar, and tighten the neck fastening of his Cape, in a vain attempt to keep out more of the penetrating cold, which made Shepherd's eyes water and nose run.

'Could do with a wooly hat rather than this stovepipe,' said Beddows. 'It would be a damn site warmer and more comfortable; and a nice wooly scarf for that matter too!'

'I've got ice crystals on my moustache,' said Shepherd, wiping his top lip.

'What moustache?' laughed Beddows. 'Bum fluff doesn't freeze - it's not thick enough.'

'Tonight,' stated Beddows, 'you may finally get to christen your night stick, as we will be going deeper into the Rookeries than the Irish may care for, and we may find a little resistance to our nosiness,' he explained, aware that Shepherd had not yet shown his skills or moral fortitude in a confrontation.

Shepherd felt a slight film of sweat break out, starting under the rough shirt collar with which he had been issued, and which trickled down into the small of his back.

It could be anxiety, or it could be that he also wore a fetching black cardigan under his tunic, that his Aunt Sarah had just finished for him, together with the extra pair of thick woolen socks that now gave his feet a little more warmth and protection.

'Okay, Beddows,' replied Shepherd. 'You do trust me, don't you?' unaware as to how much Beddows knew of his prowess as a pugilist.

'Course I do lad. You're a chip of George's old block, I'm sure. Just don't let the scum scare you off. Stand firm, and give them something to respect. If we turn away, it just gets harder to go back the next time,' said Beddows. 'Hit them first, and hardest!'

'Might be getting colder, but the old town gets smellier every day,' grumbled Beddows. 'Too many knackers' yards and sausage men - shouldn't be in the town they shouldn't, should be in the sticks. Shit hole, that's what Leicester's becoming!'

'You're in a bad mood tonight, Beddows,' observed Shepherd, noting Beddows mood changing with every yard nearer they got.

'Just getting myself ready for the Rookeries, lad - getting a bit more fired up.' Beddows sighed.

As the two men crossed Silver Street and made their way towards East Gates, a rather large and new 'Growler'- a four wheeled cab, with shiny, new, black lacquered bodywork, and pulled by two stunning chestnut horses - slowed noticeably as it passed by them.

The driver never looked down from his elevated seat in front of the carriage, but dark velvet curtains which covered the windows, twitched once or twice, and Shepherd was convinced the occupant was observing them closely.

Once passed by, the driver called out to his horses, and at a trot they disappeared into the murk, along Cheapside.

'I'm sure we were being watched just then,' said Shepherd, feeling rather exposed.

'You're getting twitchy, my lad, it's probably just some toff coming away from Manky Lils' and making sure we weren't interested in his Growler,' replied Beddows.

'Perhaps you're right,' said Shepherd, as yet another bead of sweat ran down from his collar and sent a note to his straining bladder.

'Should have had a piss before I left the station - too much tea,' he joked.

'Do what everyone else does lad, find the nearest entry,' chuckled Beddows. 'Nobody will notice a bit more piss - they're too busy stepping over everyone else's shit. Empty your bladder now, never good to fight with a full bladder,' Beddows laughed, speaking from personal experience.

Shepherd slid in and out of the next entry, post haste, just as Beddows recommended, and felt much relieved.

Churchgate came into view, and the streets were, yet again visibly much busier than the previous two nights.

'Thursday night's always a busy one - don't know why? But it always is - and they haven't been paid yet!' said Beddows.

Churchgate and Lower Churchgate attracted many drinkers to the large numbers of hostelries, which, much like Belgrave Gate, made it a problem area for drunks and violence.

There were 246 Public houses and 94 beer shops, to the best of the Police's knowledge, in the Borough, serving the current population of about 60,000 residents and lodgers. Beer and Gin were by far the safest drinks available at the time, with the cleanliness of local water supplies being so questionable.

The working population had developed a taste for them on a monumental scale, and with new laws prohibiting the sale or consumption of alcohol past eleven at night, they were prone to hasty and heavy consumption and drunkenness often resulted, many having worked a fourteen or sixteen hour day and only finishing their labours at nine or ten p.m.

'The Cricket Players'; 'The Crown and Cushion'; 'The Fish and Quart'; 'The Malt Shovel'; 'The Northumberland House'; 'The Stonemasons Arms'; 'The Sun'; 'The Victoria' and 'The Windmill'. The list of Inns and change of title was added to almost weekly.

A bit like the butchers shops, there always seemed to be more than anyone actually needed.

As Beddows and Shepherd walked down towards the Rookeries, all the pubs were in full flow, with many of the factories nearby now letting out their workforce. The sound of cheap pianos and singing came from the odd one or two, whilst from others came the signature shouting and breaking glass and wood!

The road became so well lit with the light from their windows and the many gaslights, furnishing their pavement entrances, and meant it was almost like daytime, even with the mist.

Another hour and many more would be fighting drunk, rapidly swilling the array of beers and porters that were so popular with the parched workers.

The new Constables had become fair game for daring to prohibit their enjoyment.

But this would not be within Constables Beddows' nor Shepherd's remit for tonight.

*****

Beddows initially shook the wicket door to the front of the entrance to Pawley's yard.

This merely attracted the night watchman from Star Foundry, who had begun locking up for the night, leaning out of an upstairs window, before bellowing 'Bugger off', assuming it to be drunks trying his doors. 'Sorry Constables, thought you were drunks,' he mumbled, waving a small candle lamp in front of his face.

'Not any more,' laughed Beddows in reply. 'Seen anyone coming or going today?'

'Only just got here - can't say I have,' said the elderly figure.

'Can't say or won't say, you old sod?' said Beddows, shaking his head, and knowing that old man Harris slept at the front of the foundry, in a room off the front 'area' – the lower yard.

'Mr Beddows, what are you implying? Don't pay to stick your nose in down here. It don't take long for certain people to take offence, and I want to see my 60th in one piece,' Harris moaned, before pulling the window to and securing the Foundry.

'Seems like everyone knows you, Beddows, and you seem to know quite a lot of people down here,' said Shepherd.

'That's what working a beat does for you - for good or bad,' Beddows replied. 'Some will try and help, some are too scared to help, and some don't give a 'monkeys'. Make it what you can lad, make it what you can.'

The pair walked slowly past 'The Fish and Quart' - already full to the gunnels; on, past drinkers who had spilled outside onto the corner of Churchgate and Mansfield Street, who gave them the usual jeers and taunts, then round towards Short Street.

The gates at the rear of Pawley's yard appeared to be forced and ajar, and inside a fire burned and flames were clearly spreading, with something in the middle of the yard well alight.

'Quick, Shepherd – sound your rattle! We need some help,' said Beddows, knowing he had left his behind in the Station.

Shepherd reached into his cape, and released the heavy wooden rattle from his belt, before spinning it around, above his head, on its coarse handle. Beddows wished he could do likewise with his, as he would fail any 'appointments' checks if they made a point later, but it proved bulky and often got in the way - and so often remained left behind.

Constable Ward, who lived in Butt Close Lane, just opposite the Star Foundry, had been patrolling in the proximity of 'The Cherry Tree' Inn - very close probably, and the first Constable to respond, closely followed by Constable Wheatley, who had been patrolling on nearby Burleys Lane.

'Send for the Fire Company,' shouted Beddows, 'this will spread quickly if we don't stop it soon,' and taking charge of the other Constables.

Two keen young urchins nearby, no doubt desperate to watch the firemen at work - which remained an unusual event, ran off to the Midland Counties Fire Office in Market Street, where two fire engines were retained, and seemed to return far too quickly to have delivered the message.

The Midland Counties Fire Office Force consisted of a Superintendent, two subordinate officers, and twenty-eight firemen. The duty shift lived in the Fire Office buildings so were always available to turn out, and surprisingly, they could do so in double quick time.

Both engines were state of the art four wheeled horse-drawn wagons, with lined water tanks on top, the units painted red, with the company crests thereon. They carried three or four short ladders, and they pumped the water out by large handles, manually, and under pressure, through their hoses.

Within five minutes, the sound of horses' hooves, and bells could be heard descending Churchgate.

Beddows and Shepherd stood back inside Mansfield Street, and watched as the firemen prepared to attack the fire.

The Inspector of Engines constantly shouted orders at the men, and in comparatively little time they had extinguished the fire, preventing its spread beyond Pawley's meager enterprise.

'Constables, over here,' called Inspector Martin, the senior fireman in charge. 'I think you will want to see this.'

Smoke still hung or drifted about on the swirling mist, but the smell, instantly recogniseable to the nose of Beddows indicated the nature of the fuel on the fire, and Shepherd also thought he detected a recent familiar stench.

In the yard, and now partially burnt out, lay an ageing wooden cart, most of which the fire had devoured, blackened and spread over the rough ash floor of the yard.

In the debris to the left of the bed of the cart, lay a small, badly burned body. The only identifiable part looked like a decomposed, bloated leg, which appeared to be that of the young boy from the river, and which the flames had not devoured.

'Looks like our corpse has returned - and someone's tried to save the need for burying the poor little sod,' said Beddows, peering through the dim light from hand-held lamps that had been brought from the fire engines.

'So much for hiding the corpse somewhere safe,' said Shepherd, somewhat in disbelief.

*****

With Tanky Smith and Black Tommy not readily available, Beddows had sent for a Sergeant.

Aware of the absence of Detective Sergeants Smith and Haynes, Head Constable Charters yet again chose to attend the scene.

115

'Can't I leave you two to do anything without another disaster occurring?' said Charters, with a shake of his head. 'Am I correct, and someone has tried to dispose of evidence?'

'Sort of, sir,' responded Beddows, 'but this time they've brought something or someone back first. Looks like our corpse, or rather, what's left of him.'

Charters looked at the yard, noting the position of the cart, and the extent of the fire centred around it. Still visible below the remains of decomposing leg, a small section of grey tarpaulin had also been left as evidence.

'Not much left for Coroner Mitchell now, boys?' said Charters, in a jocular manner.

'Clumsy job though,' said Beddows. 'Not got rid of the evidence properly at all. What I am really interested in now, is where we might find the missing Mule. What's the betting it's back in Delaney's yard? That would be an interesting twist,' he suggested to Charters.

'Let's go and have a look then, shall we?' said Charters.

'Constable Ward, you stay here with this mess, whilst we have a gander a bit deeper into the Rookeries' ordered Charters.

'Sir, what about the leg and what's left of the body - all the bones and stuff?' said a green looking Constable Ward.

'Find something to wrap or box it all up in - and then take it back to the Station. Don't want to lose this again do we?' Charters smiled.

'I shouldn't try and use any of Pawley's coffins though. They won't get back as far as the station before it falls to bits,' Beddows quipped.

'And don't leave it lying around where my good wife is going to be made ill. There's a large metal coal box at the back of the station scullery, put it in that, then lock it all away in one of the cells. One of our good doctors will have to confirm that it is the boy,' Charters directed.

Charters, Beddows and Shepherd made for an unusual sight - three Constables - walking abreast along Mansfield Street, making a beeline for Delaney's' timber yard which occupied a small space between Sandiacre Street and Abbey Street, just beyond the almshouses at Cock Muck Hill, and opposite Baker Street.

Constables would normally only patrol singly; unless they were a pair 'in company' as with Beddows and Shepherd, or a Sergeant and a Constable after a point; but three? Unheard of!

Beddows felt genuinely sorry for the aged occupants of Cock Muck Hill.

The six alms houses were meant to be salvation for a limited number of the Parish poor, supported by the Guardians.

As the Irish had poured into Leicester, the Rookeries took shape, swallowing up Cock Muck Hill, and isolating the frail old Leicester folk, within the midst of a secretive and protective Irish community.

The three men arrived at Delaney's Timber yard at about half past ten.

The gates were locked and padlocked through a large chain, but a small light burnt in a hut that had been constructed just in from the gates, and the door to which left ajar.

Out in the fog, distant Irish voices could be heard, calling out a warning that the Crushers were close by.

Stood next to the hut, a scabby mule, which looked rather sweaty, with pale sweat marks drying on its flanks where straps from its harness had sat, looked like it had recently been worked hard.

'You in the hut - open up!' called out Beddows, as together with Mr Charters and Shepherd, the three men peered over the wooden fence and into the yard.

From their vantage point, a large figure could be seen sat inside the door.

Even in the mist and darkness, obviously this was a huge man, well over 6 feet tall and more, and probably as wide. Dressed in shabby trousers and a dark stained shirt, that probably hadn't seen a wash for years; he sat motionless.

'Open up; Police Constables!' called out Beddows, but the man didn't move at all.

'Over the fence then, lads; have your truncheons ready. If he does wake up, heaven help us,' said Charters.

Shepherd clambered over with ease, but the older men made heavy going of the climb, making sure their cumbersome tunic tails did not tangle, and Beddows could now feel splinters where there shouldn't be splinters, and he had a notion he had just heard his breeches split or tear.

As the Constables moved towards the hut, it became apparent as to why the man had not responded; the dirt was recent, and was interlaced with the man's own blood.

A large, depressed, open wound to the top of his head could now be seen, and the man was clearly dead.

However, an obvious and distinctive lack of blood, suggested this was not where he had been killed.

As the three men became acclimatised to the light in the hut, the size of the head wound became more visible, and an open fracture of the skull had exposed part of the man's brain.

A throat wound, not quite as apparent in view of his head lolling onto his chest, became visible, and as Beddows lifted the man's chin, the enormity of the wound shocked all three men, reaching almost from just beyond his Adam's apple on one side, and round to the ear on the other, cutting the lobe, and so deep that the head lolled back alarmingly, and with little resistance, when moved.

A short length of rope loosely draped around his neck, hung like a spent noose.

'If this is the man that Pawley took with him, and he has set fire to the body on the cart, and made a mess of it, he's come back here with Delaney's mule, and somebody's silenced him. We know Pawley had been threatened,' suggested Charters in his gruffer Geordie accent.

'Looks something like that to me, sir,' said Beddows. 'Although, if he didn't bring the mule back, whoever killed him probably brought them both back together, and that would explain his being murdered someplace else.'

'So, if this is all connected to the dead boy, somebody's really frightened, and they are being extremely ruthless, setting fire to the body, and killing again,' said Charters.

'Sir, something's been bothering me since I saw the first corpse, and I now believe I know what it is. Physician Wilson I believe has caused some confusion,' said Shepherd.

'And how so is that?' said Charters.

'He described having seen a body in Anatomy who had also been murdered. He said that the killer had held the man from behind and cut the throat from left to right, and so therefore would be right handed. I couldn't initially recognise the problem but the cut on the boy looked similar to this, if not the same.'

'Go on,' said Charters.

'The short side of the wound starts on the right side of the throat, and extends across the throat and tails off towards the left ear, which on this one is also cut. The killer is left handed if he cut him from behind, the knife being pulled towards the ear as it finished cutting , so by somebody left handed!' suggested Shepherd.

'An interesting observation, young Mr Shepherd, and worth looking at further with another Physician,' said Charters.

'But why the blow to the head, and the rope?' said Beddows.

'He's a big bugger, and on the strong side. Look at the damage to his fists. This man has been a fighter, or still was, until recently - and built like a bull,' said Shepherd...'and I think I might know what caused the head wound, too, sir.'

'And?' said Charters.

'The man has been pole-axed - just like you would a beast - to stun them, just before you slaughter them, by cutting their throat. This man has been slaughtered. A pole - axe will make that fracture as it penetrates the brain. A slaughter man will tether a beast or chain it first, then strike it with the pole-axe when it's constrained,' said Shepherd.

'That's a wicked way to kill someone, sir,' said Beddows, 'wicked - but gives us some idea as to who we might be looking for. Spoiled for choice with slaughterers in the Borough at present, some dodgy Irish ones included.'

'This is all rather much an assumption, but it makes sense. Let's get a different Physician down here and see what we've got and what he thinks to Mr Shepherd's observations,' said Charters. 'We could do with either Mr Buck or Mr Barclay if they are available.'

*****

John Buck and John Barclay had both been appointed Medical Inspectors for the Police. This role allowed them to inspect the major threats to health that burdened the Borough, and they had powers to close down premises, and get things cleaned up.

They were both used to working closely with the Police, and John Buck also, as a General Practitioner, had been licensed to undertake Post-mortem medical examinations that would give far more detail as to how deaths occurred. He had previously been invaluable in this still emerging practice.

John Buck was at his address at 1 Lower Charles Street, together with a colleague, Thomas Hamilton, who had just come to Leicester, also a qualified Surgeon General Practitioner, and was presently being groomed to work with Buck, at Leicester Royal Infirmary, where Buck held a resident Surgeon's post.

'We have a murder in Mansfield Street, Doctor, and Mr Charters would like your attendance,' Sergeant Wright from the night shift explained.

'My colleague and I will be along shortly, once we have our equipment,' replied Buck, ushering Hamilton towards two black leather bags, side by side near to the front hall coat stand.

Hamilton, young and dashing, with blonde curly hair, and bright blue eyes, which seemed to glow when entertained with the prospect of attending a murder, was about 5 feet seven inches tall, and of wiry build, and elegantly but stylishly 'dressed down' for his work.

Buck, on the other hand, a little older at about 30 years of age, and taller at about five feet ten, with an early receding hairline, an oval face, and the fashionable large sideburns and he also seemed elegantly 'dressed down' for work.

*****

At five to Midnight, a cab pulled up outside Delaney's yard, which was now lit up a lot brighter, thanks to extra lamps that had been borrowed from Mr Carnell, the Ironmonger, round In Belgrave Gate. Buck and Hamilton dismounted from the cab, and told the driver to wait.

'Good evening, Mr Charters,' said Buck. 'May I introduce you to my new colleague, Mr Hamilton, who is joining the Infirmary? Interestingly, he has become one of the country's most proficient new medical examiners, and has a good eye within Post-mortem examinations.'

'Welcome to you, sir,' said Charters. 'Please don't think that murder is a frequent occurrence in Leicester, as it may seem, if you have read the papers this last day or so - but we appear to have a little problem on our hands at present. Come this way please.'

Charters led the two men to the corpse in the hut, and introduced them to Constables Beddows and Shepherd.

'Young Shepherd here has a theory about our killings, and it will be interesting to hear what you gentlemen think,' said Charters.

'We can make a cursory examination of the body here, but it is too dark and too exposed for how I think a Post-mortem should be done. We will look at all the evidence, and then complete a full Post-mortem for Mr. Mitchell later on in a proper examination room. We will need the body taking to The Infirmary to my rooms,' said Buck.

'What a brute!' said Hamilton. 'A comparative giant of a man!' at which he took out a measuring tape and began to measure the man's height. 'Six feet four or so he would be standing up; and about three hundred pounds.'

'There are two obvious major wounds, either of which could have killed him - or both of course. We will know more when we dissect him,' said Buck. 'Looks like a blow to the head to stun him, or that would have killed him, then cutting the throat finished the job off and make sure he's dead. Don't know about the rope yet, doesn't look like he's been hanged.'

'That's what our young Constable Shepherd here thinks,' said Charters.

'Interesting head wound! You need to look for a weapon, something that could be wielded, with a pointed head or projection from the handle. Something like a large lump-hammer. Again we'll know more later on,' said Hamilton.

'I was thinking about a slaughter mans' pole-axe, Doctor?' suggested Shepherd.

'Could well be,' said Hamilton.

'Who's a clever boy then?' Beddows mocked Shepherd, tapping him on his back, now showing signs of great observation and deduction. *'A natural Detective,'* Beddows thought.

'We could do with getting this man wrapped up or boxed and taken back to the Infirmary - my cab is not big enough,' said Buck.

*****

At about one a.m., Charters, Beddows and Shepherd were gathered in the private rooms of John Buck at the Royal Infirmary.

Shepherd had not been into the Infirmary before, and was surprised at its size and capacity, considering it was run purely on contributions of benefactors around the Borough and County, or so he had read.

Buck and Hamilton had a small but sparsely furnished room at the rear of Buck's office, and in it stood a long, heavy, solid wooden table, like a large butcher's block, on which lay the body of the dead man from Delaney's yard.

The floor had been liberally covered in saw dust, and in the corner stood a container of water. The room struck Beddows as much like a butchers shop would look.

'We are about to begin our dissecting, if any of you gentlemen would prefer to leave?' Buck smiled.

He and Hamilton wore the same attire in which they had attended the scene, but had each donned a leather apron, which shielded much, but not all, of their chests and legs.

At the foot of the body stood a small table with a note-book and a tray with tools, including saws, drills, and precision sharp thin knives, together with some large and ugly looking shears, which reminded Shepherd of lopping shears from the farm nearby to his home.

'I think we shall be alright, Mr Buck,' said Charters, 'or we should be by now.' As a hardened former Detective himself in the Metropolitan Force, and familiar with Post-mortem examinations, he would now be interested to see how Shepherd faced up.

The body was that of a large white male, over six feet four inches tall, of very heavy muscular build. The head was shaven bald, and an open fracture of the skull was visible at the rear and crown of the skull, which appeared to have a 'diamond shape' entry wound, and a significant depression of the skull bones allowing the brain to be viewed.

The neck appeared scuffed and the marks were in keeping with a lot of movement of the rope, still in situ, and suggested it had been employed as a means of security and not of hanging or strangulation.

There was a long and shockingly deep incision to the throat, which commenced two inches to the right of the man's larynx, and ended, exiting over and across the dead man's left ear lobe.

The body showed signs of grazing on both knees, and stomach, and the whole body covered in bruises, suggesting a sustained beating.

Several knuckles on both hands appeared to be broken.

'Let's have a look at this head wound first,' said Buck, reaching for the tools of his trade, and inviting Mr Hamilton to the table.

Hamilton took a slim, long bladed knife, and made an incision around the man's scalp, pulling the flap he had made forward, over the wound and over the dead man's face, revealing the skull.

Shepherd looked decidedly green for a few seconds, which both Charters and Beddows noted. Beddows quickly spoke. 'Want a bit of pork pie to settle your stomach, Shepherd?' grinning broadly. *Not that Beddows was feeling the least bit squeamish himself.*

Shepherd looked towards Mr Charters, then at Beddows sternly; 'I'm fine, just a little warm, after the cold air outside,' he lied, manfully.

'There are a series of expanding fractures from the centre of the main head wound, which radiate out almost in four diagonal directions, together with some small fragmentation of the bone around the point of impact. This has been the result of a massive impact with a heavy pointed object, with a square of diamond shaped pointed head,' explained Buck.

'The exterior of the brain has been perforated, and the wound extends to a depth of about three inches through the mass of the brain. This blow alone would have or could have killed this man instantly,' he said. 'Let's get the top of the skull off and take a closer look,' starting to work delicately with the saw in his right hand.

'The rope burns are just loose friction burns,' said Hamilton. 'He was not hanged, in my opinion, but tethered, such as you would a beast.'

The men then examined the wound to the dead man's throat.

'The wound has penetrated the full depth of the skin across the larynx, which has also been severed, brutally. The lightest incision is two inches to the right of centre of the larynx, and the wound gets deeper to the full depth, across the larynx, and through the left side of the throat and then through the left ear lobe, where it appears to be drawn off and exits the body - In my opinion,' said Buck.

'If this man has been held from behind, you are looking for a left -handed killer. It would be almost impossible to create exactly the same wound from a slashing type attack from in front of the man. This wound would or could also have killed him, but he would have taken some minutes to bleed to death. Most of the blood on his clothing is seepage from the two wounds rather than slow blood loss, so he would likely have died instantly from the blow to the head, and the throat cut to make sure he was dead.'

'I would concur with that observation, also,' said Hamilton, much to Buck's relief.

'So Shepherd's hypothesis regarding a *slaughtering* appears to be sound?' suggested Charters.

'That would sound plausible and most likely to me,' said Buck 'and given the lack of blood at the crime scene, slaughtered somewhere else.'

'He has recent cuts and grazes on his knuckles - and the knuckles and fingers on his right hand are smashed to pieces. Looks like he tried to defend himself, or he had fought recently. If you discard the bruises as evidence of his Pugilist status - they are probably slightly older than the fatal injuries, and there is a lot of old damage to his other hand also,' said Hamilton.

The men took note of the man's tattoos, in the event that someone might report him missing, or be able to identify him. Charters and Beddows anticipated that they would be met with blank looks from within the Rookeries, but someone amongst their snitches might come up with a name.

His body displayed an array of different sized shamrock leaves, which heightened the likelihood that he was an Irishman.

Two women's names, 'Eileen' and 'Siobhan' had been crudely scratched through, suggesting past amours and further Irish connections.

'Fancy forever' indicated an obvious link to the pugilists, Shepherd suggested.

'Property of Black Annis' had been tattooed in larger, deeper lettering across the man's back, and between his massive shoulder blades.

'Our man is into witchcraft, or of a coven?' suggested Buck, smiling inquisitively, connecting the tattoo to the legend of the Witch of Dane Hills.

Buck and Hamilton continued to complete a full Post-mortem examination of the man, making a 'Y' shaped incision, from the top and front of each shoulder to the sternum, and then down from the sternum to the crotch, before crunching through the rib-cage with the shears which Shepherd had looked at earlier, and removing the sternum and adjoined ribs, thus allowing them access to the internal organs.

'He has had a damn good feed before he died, and it's not your normal Rookery mush. There are big chunks of some sort of meat, probably steak, and potatoes, and they had not been swallowed long before his demise,' said Hamilton.

'His liver is enormous, and his bladder is full to bursting; a big drinker I would suggest,' said Buck, 'and well looked after by someone.'

After the routine examination of the guts, Hamilton rolled the man onto his side. 'Well I'll be!' he exclaimed

'Gentlemen, this man may be big, he may be considered a giant, and he may have been considered such a threat that he was executed beast style - but he has also been buggered - although I cannot say whether that occurred during, or just before his execution, but soon around time of death. I would suggest from the state of his backside, that he has been a practicing sodomite for some time.'

'So,' said Charters. 'We have a giant of an Irishman, who could knock all three of us out in one go, who has been tethered, pole-axed, and slaughtered, and before, during or after, has been sodomised. I dread to think what our killer is capable of, but he looks a fearsome adversary.'

'If he has been a practicing sodomite, it is interesting that this may connect further to our friend Salt and his associates,' added Beddows.

'We need to find him next, and that irritating Sergeant Roberts. I take it as we have heard nothing yet from the esteemed Sergeants Smith and Haynes that they are still trying to track him down,' suggested Charters.

'And thank you, Gentlemen, for your most illuminating examination,' said Charters. 'By the way, we have a second body, or rather badly burned remains of another of our current victims, which we would like you to have a look at if you would. He had been seen previously by Physician Wilson, from the Newarkes,' he added.

'Not Joseph Wilson, by any chance?' enquired Hamilton, incredulously.

'That is his name, sir,' replied Beddows.

'Arrogant, pompous and careless Physician, may I warn you, Mr Charters,' said Hamilton. 'Came up from London just a few months before I did, and moves in posh circles - has posh backers. But I cannot understand why, as he is a terrible Surgeon.'

'On what basis can you say that, Mr Hamilton?' enquired Charters.

'When we were at Guys, he conducted a Post-mortem on a classy young female prostitute that had been murdered in the grounds of one of the College halls. He deliberately misled your Colleagues in London, and they suspected he was in the pocket of an Irish Businessman, the Police's prime suspect, but he proclaimed inexperience and made a bit of a fool of himself. Would have still been in London and earning a pretty penny no doubt, rather than coming to the provinces - not that there's anything wrong with Leicester, of course,' Hamilton blushed.

'A strange co-incidence?' said Shepherd. 'A dubious Physician; misleading guidance regarding the killer's dexterity; what are the chances of that happening?'

'*We* sent the locals to fetch a local Physician,' said Beddows, going through the events of New Years day again in his own memory.

'So we did,' said Shepherd, 'but he took a long time coming, and didn't seem that keen to help as I recall - wouldn't do a Post-mortem.'

'Another necessary line of enquiry, I would suggest,' said Charters. 'I'm running out of Detectives.'

'I take it you'll be keeping me and Shepherd on this case then, sir?' said Beddows, now confident that they were back in Charters' good books.

'Do I have any choice?' Charters responded. 'Now, off to bed with you, as I want you back in the Station by eight o'clock in the morning. I feel we are in for a busy day.'

*****

Eight o'clock a.m. on Friday the 4th of January, and the fog had reduced to a light mist, and there were weak rays of intense, white sunlight, trying to burn their way through the diminishing, but as ever, sulphurous, blanket lying over the Borough, giving the visible disc of the Sun itself a yellow tinge.

When Beddows and Shepherd arrived back in the station, they were ushered in to Charters' office, where a pair of bleary eyed Detectives sat, tea in hand.

'Looks like you two have had a bad night?' laughed Beddows.

'Haven't seen a bed in two days,' said Tanky Smith, stretching and rubbing his eyes.

Black Tommy's head dropped and he suddenly sat upright, clearly in the throes of nodding-off, much to the amusement of Shepherd.

'Not bleedin' funny from where I'm sitting,' grunted Haynes. 'Your bleedin' Job and we get the rotten bit. You owe us a wet when we get done next.'

Both were dressed in labourers clothing, and smelled of rotting vegetation, from somewhere they had obviously been keeping observations. Tanky had acquired a full beard and Black Tommy a large bushy moustache, and had matching flat caps - never looking the same twice.

'Well, gentlemen,' said Charters. 'Now the fun part begins.'

'Today, I want to arrest Mr Salt, as he is now a more apparent and valuable cog in our enquiry, and that is your job,' Indicating to Beddows and Shepherd.

130

'I believe he is actually in the Mayor's parlour, as we speak, with Thomas Nunnelly, his worship The Mayor, and some hoi polloi from the Midland Counties Railway Company. Would be a rather embarrassing time to arrest him would it not? Perhaps if you popped your head in, and asked him to come and see you when the meeting finished, if he would be so kind?' suggested Charters.

'That will get the tongues wagging,' replied Beddows.

'As for my sleepy eyed Detectives, I want you to get the next Locomotive to London, and go and see our Colleagues at Scotland Yard. Get some money from the Station Sergeant, and get a few things, I expect you'll be down there a couple of days. I want to know everything there is about Physician Joseph Wilson and the case of a murdered prostitute near Guys Hospital last year,' said Charters.

'Yes, sir,' said Smith.

'I would like to know the suspect; Wilson's backer - we've been told he mixes in high places. It may be a co-incidence, but I want to know before we go and talk to him next. The good news is you can have a sleep in the carriage, so long as you wake up when you get to the other end. We will send a telegram to let them know you will be arriving,' directed Charters.

'You can rely on us, sir,' said Smith.

'And can I suggest a shave and a wash before you get *properly dressed* for our friends in London? I have a meeting with the good Thomas Thompson shortly, who will tell me all about these adverts and our missing Children, lest we forget that they are the reason that we are making all these other enquires,' Charters emphasised.

* * * * *

131

Constables Beddows and Shepherd donned their Top Hats and in best presented uniform, walked across the yard towards the Mayor's parlour, on the ground floor at the far end of the yard.

The yard side of the Mayor's parlour was adorned with ornate leaded windows, which pre-announced their arrival to a visibly sheepish Salt.

Beddows knocked on the door to the parlour, and awaited approval to enter.

'Come in,' came a robust voice, which turned out to be his Worshipful Mayor Nunnelly himself. 'I take it this is something of some great importance, to disturb Borough business, Constables?' he grunted, looking over his glasses, precariously perched on the end of his nose.

Salt sat in a little built-in desk and chair in the far left corner of the room, taking notes, by the look of it, whilst the Mayor and some posh looking gentlemen perused large drawings and maps spread out on the large desk which filled the centre of the room.

'It is Mr Salt we wish to speak to, your Worship; and of a matter of some gravity, as he is well aware. However, Mr Charters appreciates we must not impede Borough business, so after the meeting we would be obliged if Mr Salt would stroll over to the station and avail himself to us upon his return,' Beddows proposed.

'Some gravity? What's all this about, Salt? I hope we're not in for another Workhouse embarrassment?' Nunnelly sounded skeptical.

'I'm sure not,' said Salt, sheepishly, his hooked nose pointing at the floor, avoiding the direct gaze of the Constables.

'Oh Mr Salt, I didn't recognize you; thought you must have just popped out of the room for a while,' Beddows said sarcastically. 'We'll be seeing you after the meeting then, Mr Salt?'

'Good day to you, officers,' concluded Mayor Nunnelly, indicating some degree of annoyance and embarrassment at the interruption.

'I shouldn't like to be in Mr Salt's shoes, with his Worship. Bet he gets the grand inquisition before we get our hands on him,' whispered Beddows.

*****

Whilst the Constables had been with the Mayoral party, Mr Thomas Thompson had arrived for Mr Charters, and taken by him to his personal abode, across at the rear of the yard.

'Tea, my dear Thompson?' said Charters. 'I know you newspaper chaps have a reputation for hard drink early in the day, but I would hate to offend and not offer something stronger, should you prefer?' teased Charters in his broad Geordie accent

'Never before Eleven, Robert, not even with other hardened drinkers!' replied Thompson.

'Touché,' smiled Charters. 'And what, prey, have you managed to ascertain for us from your advertisements?'

'Have you any idea how far we have gone back, and how many advertisements match your request?' said Thompson.

'Ten? Twenty?' said Charters.

'There are over thirty similar advertisements, averaging about one each month, for the last two years or so,' replied Thompson, 'and they are all strikingly similar'.

'And in what way are they similar?' said Charters.

'The adverts all start off with 'Wanted; respectable woman wanted for young child', each and every one of them,' replied Thompson.

'The strange thing is, the advert asks interested parties to make contact with a Mrs O'Crowley and the address is given as Blaby Workhouse, at Enderby,' said Thompson. 'Here, I have had them all copied for you, with the date, source, and wording. I hope they will be of some help.'

'I am sure they will prove significant. When was the last advertisement placed?' said Charters.

'In our Saturday edition, on the twenty-second of December last; nearly two weeks ago,' replied Thompson.

'About the time our recent victim would have met his demise; Interesting!' said Charters.

*****

Detective Sergeant Herbert Kettle, the other *reliable* Detective in The Borough, worked regularly with Tanky Smith and Tommy Haynes.

Charters had called for him to take charge of the latest murder, and in particular to look into the Irish Slaughter House trade, and slaughter men with a history of violence, here In the Borough, or back in Ireland, and possible connections with Delaney's Yard, or the suspects Pawley and Salt.

Kettle had a number of trustworthy snitches who had helped out previously with Irish crime enquiries.

Charters felt comfortable that he had most bases covered, with the exception of Sergeant Roberts, currently still *absent*.

*****

Charters sat at his private desk, in the house at the rear of the yard, quiet and away from prying eyes and ears.

He had set up on his wall, a large blackboard, and a supply of white chalk.

He wrote on the board, the names of his present suspects, Pawley, Salt, Roberts and Wilson.

He had two victims which he marked as v1 and v2.

He had three crime scenes, The River, Pawley's workshop and Delaney's yard.

He had a tenuous link to Blaby Workhouse and one Mrs O'Crowley.

He had a tenuous link to an Irish businessman and a murder and a possible 'v3' in London.

He began to join up each suspect with each victim, scenes, and any known associations he could determine.

He felt sure Pawley, a relatively minor player, had been coerced into disposing of the body.

He felt confident that Salt would prove to be involved up to his neck, as would be Roberts, but could not see Salt as a killer. And, Roberts evidently corrupt, for sure now; and those two were probably in each other's pockets, but Salt would be easier to break presently, he thought.

Now he needed to bide time for the information from Smith and Haynes before he could ascertain to what degree, if any, Wilson might be involved.

Who would pay eight guineas just to have a body stolen?

Who he really wanted to identify, as a priority, was the man with the money behind all this. He wrote *'Eight Guineas'* at the centre of the board, in thicker lettering, and drew a circle around the words.

*****

Beddows sat in the corner of the yard, out of sight of the rear entrance to The Mayor's parlour.

Shepherd had gone out onto the corner of Town Hall Lane and St Martin's West, where he could see a front door to the side of the Great Hall , now rarely used, and also the bottom exit from steps, which led down from the Library and the upper floor of the Town Hall.

Beddows had briefed him earlier what to be on the lookout for.

Beddows had become aware that the meeting that had been taking place in the Mayor's parlour had ended, and he had seen His worship Mr Nunnelly take his visitors through towards the Great Hall, and by the stairs up to the Borough Offices above.

He had also seen Daniel Salt scurrying around the mayor's parlour, pacing backwards and forwards, contemplating his next move, holding his head in his hands more than once - before moving from the room and upstairs, and out of Beddows' sight.

Shepherd first became aware of a familiar figure, slipping out of the rarely used door at the side of the Great Hall and onto Town Hall Lane, the clock just chiming Midday.

Shepherd stepped out and across Salt's path, as head down, he scurried towards the centre of the town. This, the first time Shepherd had seen him dressed as a man, and in a grubby suit with tails, faded grey shirt, and a stained neckerchief, he considered he looked shabby for a Borough official.

'Going somewhere are we, Mr Salt? I thought we had an appointment?' said Shepherd.

'Constable Shepherd, I thought Mr Beddows had meant *any time* after the meeting had ended,' said Salt, lying through his teeth.

'Daniel Salt, I am arresting you on suspicion of being involved in procuring persons to steal a body, by means of a burglary, at 'The Bakers Arms' and I require you to return with me to the Police Station to answer those charges,' said Shepherd, grabbing Salt by the scruff of the neck and marching him back through St Martin's West and into the Station.

Salt looked as pale as death itself, Shepherd noticed.

'Don't know what you're on about Constable, but wait until the Mayor finds out about this,' said Salt.

'I'm sure Mr Charters will be advising his worship, Mr Nunnelly, and probably, right now,' said Shepherd. 'I understand he already has had cause to question your honesty?'

'That was a long time ago, and nothing was proven,' responded Salt, sharply.

'Not that time perhaps, but this time you are not going to be so lucky, me thinks,' Shepherd smiled, shaking his head.

Beddows walked in, also smiling broadly, just as Salt was presented to Sergeant Sheffield.

'Well done lad, always nice to feel your first collar - especially when it's got such a scrawny little occupant.'

*****

Herbert Kettle had made his way down to 'The Artillery Man' in Humberstone Gate, the heart of animal keeping and slaughtering in the town centre, and location for a large number of the most productive, such as Cooks Yard, Pickering's Yard and Plough Yard.

There were still far more pig keepers than Kettle could understand, with so many pigs slaughtered, and so few of the population that could afford proper pork meat.

The cattle and sheep were more often bought at the Cattle Market on a Wednesday, and herded through the Borough to whichever Slaughter man would be contracted to kill them.

There were twenty-seven Butchers shops within two hundred yards of the Cole Hill and Assembly Rooms, each of whom bought the animals to be slaughtered, before butchering them for sale in their shops.

'Just who is eating all this meat?' puzzled Kettle, aware that even on his Sergeant's wage, he could not afford expensive cuts, and more often than not he was not that keen, having seen the way some of the meat was handled.

Kettle bought two pints of warm foaming bitter, and went and settled in a booth at the back of the pub, with his back against the rearmost wall, and from where he could see all of the comings and goings.

Detectives should have been born with eyes in the backs of their heads as well as the front, and then they could have sat anywhere. But a back wall gave added safety; and Kettle felt comfortable here.

He quickly examined the change he had been given, knowing that it would not be unusual for the staff to take a little extra coin for themselves - even from Policemen.

Shortly, a stocky figure crossed the bar, bumping in to several disgruntled drinkers, before settling into the bench opposite Kettle, his wide girth making it difficult to squeeze through the small gaps left between the seated groups around the small Copper topped tables.

'How do, Porky?' said Kettle. 'Looks like you've had a busy day?'

Elijah 'Porky' Black, was a local pig keeper, and lived above his pigs in a two roomed hovel in a small, pokey yard off St James

Street, number 3a, or, as *he* referred to it, 'his little bit of Heaven'.

Porky by name and by nature, he stood only about five feet four inches high, but appeared wider than his height. Red faced and always cover in angry pustules, with bushy grey sideburns and thinning hair and immensely muscular around the arms and chest, as befitting a man of his trade. His flattened and broad nose added an unfortunate twist to his nickname.

Porky, covered from head to toe in blood and gore, had obviously put one or two of his pigs to the knife. His hairy forearms were matted dark red, and smelt of blood and innards, from where he had reached into the throat after cutting it, to grab the pig's windpipe and breaking its neck - his preferred way of putting the pig out of its misery.

Oddly, he looked more in keeping with the other drinkers, most of who appeared to be slaughter men or butchers, and it was Sergeant Kettle who looked out of place, and unusually clean in contrast with the other clientele.

'What do you know about our Irish friends, and their slaughter men?' said Kettle.

'Don't have much to do with them Mr Kettle,' replied Porky. 'Bad buggers those Paddies - treat their animals all wrong they do. Won't hear a friendly word said about them along the gate here; they all hate them; vicious bastards they are!'

'What about our lot down here. Any of them scare you the same way?' said Kettle.

'Our slaughterers are all gentlemen Mr Kettle - humane and quick -just like me. All learned from the same teachers, suppose,' grinned Porky, his few teeth, broken and bad, emphasised by his bad breath whenever he looked at you and spoke, or more often than not, grunted.

'Who would be handy with a pole-axe?' said Kettle.

'Any of them what's killing cattle. Need to stun them big buggers first - not like the pig and sheep slaughterers. Mind you, the Paddies use them to put down their nags too - when they're too old or have stopped earning them coin at the races. Never buy meat from near the Rookeries, Mr Kettle, probably not what you think.'

'Any of the Leicester slaughterers involved with 'The Fancy' at the moment?' said Kettle.

'One or two has had fights with 'em, one or two has done alright and made a few shillings. One or two of them has forgotten that they were Irish once. That Dick Cain, him that runs 'The Castle' in Gallowtree Gate, he's got a few good sorts that train or spar down there, and who are still well in with them.'

'Thought he was all dead straight these days and giving his fists a well-earned rest?' said Kettle.

'Might have stopped fighting, and runs a nice Inn, but like I say, he's got some good lads that will have a crack at them,' said Porky.

'Anyone from the slaughterhouses got any bad blood with the Irish going on?' said Kettle

'Bad blood?' said Porky.

'Bad enough to brain one of them?' said Kettle.

'Them Paddies does that to each other, don't need any help from our lads' laughed Porky, spitting warm ale over Kettle's face, simultaneously blowing it out of his nostrils, nearly choking to death in the process.

Several drinkers stopped for a moment and watched Porky coughing and spluttering, before carrying on drinking.

'Look at that lot Mr Kettle, wouldn't even help a mate of theirs get his breath back, nosey bastards. Could do with another 'fore I get back to me pigs - any chance?' he grinned.

'You've not really helped me much yet Porky; you're getting a bit deaf me thinks. Perhaps I should put *you* out to grass?' said Kettle.

'You ain't asked me the right question yet though have you?' Porky grinned.

'What questions is that then, me old duck?' whispered Kettle.

'Who would want to kill some *particular* big Paddy, with a pole-axe?' whispered Porky.

'Who would?' said Kettle in an equally low voice.

'Word is it is Black Annis, *making someone else disappear*; s'what they're saying down the Rookeries this morning. Dumped him down by Cock Muck Hill so I hear, opposite me ma's house,' grinned Porky.

'Black Annis is a myth; it's a story that's been told for years around here - stop kids wandering off,' said Kettle.

'This one's Irish, so they tell,' whispered Porky.

'Sounds like you don't need that second pint. You had a few for breakfast as well?'

'Honest Mr Kettle, me old Ma came by this morning and said they were shouting all over the Rookeries that Black Annis done it again.'

'Is that so? Black Annis? The legendary hag of Dane Hills?' said Kettle.

'Fancy some nice bangers Mr Kettle, the skins are that warm they're still wriggling and twitchin' - best in the street?' said Porky.

'Next time; perhaps,' at which point Detective Sergeant Kettle made good his escape, retching at the mere thought.

*****

The clock on St Martin's had just struck half past twelve, when Beddows and Shepherd escorted Daniel Salt into the office, now vacated by Mr Charters.

'I hope this won't take long, Constables. I have some rather important business with William Biggs esquire at about two-thirty,' said Salt, attempting to regain some composure.

'I think perhaps Mr Biggs will understand when he talks to his worship, Mr Nunnelly,' said Beddows. 'I also shouldn't worry about any future appointments, least not in these buildings.'

'So Mr Salt, what have you heard about your friend Mr Pawley?' said Shepherd, seeking some early signs of fear leaking.

'Mr Pawley? Oh, the man from the other night, I knew I knew his name but I am not that familiar with him,' Salt replied, desperately hoping they would be convinced.

'But Mr Salt, it was only the other morning when you and he were up to a bit of 'Three penny business' behind 'The Globe' and you told us you and he had won some money from a night together down at 'The Stokers Arms',' said Beddows.

'That was just a one off occasion. I hadn't known him before that night,' Salt replied.

'That's not what Mr Pawley has been telling us, Mr Salt. And wisely so - to save his scrawny little neck,' growled Beddows, already bored with the little man's arrogance.

'Well he's been telling you lies,' said Salt, spitting out his reply.

'That morning we stopped you, where else did you go after we let you go?' said Shepherd.

'I don't know where he went, but I went home to bed. Slept like a baby I did,' said Salt, digging himself into a deeper hole, from which he would struggle to climb out.

'What if we told you that you are a persistent little liar, Mr Salt, and that you probably can't even lie straight in that little comfortable bed of yours,' said Beddows, growing redder in the face , question by question, his blood pressure rising.

'You can't bully me again; I shall complain to the Head Constable. He is an acquaintance of mine,' blurted Salt.

'Funny that,' said Shepherd. 'It was Mr Charters who was so keen to have you brought in for this matter - very anxious he is to see you hang.'

'See me hang? What are you talking about man?' said Salt.

'That's what they do to liars *and murderers,*' said Shepherd.

'How's Mr, sorry, *Detective Sergeant* Roberts these days?' said Beddows.

'Who?' said Salt, gulping hard, sensing that the Constables already knew far more than he had imagined.

'Or is it 'sweetie'? Do you have a nice name for Mr Pawley for when you are tupping him, too?' said Beddows, crudely.

'I don't know what you mean. You're disgusting; you make me feel sick,' said Salt, stalling.

'Cut out the shit, Mr Salt, your lies are falling apart, every time you open your mouth you make matters worse. Why not just tell us what we want to know?' said Shepherd.

'How can I tell you something, when I don't know what you're talking about?' he replied.

'Who gave you eight guineas, to pay off Pawley?' said Beddows.

'Eight guineas; four to get him to do the job, and four to him when the job was done and you had made sure it was done. The four guineas that Mr Pawley tried to hide when you and he were caught out,' said Shepherd.

'That was from 'The Stokers Arms', I told you, a fancy dress prize,' said Salt, his voice becoming more rapid and high pitched; almost effeminate.

'Do you know, Mr Salt that you are starting to really annoy me now? Do you know how we get confessions from lying little shits who don't talk. Would you like me to give you a little demonstration?' snarled Beddows.

'Careful Beddows, you know what happened the last time you lost your temper. That poor man is still in The Infirmary. They say he will never be able to walk or talk, ever again. And his poor wife,' winked Shepherd, who was now getting familiar with Beddows' little ways.

'Then there was that other man before, he said you couldn't do that, when he lied - Billy Hubbard - and look what happened to him!' said Shepherd, hitching an imaginary rope high above his tilted neck, and jerking it upwards.

'They left him swinging there for hours, in front of the Borough Gaol they did,' said Beddows. 'He was just like you. Could have saved his neck, but lied. Didn't help him, so won't help you.'

'There hasn't been a hanging in the Borough in five years Mr Salt. So, they will love to see your scrawny little body swinging there. Always cheers up the poor people of Leicester. Bit of something different to watch, a good hanging,' said Shepherd, building up that imaginary image, which was no doubt starting to worry Salt.

'Lying about a capital offence is always bad news. We can always beat it out of you, but the bruises don't look very good in court, them as they can see,' said Shepherd.

'Sir Robert Peel's rules say that you cannot do that,' said Salt.

'Sir Robert bleeding Peel isn't here to watch; is he?' responded Shepherd.

'I think, Mr Salt, it is time we had the truth, cos If I don't hear some of it soon, I'm going to send my friend here out of the room and there will be no witnesses, and I know how not to leave *visible* marks,' said Beddows, convincingly.

'Since when has stealing a body been a capital offence anyway?' said Salt, tripping himself up at long last.

'Who said anything about stealing a body? I don't think I did, Mr Shepherd, did you?'

'No, Mr Beddows, nothing at all,' said Shepherd.

'So what body is this, then?' said Beddows, moving in closer on Salt, leaning forward towards the nervous prisoner.

'I am assuming this is something to do with the body that Pawley stole? Sordid little man he is. He fiddles with them when they're dead you know. That's what this is all about. He was going to give me four guineas if I promised not to tell. That's what those four guineas were for,' said Salt. 'I might prefer men's company to those disgusting Dollymops and Bunters; and I may like the feel of women's attire, but he was going to fiddle around with that dead boy. Outrageous!'

'So, Pawley was going to steal the boy's body for his own perversions?' said Shepherd, clearly unconvinced.

'Exactly,' said Salt.

'And how did he come to find out about the body, may I ask?' said Beddows.

'I had been in the Dolphin, just before I saw Pawley. Your friend Sergeant Roberts was in there, pissed as always, chatting all us 'girls' up, saying how he had been down to the most disgusting dead boy in The River - trying to make us all Whiffy,' said Salt.

'Whiffy?' said Shepherd.

'Sick, poorly,' Salt replied.

'And so you told Pawley?' said Shepherd.

'Yes,' Salt replied.

'And what did Pawley say?' said Beddows.

'He said, if I didn't give him four guineas, he would make sure the Mayor would find out about my little *dalliances,*' replied Salt.

'And when we caught you both in the yard to The Globe?' said Beddows.

'What about it?' replied Salt.

'What were you doing there?' said Beddows.

'Like I told you, telling him about the body,' said Salt.

'Why go down an alley, to tell someone about a dead body, when the man is trying to demand money from you with menaces?' said Shepherd.

'Because we heard someone coming - must have been your hobnails.'

'So you are trying to tell use, that all you did was overheard Roberts, and told Pawley because you knew he was into dead bodies, like you are in to other men, and he had the four guineas off you for telling him, because he was going to tell the Mayor about your own perversions if you didn't pay up?'

'Exactly,' replied Salt.

'Mr Salt, I don't believe a fucking word of it; try again,' said Shepherd, starting to sound rather like Beddows.

'Shepherd, best you leave the room, as Mr Salt and I are about to have a little dance and I don't want you getting involved, understand?' growled Beddows, yet again.

'Okay, Mr Beddows, whatever you say,' said Shepherd, winking discretely.

'Shepherd, stop, please don't leave me with this animal,' pleaded Salt.

'Well then, tell him the truth and stop messing him about,' said Shepherd.

'Last chance Mr Salt - last chance, I promise you,' growled Beddows.

'It was Roberts,' Salt blurted.

'What do you mean - *it was Roberts*?' said Beddows.

'It was Roberts told me to have the body removed, lost, disposed of; his words,' said Salt.

'Why should we believe this story?' said Shepherd.

'Because what I am going to tell you will not only put me in danger, it will put all of you in danger. And I need you word that you will protect me if I tell you what I know.' Salt began to cry, tears appearing on his cheeks.

'Try us,' said Beddows.

'In this Borough, there are some powerful and influential men, incredibly powerful, and some of them have the influence to get rid of people who get in their way. Your Sergeant Roberts is one of them,' Salt said.

'And?' said Beddows.

'On the night you caught us, I had been in 'The Dolphin' and I did see Mr Roberts - that bit is true.'

'Carry on,' said Beddows.

'Roberts had investigated me when the Union Workhouse unpleasantness occurred. He got some evidence against me, but traded it for some *gratuities* and has done so ever since.'

'Carry on. You've become one of his snitches?' said Beddows, unsurprised.

'Not just a snitch, but when I hear about planning applications, and there are some extremely large scale development projects going on in the Borough, I let Roberts know, and he can let some of those other most influential gentlemen know, and they can make a nice fortune every now and again by gaining such an insight, with a little inside help'.

'And what does Roberts get?' said Shepherd.

'I suspect he is in the pocket of most of these people, judging by his lifestyle. You think I am not nice, and have strange habits, but your Mr Roberts has what he wants, and who he wants, whenever he wants, women, men, boys, girls - and he throws them away like old rubbish.' Salt shuddered.

'So what happened that night?' said Shepherd.

'Roberts told me there was a nasty body in the back of the Bakers Arms. He had been asked to arrange for it to be disposed of, before anyone could make anything of it. He told me it would be worth my while, and that there was also some coins for whoever I got to do it,' replied Salt.

'And?' said Beddows.

'I was owed a favour or two by Pawley, the little cheapskate. He has been getting a bit more work for Parish Coffins than he might, of late. They are cheap and nasty, but he charges us more than it costs him and him and I have a little business out of it that we both prosper from.'

'Go on,' said Shepherd.

'So, I told Pawley I needed to speak with him. We met in town, long before you stopped us. I had already made the proposition to him, and paid him four guineas up front to steal the body. That was the four guineas he had in his pocket and he was to get four guineas later when the job was done.'

'And how did he say he was going to get rid of the body?' said Beddows.

'He has an arrangement with an associate out of the Borough. There is quite a trade in children, even today, and when they are done with, there needs to be somewhere to dispose of them. Welford Road is too obvious, and the paupers' grave and Parish grave is constantly being checked, so he takes his down to Enderby, and they get buried in a field somewhere over there.'

'Say that again; a trade in children? Disposes of them when they are done with? D'you mean this is not the first?' said Beddows.

'Every month or so, I would say. But not like this one. Someone wanted this one done quickly, that's why the eight guineas were put up by someone. Pawley told me that the boy's throat had been cut and he had been murdered. Roberts must have known this, if he hadn't done it himself. But eight guineas - that must have been one of these men I tell of,' said Salt.

'Who was to help him?' said Shepherd.

'Roberts said he would send a bloke round from the Rookeries who he knew. He had moved a few bodies with Pawley before,' said Salt.

'And what about these other children?' said Beddows.

'As the Industry in the Borough advances so quickly, there is a need for a cheap and reliable workforce. Lots of families can't afford the children they have borne, so put them up for sale. They make for chimney sweeps' boys, fluff pickers, shuttle minders, a whole manner of opportunities for free labour, and, worked to the bone, not all of them survive, the state they're in. But, as Roberts says, if they don't know they've gone, nobody is going to miss them. So rather than bother the Union or the Parish they dispose of their own,' explained Salt.

'Do you know a Physician called Joseph Wilson?' said Beddows.

'Do you mean Mr Robert's brother-in-law? He is his wife's brother, another of the group of whom I speak, the high movers.'

'Robert's brother-in-law?' said a clearly surprised Shepherd.

'Yes, Roberts' wife's brother,' affirmed Salt.

'And where do these upstanding Gentlemen you speak of, gather to do their business, Mr Salt?' said Beddows.

'You might wish to take a closer look at The Stokers Arms,' said Salt.

'I'm going to sit you down in a cell again Mr Salt, just for a short while, I think Mr Charters needs to hear about all this. And, by the way, I'll let Mr Biggs know that you are currently indisposed,' said Beddows.

'The Stokers Arms' sat in the middle of Belgrave Gate, opposite 'The Fox and Grapes' and had a reputation as the centre of Variety entertainment in the Borough, for those with less means than could afford 'The Theatre' or 'The Old Cheese' and that wished to have a little fun and frivolity to brighten up the dreadful lives most of them lived.

A large public Beerhouse; it comprised of a saloon bar and a private room - where customers could be entertained by singers, dancers, magicians and variety acts.

As part private, the Police and Magistrates had little influence on what went on in the private section.

Tom Pattersby had been the respectable Landlord during 1849, but had been displaced, and somewhat quickly, by new owners, the identity of whom proved extremely difficult to establish.

It was however clear that this was Irish influenced, if not Irish owned, and 'The Stokers Arms' had become favoured by many of 'The Fancy' and the more affluent or moneyed Irish population.

The new Licensee Michael McCormick, never a friend of the Police or of authority, ran an unruly house, or at least an unruly public bar, which the Police frequently had to attend.

Non-Irish residents were welcome, but these tended to be by *select* membership, and membership tended to be based upon money and business.

*****

Monday the 7th of January 1850.

Detective Sergeants Smith and Haynes had returned earlier in the morning from London, and were now fully briefed on Physician Wilson, and his past involvement in the murder of a high-class prostitute, close to Guys Hospital.

They had also had an opportunity to experience first-hand the joys of London life, and were both feeling a little the worse for wear, but had enjoyed the *first class* view from the Locomotive - soot, cinders and all!

Robert Charters gathered his officers in the private office in his house at the rear of the yard.

None of them had ever been in before, and Mrs Charters had made everyone tea, served in fine china cups and saucers, together with homemade shortbreads, before Head Constable Charters dismissed her formally.

In the room were Smith, Haynes, Kettle, Beddows and Shepherd, who was already being treated with suspicion by longer serving colleagues for the way in which he had been extracted from the mundane and dangerous duties they endured, for these *special enquiries*.

Charters spoke to the assembled men.

'When I took on this job from Mr Goodyer, I was told that he had rooted out the bad apples, and I was taking on a body of trust-worthy and devoted Sergeants and Constables, each of whom he would vouch for. I am sad to report that I find too large a number of your colleagues still to be weak of heart or weak of integrity, and who turn a blind eye to dishonesty and corruption...

...It seems we have at least one bad apple in our numbers, and some sheep who may follow him, and whom, I intend to remove. First we need to get rid of the rotten - our Detective Sergeant Roberts...

...We have now charged Mr Pawley and Mr Salt with various offences of Theft, Burglary and conspiracy to commit such crimes, but cannot presently implicate them in either of our murders. Mr Salt may yet become further implicated, but he is already asking to turn queen's evidence and save his own neck if that day arises, and he will no doubt help us hang Roberts if that becomes the case...

...Sergeants Smith and Haynes, what have you learned about Physician Wilson and his murky past?'

'Wilson came to note in May 1848, whilst an apprenticed General Practitioner at Guy's Hospital in London. A young prostitute, Margaret Byrne, aged seventeen years, was found with her throat cut in the grounds of the Hospital. Wilson was asked by colleagues in the Metropolitan Force, to give his opinion as to how the wound had been received, on the endorsement of Professor Kilpatrick, a senior Professor at Guys, who was Wilson's backer as an Anatomist,' said Haynes.

'And?' enquired Charters.

'Another Professor of Anatomy, named Tucklewood, heard of Wilson's evidence and on review, found it to be most flawed. Wilson had implied that the murderer would be right handed, based on depth and extent of the fatal wound. In fact the most likely scenario demonstrated a left -handed killer and who attacked from behind. This threw the Metropolitan officers, as they had concentrated on one specific suspect for so long, once the facts were announced, the case fell apart. They suggested that Wilson probably knew the killer, or had colluded to assist in his elimination, and probably got a back-hander.'

'Did the Met identify the suspect?' asked Charters.

'The man they had in custody was an Irish businessman called Martin O'Shea. Once he had been released, he disappeared off the face of the earth, and they now think this name and identity had been falsely created. Wilson told them he had never heard of a Martin O'Shea They still have no idea as to his real identity,' said Smith.

'And how did Wilson end up here?' said Charters.

'He moved out of medical school rooms shortly after and into a nice house off Harley Street, but before he could ply his trade, became openly disgraced, and his credibility blown. He left London under a large cloud,' said Smith.

'Are you two gentlemen aware that we have now established Physician Wilson, to be Sergeant Robert's Brother-in-Law by marriage?' said Charters.

'You're having us on, Sir; surely not?' said Smith.

'No Sergeant Smith, I am deadly serious; and I now suspect Wilson may have a lot more to offer us than we had originally imagined,' said Charters. 'He and his Brother-in-Law are my next targets. I want them both - but we also need to know if Wilson has followed the killer from London to our Borough, or whether he is in the keep of more than one killer?'

'How do you want us to pursue this end of the investigation?' said Haynes.

'It has been suggested that some answers may be found in 'The Stokers Arms' and we need to get someone in there, or we need one of our snitches who is already in there to help us' said Charters. 'Any of you got eyes or ears down there already?'

'The problem we have always had there is the nature of the members in the private variety rooms. All high to do Irish or

Gentry, or budding businessmen with investment opportunities, but we can't get through the door to see what goes on,' said Kettle.

'Right then, we need to get someone on the inside of those premises. Get out there and find a way in,' said Charters.

'But be most careful. We know who goes in, and I know there are one or two Lords and Ladies, MPs, Major Landowners who put money into the Borough and The County, so tread delicately. I don't want a controversy along the way, if it can be avoided.'

'Are Shepherd and I still required, sir,' enquired Beddows.

'You started this mess, so I want you both here when we clear it up. You've done a good job so far - you never know, one day you might get to be Detectives yourselves,' Said Charters.

'Not dressed like that and in those hobnails you won't,' laughed Smith.

'Sorry, sir, my little joke,' Smith added, recognizing the look in Charters' eyes.

'But very true. Go and get some plain clothes on, now!' instructed Charters.

'Have you all got snitches in mind?' said Charters.

All replied - 'yes'.

'Even you Shepherd, already?' Charters queried.

'Well actually, sir, I have one or two people I know from back in Nottingham who are here in Leicester, and might have an inroad on the Irish side,' replied Shepherd.

'Be most careful lad. No stupidity, give nothing away, and promise nothing you can't deliver - understand?' stressed Charters.

'Very much so, sir,' Shepherd replied.

'Off you go, all of you, I want you back here to me when you have some news for me.'

*****

Beddows left for home to get some 'plain' clothes. He hoped he would be reimbursed for using his own clothes, which were actually quite a limited offering, and suitably informal.

Before Shepherd could leave for his Aunt's house, Tanky Smith grabbed him by the arm, and pulled him quietly into the Courtyard.

'Look lad, from what Beddows' told me, you're a bright lad and there's hope for you yet. I know you've got an axe to grind over the death of old George. But don't go getting yourself out of your depth, understand?'

'Yes, Sergeant,' replied Shepherd.

'I know about your Irish mate - just be careful. He might be okay with you, but you don't know who's watching him, and that 'Fancy' are a bad lot to mix it with,' said Smith.

'How do you know about him?' said Shepherd.

'That's why I'm a Detective and you're only just plodding a beat my good lad. It's my job to know these things,' laughed Smith.

*****

Shepherd walked down Oxford Street towards the welcoming entry to Twizzle and Twine passage, and the warmth of his Aunt's house. It seemed pleasant not to have the fog around, and the winter sun tried hard to warm up the enlivened, scurrying, people along the route.

He passed by Mr Flowers' house, noting the door shut, and the curtains likewise, which suggested Flowers could be away painting. His mind diverted to the lovely Sally, and he stood still for a moment and day-dreamed.

His mind often went back to that first session of life-study, where the Beautiful Sally had sat, naked as the day she had been born, for a chosen group of local artists. With her relaxed and natural beauty, Shepherd had compared her to the nudes of the Great Masters.

Far from the curvaceous and fleshed out cherubs of their studies, Sally was slim and sinewy, and when her long hair cascaded over her shoulders and brushed across her little pink buds, causing them to harden under its soft caress; and the sigh that followed, and the swell of her breasts, and the soft downy hair between her thighs; and the moist pleasure it must conceal. Ah, Sally!

Shepherd snapped back into consciousness. He felt that manly stirring again and a fear that it would be obvious to passersby, and he directed his thoughts back to catching murderers, diverting his circulation to where it would be better currently employed.

*****

Head Constable Charters strolled sedately around to The County Police Headquarters, which had been given large three storey premises in the Market Place South, adjacent to 'The County Rooms' at the corner with Hotel Street.

As with the Town Hall, Frederick Goodyer also had living accommodation provided within the building, which also housed accommodation for Goodyer's deputy and his family, a muster room and offices, plus two cells. The County Courts were held in the building sandwiched between the Police Station and County Rooms.

Charters agreed to meet Goodyer in Goodyer's private rooms, given the sensitivity of the matter to be discussed.

As Goodyer was not governed by The Borough Watch Committee, but instead, by the County Police Authority, his title was Chief Constable, as opposed to Head Constable within the Borough, but both did the same job.

'Good morning, Robert,' greeted Goodyer 'what is so secretive to merit such a private meeting - some scandal?'

'Of sorts, my dear Frederick; a scandal involving one of your old officers, with a hint of corruption, and unpleasant fronds of growth out into the County, that may impact on you and your Constables,' said Charters.

'And who is involved this time?' questioned Goodyer.

'Detective Sergeant Roberts,' said Charters, 'or as he probably should be referred to *Defective* Sergeant'.

'Ah, never could get to the bottom of him. Good thief taker but always on the fringe of the underworld of the Borough, so not totally surprised!' acknowledged Goodyer.

'Overstepped the mark this time - got himself implicated in our recent murders by sound of things,' disclosed Charters.

'And how is this going to impact on the County?' said Goodyer.

'What do you know about Blaby Union Workhouse at Enderby?' said Charters.

'Bit of a growing but essential need over there,' said Goodyer. 'Has about three hundred and fifty or so poor in need of accommodation, at any one time, often young children, as most of the area are poor frame-workers and like here, the families struggle to keep them.'

'Who is in charge at the premises?' said Charters.

'I believe it is an Irish woman, Mrs O'Crowley if memory serves - who is the appointee of the guardians there. Some big patrons though, Charles Lorraine Smith when he lived at Enderby Hall, and more lately Richard Mitchell, now of the same abode. Both been MPs and High Sheriff as you know and major landowners of the district. The Lord of the Manor of Whetstone also normally has his fingers in the upkeep; but they are all highly respectable and their charitable support beyond reproach,' replied Goodyer.

'Has the place ever come to notice before?' said Charters.

'Not to my knowledge,' said Goodyer.

'Well looks like it might this time,' said Charters, going on to explain about the confessions of Daniel Salt, and the story of concealed burials and the disposal of victims nearby.

'I have a trustworthy Constable over there, Constable Parks, up on Mill Hill, I shall seek his current knowledge,' said Goodyer.

'And what would your views be on one or two of my lads having a nose around with your Constable Parks?' said Charters.

'Not a problem with me old boy, so long as they're civil to my Parishioners,' smiled Goodyer. 'Do some of them good to see how you Borough Boys work. Nicer out in the sticks, not so smelly or scruffy, and with nice fresh air in the main!'

*****

Shepherd made his way into the main bar of 'The Castle Tavern' in Gallowtree Gate. At half past ten in the morning already full with market traders, cattle and horse traders doing a bit of haggling for the next sale, and the usual seedy characters that the Borough attracted at that time of day.

There were more than a few hard looking men, and a strong contingent of Irish voices amongst those there. One or two bore recent cuts and bruising, suggesting their membership of 'The Fancy' and no doubt there were their backers and the men who made money running books on their fights.

Kavanagh stood behind the bar with Dick Cain's mother, Mary, as poor as a church mouse, for all her son's efforts, and who lodged in Abbey Street amongst the Rookeries. Irish and a former nurse, she had married William Cain, a Leicester Irish frame-knitter when times in Leicester were prosperous, but then went back to Ireland where Dick had been born.

Kavanagh saw Shepherd approach and pointed to the side of the bar, where he met him, and they shook hands.

'Well if it isn't the ginger giant himself, Sam Shepherd. How are you doing my friend? Long time, no see,' said Kavanagh genuinely.

'Good to see you also, my friend. Is there somewhere we can talk in private?' said Shepherd, keeping an eye on the faces surrounding the corner of the bar where they spoke.

'That sounds like something dodgy. Not into fight-fixing or anything like that you know, we run a legitimate pub here,' Kavanagh laughed.

Kavanagh took Shepherd up the rickety staircase at the back of the bar, and into the 'training room' where a ring had been set up, with ropes and all the trimmings of a fighting booth, although many a fight still took place in clandestine locations with only the crowd marking the confines of the fighting area.

Presently, talk of a move to contain a prizefight and rumours of harsher rules, *even gloves*, were rife in the 'sport'.

The existing rules – 'London Prize ring rules' of 1838 were 'flexible'.

A round ended with a man downed by punch or throw, whereupon he would be given 30 seconds to rest and eight additional seconds to *'come to scratch'* or return to the centre of the ring where a 'scratch line' had been drawn and square off with his opponent once more.

Consequently, there were no round limits to fights. When a man could not *'come to scratch'* he would be declared the loser and the fight would be brought to a halt.

Some took advantage of the 30 seconds rule, and feigned minor injury to gain time to recover, and fights went on for seemingly ridiculous lengths of time.

Shepherd had learned to fight under these rules.

'I could do with a spar,' said Shepherd, scanning the room and taking in the smell of rope and liniment, most of which was originally meant for horses and treating their injuries.

Kavanagh swung a huge hay-baler right hand, which Shepherd saw coming, and as he ducked he struck out with a well timed left jab. Neither blow hit, nor were they meant to - the men laughed and embraced each other, as good friends and adversaries do.

'So what are you doing in Leicester my ginger headed friend?' said Kavanagh.

'I'm not ginger, let's get that clear for a start,' grinned Shepherd 'and I am here on business.'

'What business might that be my friend?' said Kavanagh.

'Declan, believe it or not, I am now a Constable, here in this Borough, as was my Uncle George as you may remember,' said Shepherd.

'I hope this is not official business then,' said Kavanagh 'and don't let the crowd downstairs find out who you are, talking to me, they're a suspicious bunch, and not to be tangled with if I was you. Some bad boyos there are,' he warned.

'Declan, we have had two murders in the Borough of late. There is talk that somebody in the Irish community is behind at least one of them, the victim of which appears to have been a fighter,' explained Shepherd.

'And how can I help you?' said Kavanagh.

'First, we need to find out who the dead man is, or rather was. A massive bloke he was, about 6 feet six tall, with a bald head, and heavily tattooed. About three hundred pounds he weighed,' said Shepherd.

'I might know of such a fighter of old,' said Kavanagh 'but, he hasn't fought for over a year or so - came over here as a Bruiser for one of the local business men.'

'A name?' said Shepherd.

'The Bruiser? He boxed as *Black Mountain Riordan*, not as he came from the foot of the mountain, but because of his size. Was a bit on the slow side - of brain and foot - and was easy for good fighters, but a hard bastard he was. Been punch drunk for some time now. Not seen him around for ages. You might find he has been locked up once or twice though, few years ago - Jimmy O'Riordan,' he replied.

'Who did he work for?' said Shepherd.

'Are you trying to get me killed, my friend. I think I've told you more than enough. He was a journeyman of late. Worked for whoever paid the best coin for hard labour. Can't tell you anymore than that - don't want this place burning down or Mr Cain and his family harming, do I now?' said Kavanagh 'And you mind your back with this one!'

'You're a good man Declan, and I won't bother you again,' said Shepherd. 'You've told me more than enough, and we have more than we did a few minutes ago.'

'You don't want me to fix you up with a scrap then? Mr Cain's got a couple of good boys on the go - give you a good hiding, and would probably enjoy it if they knew what you did for a job,' laughed Kavanagh.

'Not just yet, thanks,' said Shepherd. 'Don't think I'm fighting fit just at the moment. Give me a bit of time. But if you ever fancy a spar?'

*****

Shepherd asked some of the longer serving officers if they had ever heard of Jimmy O'Riordan, but most just turned their back on him. A few hours later when Black Tommy came back in, Shepherd received some new information.

'Is that the bloke from Delaney's yard?' said Haynes.

'Didn't you know?' said Shepherd.

'No, Mr Charters hadn't said, and I was too busy with the London end and Physician Wilson' he replied, 'as was Tanky. Bugger me! Jimmy O'Riordan pushing up the daisies at long last!' exclaimed Haynes.

'What do you know of him?' said Shepherd.

'O'Riordan was a really bad bloke back in the old days, just after the Force had formed. He put a lot of the blokes who resigned on the floor. Scared many of them to death he did. That's why a lot of them left. Some of those Bruisers or their Fancy was harder than anyone they'd come across before. Tanky had him one night and broke his stick on his noggin, and the bloke just stared at him,' said Haynes.

'And I take it he has not been around much lately?' said Shepherd.

'I thought he had gone back to Ireland. He used to be a bruiser for a bloke called Sean Crowley, a bookmaker from County Cork or somewhere like that. Not been in Leicester for years I thought,' explained Haynes. 'That bugger Roberts would have known him - right time period!'

'Think it's time we updated Mr Charters?' said Shepherd.

'Good lad. Let's go and give him the news,' said Haynes.

*****

Shepherd left the station about one o'clock, and set off towards High Cross, where he had arranged to meet Beddows. Unusual for Beddows to be late, Shepherd walked along Burley's Lane and towards Burgess Street, where Beddows had been making his own enquiries.

'When will this damn fog lift?' he thought, peering hard into the murk, trying to avoid on-comers who would appear, as if out of nowhere, and have to try and avoid Shepherd likewise.

As he crossed by the County Gaol and 'The Duke' on the corner of Cumberland Street, he became aware of several sets of footsteps behind him, running.

He turned to his left, and as he did so, he was struck a hard blow to the back of his head, and he fell to the ground.

The pavement felt wet, sticky and smelled of the Borough, but today he could actually taste it, as his mouth brushed the floor. *'Why did everything in this Borough have to smell or taste of shit?'* He thought.

Stunned, he tried to push himself up off the floor, only to feel a hard kick in the ribs, and briefly caught sight of a boot which

164

appeared in front of his face, smashing into his nose and teeth, sending him sprawling sideways, spitting blood and teeth.

Kicks rained in all over his face and body, and a brutal blow caught him square in his crown jewels, prompting him to vomit profusely, and curl up in a ball, *which probably saved his life*, as his natural instinct had been to tuck his head behind his hands and protects his head from the onslaught.

'There must be passersby?' thought Shepherd. 'Why is nobody helping me?' before remembering that by wearing his own clothes, and was not obviously a Policeman.

Also, the density of the fog meant it possible that people could be walking within six feet of the assault and not see it, although they could probably hear it!

'And let that be a warning for yer, yer Feckin' pig. Keep yers Feckin nose out of Irish business, and feck off from Leicester else yers a dead man,' Shepherd heard through the banging in his head and the pain that blanked out most other thoughts, before he slipped into the darkness.

*****

Shepherd opened his eyes, but then decided he was dreaming, or he had died and gone to heaven. Above him stood Sally, gently touching his bruised and battered face, wiping away blood and dirt, and he became aware that pain seemed to surge from all corners of his body.

'You've decided to come back to the living then?' came the soft voice.

'Where am I?' said Shepherd, squinting through half closed and swollen eyelids, and unable to make out other detail in the light behind Sally.

'At your Aunt's,' said Sally. 'Beddows brought you back here and summonsed Mr Hamilton, who's been caring for you these last few hours. I was on my way to Mr Flowers' and walking by when you arrived, but there was nobody in - so I said I would help.'

'Bless you, Sally, bless you.'

'Scared us all to death you did, lad,' came the gruff but recogniseable and welcome tones of Beddows, who had found Shepherd out cold on the street.

'I had come to look for you,' said Shepherd.

'And I had been sent to Abbey Street to find you - courtesy of some young whipper-snapper. Obviously didn't want us together, so someone at the station sounds like they've stitched us both up, scum,' muttered Beddows.

'How are you feeling now, my young friend?' Shepherd recognized the voice of Mr Hamilton.

'Got a few nasty cuts and some teeth missing, and a few cracked ribs by the feel of it; you'll be sore for a few days,' said Hamilton.

'Thank you, sir,' responded Shepherd.

'Call me Thomas, or rather Tom. Physician or Doctor sounds so old and formal; and we look like we are fated to cross paths, so it may as well be on friendly terms?'

'Thomas; Tom; thank you again,' said Shepherd.

'And Sally; how did you know where I live?' said Shepherd.

'Why Mr Shepherd, a lady likes to know a bit about her admirers,' she replied, 'and you look like you need someone to look after you. Where's your Aunt today?'

'Gone off to Sutton to stay with my mother for a few days,' he replied.

'Well there you go then, Samson Shepherd, I shall look after you. You'll be glad I did one day,' she smiled. 'And we're going to have to do something about your trinkets, they're so swollen.'

Shepherd, lost for words, could merely blush.

'There's more to you than meets the eye, Miss Sally.'

'And you've seen more of me than most Mr Shepherd,' she teased. 'Anyway, I'll go and put the kettle on, as I'm sure you three gentlemen will want to talk shop,' and walked off downstairs.

'What happened?' said Beddows.

'I can only tell you that there was more than one - and at least one was Irish. I didn't see anything other than one boot, and I have been threatened to leave Leicester or else!' Shepherd replied.

'How have they got on to you?' said Beddows.

'Probably they saw me in the Castle Tavern talking to my contact. We got some real dirty looks. He warned me to mind my back.'

'Then we had better talk to Mr Charters about getting your young back covered a bit for the next few days, else your Aunt will never forgive me, and George will be turning in his grave,' said Beddows.

'And I will suggest that you have a day or so to recover and let *the swellings* go down,' laughed Hamilton.

*****

Later in the afternoon, Mr Charters knocked at the door. Sally let him in and introduced herself to him, in return giving him the grand inquisition as to what he was calling for, and asking what protection he had arranged for Sam.

'A feisty one you have there, Mr Shepherd, and a good looking young lady to boot,' said Charters.

'She's just a friend, Sir,' Shepherd replied.

'And that is your humble belief?' Charters smiled. 'Sort of friend a young Copper wants!'

'How can I help, sir?' said Shepherd.

'To start with; take the next day off, but be back by Wednesday if you are up to it. I'll make sure your pay is not docked,' said Charters.

'In the meantime?' said Shepherd.

'In the meantime, I have arranged a little extra security for you, and your friend - if she goes out. So don't worry about that.'

'Thank you, Sir, very kind,' said Shepherd.

'So you got us a name for our big Irishman, and that looks like it got you a kicking in return. Any ideas?'

'Suspect they were from 'The Castle' - must have made me out talking to my contact,' replied Shepherd.

'Dangerous place that Castle Tavern,' grinned Charters. 'Got a few teeth loosened myself after bit of a nosey in there a few years ago. Don't suspect your contact then?'

'My contact is a sound bloke. I would trust him completely, but there were definitely some hard, dodgy looking customers, as you might well have expected, Mr Charters.'

'Are you sure he is sound?' said Charters.

'Fought him once as a young lad in Nottingham, met him once or twice more over the years, and he's always treated me well,' said Shepherd.

'And now you are a Constable, will he feel the same?' said Charters.

'He told me to be careful. I didn't think I would need to start being careful quite so soon,' Shepherd replied.

'Did you see anyone else you knew in there?' said Charters.

'No, sir. That being said, I still don't know that many in Leicester yet,' Shepherd confessed.

'Well, as it happens, it appears that not only did Detectives Smith and Haynes know of the man O'Riordan, but Smith remembers him passing the time with our Sergeant Roberts a couple of years ago in 'The Fox and Grapes' with old Clodagh Murphy herself. So we have a tenuous connection yet again - but it is a start,' explained Charters.

'That's good news, sir, yet again, thank you for keeping me updated.'

*****

Sally appeared just after she had let Mr Charters out of the front door, carrying a bowl of steaming, warm water. The house seemed abnormally quiet. Passing pedestrians and Horses and carts were just audible outside.

'You've still got so much dirt on you, and you smell horrible,' said Sally. 'Let's get you cleaned up.'

Shepherd realised he was still bare-chested, apart from some bandages that Mr Hamilton had strapped up his ribs with temporarily. He did not have a mirror in his room, and had no idea how he looked, but he knew he could still smell and taste blood, and also, he suspected, there appeared to be a strong urine smell.

'They pee'd on you to add insult to injury, young Samson Shepherd - and I hate the smell of pee at the best of times, so let me sort you out.'

Sally wore a long flowing skirt, and a long sleeved white blouse - which she unbuttoned, much to Shepherd's surprise, and removed, exposing a short bodice which was loose fitting and exposed her small but perfect breasts when she leaned forward.

'Sally, your top!' Shepherd blushed.

'There's nothing you haven't seen and painted before, so what's all the fuss about now. If you think I'm going to get my blouse all smelly and dirty - I don't think so, Young Sir,' she smiled.

Sally placed the bowl on a stand at the side of the bed, and soaked and soaped the hand cloth, with which she began to wipe clean his face and head, gently and carefully, responding to Shepherds pain if she caught him wrong.

'You are a lovely girl, Sally,' said Shepherd. 'How come you don't have a man to look after you?'

'I have, sir, but he hasn't realised yet - think he's a bit shy - but he'll work it out one day,' she smiled.

'And what is his name?' Shepherd asked.

'I think it's Samson, young Mr. Shepherd; that's what Mr Flowers told me anyway. You silly man you, if I'd waited to be asked round I'd be an old maid. Sometimes the lady just has to grab the bull by the horn, in a manner of speaking.' Sally smiled again.

'But Sally...,' Shepherd started to say, interrupted by Sally's lips moving over his, as she kissed him gently.

'This is an unusual first walking out, Mr Shepherd, really it is,' she smiled and winked.

The smell of the soap and the warmth of the water eased Shepherd's pain for the first time, and he began to relax the muscles that had tightened to protect him, and his eyes closed in relief.

Sally washed the dirt out of his hair, and placed some mint leaves on his tongue, to rid the taste of the blood and the pavement, and downwardly she cleansed his body, off his shoulders and gently around the cracked ribs.

'Oh, Sal, you shouldn't be doing this, you are so sweet.'

'Think of it as a little gift. I am sure you will return the kindness one day,' she said, moving her hand down across his soft belly and towards the warmth of the sheets.

'Oh, Mr Shepherd, I think you have a problem. I don't think that was swollen before!' she chuckled, brushing against his manhood. 'Whoever could have done that?'

Shepherd blushed like he had never blushed before.

'I think I have a little something to get rid of the swelling,' said Sally, sliding her hand beneath the sheet. 'Oh Mr Shepherd, the swelling is getting worse!'

*****

As night fell, Shepherd slept, with Sally Brown next to him, warm and comforting, unaware that in the shadows outside, friendly eyes kept a watch on the house. They would sleep safe tonight.

Wednesday the 9th broke clear, cold and bright, and at last the fog that had lingered had finally disappeared, revealing Leicester again in its full Industrial gore.

Constable 37 Coltman, made his way from his home in Gray Street, off The Newarkes, towards the posh houses that sat between Southgate Street and Trinity Hospital.

Coltman had been approached by Mr Gerraghty, a Solicitor, who lived in one of the adjacent houses and who had announced to the Constable that his neighbour, Joseph Wright, The Physician, had not been seen for two days. Despite knocking on the door, by several of his patients who had appointments, there had been no reply.

At about nine o'clock Constable Coltman made his way around the ground floor of the house, gaining entry at the rear through the walls beyond the Hospital gardens, from Castle View.

As he peered through the lower ground-floor windows, he could see a figure of a man slumped over a desk or table on the far side of the room. The sash windows were all shut tight, and as the man had failed to respond, Coltman took out his Truncheon and smashed the glass pane at the base of the window, and reached through to release the catch.

As he pulled up the panel, the smell of death swamped his nostrils, causing him to gag in reflex, and he suddenly understood why the person had not responded.

Climbing carefully over the ragged chards of glass that wedged in the bottom sill, and careful not to hurt his pride and joys, he descended onto the plush carpet that covered the room, grinding and crunching the broken glass from the window that lay beneath his size eleven hobnails.

He could see slumped over the desk, the body of a young, well dressed white male. In the man's left hand, an ornately engraved flintlock pistol, and, looking at the man's head, a hole quite apparent above his left eye, from which the man had bled; to his horror, on the right side of the man's head, a larger wound from which the man had bled more profusely.

Coltman had realised he was also now staring at the man's brains which had oozed onto the table and were congealing with the dead man's own blood and bodily fluids.

On the desk in front of the dead man, a suicide note, white and unblemished considering the bodily damage around it, lay in clear view.

On the wall to the right of the body, more blood, brains and bone fragments were splattered across some extremely ornate and expensive, he suspected, wall covering.

Coltman went out onto The Newarkes and swung his rattle vigorously to attract assistance, before vomiting profusely over his freshly polished boots.

By ten o'clock, Detective Sergeant Kettle, and Constable Beddows had arrived at the house, having been made aware that a Physician named Wilson had been found deceased.

Beddows recognised the name and address immediately, and advised Head Constable Charters, who sent the two men to investigate.

Kettle and Beddows made a thorough examination of the dwelling, a luxurious, three story white painted town house, where Wilson had resided since he had arrived from London.

'How could a budding young Physician, own such a desirable piece of real estate as this?' said Kettle.

'We think he was bent. He had a rich backer who he got out a mess in London last year - probably the pay-off helped buy this' explained Beddows.

The inside of the house, so spotlessly clean and tidy, had been festooned with art works and curios.

There were portraits on most walls throughout the house. No doubt some were family, and were marked with assorted Wilsons across plates on the bottom of each picture. Some were quire erotic and featured naked youths and feasting and wine, and there were large elaborate figurines and busts in each ground floor reception room.

In the cellar, an extensive wine cage, full of impressive looking bottles, filled one entire wall. Kettle recognized several labels as identical to those sold by his father-in-law, at the wife's family wine merchants in Hotel Street, and which sold for over a guinea a bottle. Kettle couldn't understand though why people bought it and left it in racks, rather than consuming it?

In the drawer to the desk immediately below the deceased, a small metal box contained over Fifty pounds in £5 notes, Guinea coins, pound notes, ten shilling notes and silver coinage.

The house was secure and the doors were all locked, and windows bolted from inside.

The officers read the suicide note.

Saturday 5th January 1850   *3, Newarkes,*
                                                        Leicester.

Dear Mother, Sister, and friends;-

By the time you read this, my soul will have departed this mortal coil, and I shall be in a better place, I believe.

I have wronged you all, and brought shame to such a respectable family.

I am not just a poor Physician by skills and aptitude, but I am also a cold hearted killer, and have killed not just once, nor twice, but three times now, and can no longer live with myself.

It was I who murdered that poor girl at Guys Hospital when I was in London.

It was I who murdered a poor innocent young boy, for my own pleasure, before discarding him like some unwanted possession in the River.

It was I who killed and tormented my friend Mr O'Riordan in such a brutal and cold way.

I am afraid I can no longer live with my self- revulsion, and have chosen to take my own life in this cowardly manner, before it is taken for me.

Please forgive a wicked and depraved son and friend.

I bid you peace and health and that the world will be a better place without me.

Joseph

'So he could no longer live with his guilt?' said Kettle.

'So it would seem,' said Beddows, 'but I have another theory.'

'And what's that?' said Kettle.

'He didn't kill himself at all,' said Beddows.

'How can you be so sure? The house is locked and secure. There are no signs of disturbance, burglary or robbery, as there are valuables and money throughout the house,' said Kettle.

'Look at the body, and tell me, what do you see?' said Beddows.

'I see a young white male, of well means, and of healthy disposition, sat at his desk, with all the trimmings required to commit suicide. He has a gunshot wound to the left side of his temple which has exited over his right ear and eye, and he is dead. He has also written a suicide note, and the pen and paper are in an obvious place to be found,' said Kettle.

'And in which hand is the pistol?' said Beddows.

'The man's left hand, which is in keeping with what we have been told of our suspect,' replied Kettle.

'And the pen and ink?' said Beddows.

'To the left of the blotter and the letter,' said Kettle.

'Precisely,' said Beddows. 'Not one week ago I was with Physician Wilson whilst he wrote his statement for Mr Mitchell, and he was without doubt right-handed. He wrote with his right hand, he shook hands with his right hand, and he donned his top hat with his right hand. And where is his pistol box, or cleaning kit, or ammunition?' said Beddows.

'Good god,' said Kettle. 'I take my hat off to you, Beddows. I think it's time for Mr Charters to join us.'

*****

At about quarter past eleven that morning, Head Constable Charters arrived at the address, in company with General Practitioner and Police Medical Inspector, John Buck.

'Do you realize, gents, we have not had a murder in this Borough since 1846? But since the 1st of January it has been raining bodies down upon us,' grumbled Charters.

'Don't complain, Head Constable,' joked Buck. 'Your Sergeants and Constables are keeping me and my new friend Thomas Hamilton in pocket. So I am not complaining!'

'Show us the body then. Let's get on with it,' urged Charters.

John Buck, as he had previously done at Mansfield Street, took his time opening up his medical bag. From this, he produced a large magnifying glass.

Buck then went over to the body, and began to examine the wound to the left side of Physician Wilson's Head.

'Not looking for brains!' joked Buck. 'Don't think he had too many according to Hamilton, and most of what he had are probably on the table at the side of him, or up on the wall.'

'What are you looking for then, Mr Buck?' enquired Charters.

'I have been reading some hypotheses on gunshot wounds,' said Buck. 'Seemingly, whilst studying victims of duels, French Physicians have noted that people who have been shot at close distance, have some sort of powder burn around the wound, whereas the further away the shot, the cleaner the entry wound. One day it will be scientifically proven, no doubt, but today I just want to see what I can see. Don't get too many gunshot wounds in Leicester,' he sighed.

'And how does it look?' said Charters.

'It looks to me like it was not fired too close to his head at all, on the basis of what I have recently read. I suspect he has been shot by a third party, and someone has placed the gun in his hand and made it look like he has shot himself. However, it will not be scientifically provable at present without a supporting witness or confession,' said Buck.

'Mr Buck, you have done more than enough to persuade us. Yet again we appear to have another linked murder, but now we also have some hand-writing. We might find some more that we can compare?' Charters hoped.

'Do we know who his next of kin is?' said Buck.

'Indeed we do,' said Charters. 'His sister is married to our Detective Sergeant Roberts, no less; and the last time we looked she was not to be found, much like her confounded husband.'

'We know we have Roberts hand-writing Mr Charters,' said Kettle. 'His diary and old case notes are all over the station store, or rather, should be.'

'Right, you two back to the station and look them out. Mr Buck, I take it you will be wanting transport for Physician Wilson?'

'If you would be so kind,' agreed Buck.

*****

At the same time that Messrs Buck and Charters were examining Physician Wilson, Thomas Hamilton made a house call to Shepherd.

'Have you heard the news?' said Hamilton.

'What news, Tom?' said Shepherd.

'Your dodgy Physician Wilson is dead. Seems he shot himself. They found the body earlier, slumped over his desk at home,' said Hamilton.

'And why are you not there then, ably assisting the good Mr Buck?' said Shepherd.

'Mr Buck was doing these examinations long before me, and I doubt he needs any second opinion too often.'

'So, why the visit - House calls are expensive?' said Shepherd.

'Just want to make sure the old bones are healing - and how are the old crown jewels, still a bit swollen I'll hazard?' said Hamilton.

'Oddly enough,' said a smiling Shepherd, 'they seem to have gone down, rather well.'

'Amazing what a good old fashioned bed-bath can do!' Hamilton remarked, with a wry smile. 'You lucky sod!'

'What do you mean by that?' said Shepherd blushing again.

'I'm sure Miss Sally Brown has been looking after you well!' Hamilton exclaimed.

*****

Shepherd felt well enough to stroll in to the Police Station later that afternoon, arriving there as St Martin's clock struck one.

He had been unaware of anyone following him, albeit he had kept a constant check over his shoulders.

He had thought once he was being followed, by an old chap in a Breton jumper and old sailor's hat, who looked vaguely familiar, but he never saw him again, despite slowing and changing his pace, and one or two detours.

Tanky saw him safely into the Station without him even realising. Haynes was still tucked up keeping a beady eye on Miss Sally Brown, back at Shepherd's lodgings. Tanky would return there shortly.

Beddows sat with Sergeant Kettle and were together searching through piles of papers.

'Hello, Shepherd,' said Beddows. 'How are you feeling lad?'

'Much better, thanks, ready for getting back to work if Mr Charters will let me,' said Shepherd.

'Mr Charters is glad to have you back in the fold,' said Mr Charters, appearing from the rear door to the Muster Room.

The station looked and sounded unusually quiet, and the cells were all empty for a change, and Sergeant Sheffield looked to be having a good day - apart from running out of tobacco, whereby he gripped a cold and bitter tasting pipe between his teeth, *so perhaps not that good a day.*

'How are we doing with Robert's diary or case notes?' said Charters.

'Found his diary, and got two case notes, one from November and one from March. Hadn't realised just what a lazy bugger he is, Sir,' said Kettle.

'And?' said Charters.

'And it looks like we might have found our letter writer. Looks the same to me, and it looks the same to him,' said Kettle, Beddows nodding alongside, in agreement.

'What's that all about, sir?' enquired Shepherd.

'Looks like Sergeant Roberts has been out and about in the fog and been up to his tricks again,' said Beddows. 'Written a suicide note for his late lamented brother-in-law, and probably murdered him we suspect.'

'Sergeant Sheffield,' said Charters. 'Put the word out to all the Constables - I want Detective Sergeant Roberts arrested on sight for Murder. Anyone messes me about and fails to report a sighting of him or doing anything to harbour him - I'll have their baubles and their jobs - let them be made aware of the consequences.'

'Yes, Mr Charters,' sighed Sheffield, now even more desperate for a drag of baccy. His fellow Sergeants and their Constables would not be that easy to persuade.

Beddows smiled as he checked his own baccy, safely stowed away in his jacket pocket. He could have offered Sheffield a pinch or two, but this would make up for taking the piss recently.

*****

About two o'clock Head Constable Charters sat in the plush leather chair in Coroner Mitchell's office at 10 New Street. Alongside him sat Chief Constable Frederick Goodyer.

Goodyer had been appointed as the original Head Constable of the Borough Force, before moving to take up post as Chief Constable of the newer County Force in 1839. He had set up all the beats and logistics that Charter's men now patrolled.

An ex Metropolitan Officer, who had been recommended to the Borough Watch Committee; a calm and dignified looking man, with swept back short hair, and a large billowing moustache which linked two enormous whispy sideburns in the fashion of the day, and who had a propensity to wear bow-tie rather than neckerchief or cravat.

'Must be something rather serious, to have the pleasure of both *Head* Constables at the same sitting?' said Mitchell. 'A glass of sherry?'

'Not for me,' said Charters.

'A little too early still, for me, also,' said Goodyer.

'Don't mind if I do? Dreadful indigestion - too much game pie for lunch I suspect,' said Mitchell, pouring a large measure into a crystal schooner.

'Mr Mitchell, we are here jointly, regarding our current pattern of murders. We have new information that suggests that children are being farmed and worked to death, or are being used for depraved pleasures and then being murdered, either way, depraved practices are employed,' said Charters.

'The indication is that the murders may be happening within the Borough, and possible, also in the County, with a suggestion that there is a disposal site somewhere near to Enderby. We are currently making joint enquiries to develop the Enderby issue, but we are unsure what your guidance is for opening any site and the prospect of exhuming bodies,' said Goodyer.

'And are they being buried in consecrated or non-consecrated ground?' said Mitchell.

'We are not yet sure. There appears to be some sort of connection to Blaby Union Workhouse, but that is merely speculative at present. Would it make a significant difference?' said Goodyer.

'Historically, the cadaver is *'flesh for worms'* and, as it belongs to no one, the Church will protect it. Thus, the Church is responsible for the dead and anyone seeking to exhume a corpse from *consecrated ground* requires a faculty from the Church courts to do so. If the corpse were *not* in consecrated ground then the common law would apply and prevent exhumation, unless under the ancient authority of the Coroner, that being my good self,' stated Mitchell.

'To gain such a faculty from the Church, the *'Ordinary'* - usually the Bishop of the diocese exercising the ecclesiastical jurisdiction annexed to his office, would authorize the exhumation. In this case that would be through the Lord Bishop's office at St Martin's Church,' he continued.

'In that case, we had better find out just where this site is and whether it is consecrated or non-consecrated,' said Charters.

*****

Whilst the meeting with the Head Constables and Coroner Mitchell was taking place, Constables Beddows and Shepherd were dispatched, together with Sergeant Walter Marvin of the County Force, in one of the duty carriages provided for County Supervisory officers, to meet with Constable Edward Parks - the resident County Constable for Enderby area.

The carriage represented an exceptional luxury in the eyes of Beddows and Shepherd, as 'The Borough' had no such transport provided currently, given the proximity of its boundary.

The carriage, a two wheeled Hansom cab, had its roots in Leicestershire; the original had been designed and built by Joseph Hansom, of Lutterworth a few years prior.

Small but comfortable for a two-wheeled cab, designed to be pulled by one horse, but capable of seating four adults together with a driver, it was economical and gave the County Sergeants and Supervisors easy means of getting to their villages and County Towns.

In 1850, the old town walls still defined the main habitation and Industry considered 'The Borough'. However, the authorities had the foresight to retain adjoining fields around the old walls, to allow for expansion of both population and business.

A small area on London Road now extended up towards the gallows at Evington turn, and with some new housing emerging on the road to Humberstone, and along the road to Belgrave.

But effectively, and for policing purposes, the County began as did the countryside, with the boundaries known as 'Lordships' of Evington, Belgrave, New Parks, Braunstone, Aylestone and Knighton, adjoining Leicester Racecourse at the Borough's Southernmost point.

It was clear that Marvin had been hand-chosen by Mr Goodyer, and had similar attributes to the early Borough Officers. Taller than most of his generation, and strongly built, with large rough hands, Marvin knew he was the highest rank, and even though the two Constables were not his own to command, he had no trouble assuming authority with them.

A few well chosen questions lead Shepherd and Beddows to establish Marvin had originally been a quarryman, and heralded from Croft, where his family resided to this day, but the choice of Police career seemed a better long term prospect for him.

It had also allowed him to explore the County as a Supervising rank, and for the first time in his life he had gone beyond the immediate villages surrounding his home – and with the bonus of a *handsome Hansom cab to boot,* in which to do his exploring.

Beddows and Shepherd sat comfortably in the back seat, as Sergeant Marvin at the reins, steered the vehicle out over West Bridge and left onto the old Fosse Way, the Coventry Road, and towards Enderby, passing the verdant estates on their right hand side of Dannetts Hall and Westcotes, close to the legendary cave of Black Annis, who continued to raise her ugly head, even in the current investigation.

Once past Westcotes, the Borough gave way to 'The County' and open countryside, with Aylestone and its meadows, running the length of the rivers Soar and Byam to the left hand side and Braunstone, with its raised Parkland and Braunstone Hall, off to the right.

The Fosse Way then ran through low, flat fields until ruins of the small ancient church of Aldeby St John's came into view in the low meadows of the Soar beyond Aylestone and before Glen Parva, nestled just off the Fosse Way between the road and the river.

At the crossroads just before The Blaby Union Workhouse, whose name itself was confusing as it was actually in *Enderby*, where a left turn took you down a lane through Whestone, Marvin turned right, and travelled up the hill towards Enderby Village, past the sandpits on their right, and up towards St John The Baptist Church, the 'new' Parish church, and Enderby Hall, the home of the Mitchell family.

Constable Parks lived in a small terraced house on the left hand side of Mill Hill, directly opposite the rear entrance to the impressive Enderby Hall, at the end of Hall Walk - the 'Tradesmen's entrance', secured by two large wooden gates, and surrounded by eight feet high stone walls, through which Park's kept a careful eye on the Estate.

As the three men climbed down from the cab, Constable Parks appeared in the doorway to greet them.

'Morning, Sergeant Marvin - ready and waiting as instructed' said Parks.

'Bloody hell, if it isn't Big Sam Shepherd,' said a surprised Parks.

'Teddy Parks? It can't be,' said Shepherd, the two men shaking hands and embracing, rather too informally for Sergeant Marvin's liking, given his presence.

'I take it you two know each other?' deduced Beddows.

'Your Constable Shepherd, here, was a regular visitor to my old parents' neighbours in Normanton on Soar. How is your Uncle George?' Parks asked.

'Sadly, he died a few years ago now. He too was a Constable in the Borough Force, one of the originals - got killed as a result of the Chartist riots,' said Shepherd.

'Sorry,' said Parks. 'What a coincidence, you in the Borough, and me in the County, both Constables.'

'Good, now we've got the pleasantries over, let's get down to business,' urged Marvin.

The men convened in Park's back parlour. The House felt small but cozy, two up, two down, but substantially better quality than similar houses in the Borough, and the parlour, warm from the leaded grate and welcoming log fire.

'What do you know about the Union Workhouse lad?' said Beddows.

'Bit of a shady place - all very sad really,' said Parks.

'Enderby gives the impression of a thriving village, as with Whetstone, Narborough and Blaby. But in the main they are frame knitters and workers, and the industry is dying. The Union Workhouse has capacity for about 350 who come from as far away as Wigston and Potter Marston, and out to Sharnford and Smockington - all lost souls. You see them wandering about, like walking dead, and many of them are youngsters, just children,' Parks continued.

'And who is in charge?' said Shepherd.

'Connor Crowley, or sometimes O'Crowley, depending on his Irish of the day, he is the Workhouse Master, and his wife, Mary Crowley is the Workhouse Matron. Rough and coarse couple they are. There is a Reverend Morrison who is their Chaplain - why in such an unholy place I do not know? But he is in high demand as many pass away through poor health or exertions and he buries them. He does not have a Parish otherwise, but assists at Enderby on occasions,' explained Parks.

186

'And they are buried in their own Parish churches?' said Shepherd.

'No, the Workhouse had retained the original cemetery at Aldeby St John's - the old church in the meadows off the Fosse Way. You would have passed by it on the way here,' said Parks.

'Why is that? I remember reading something years ago about that being a closed church, just ruins, and most of the time flooded,' said Beddows.

'That's why, I think,' said Parks. 'There is little facility for paupers' graves anymore in many of the Parish churches, and St John the Baptist, here in the village won't take them. So Aldeby is ideal for them. The ground is wet and soft and they're easy to bury in the numbers that pass away.'

'Ever heard of any strange goings on around yon Workhouse?' said Beddows.

'Like what?' said Parks.

'Any gatherings, posh people, partying, that sort of thing?' suggested Beddows.

'Not to my knowledge. The place is built of local stone and is cold and dark and unfriendly. The inmates work most of the day, down at the Mill, or at the sandpits, or breaking granite from the local rock formations that the Workhouse is built of. They have no cheer at all. Connor and Mary Crowley are hard and ignorant, come from County Kildare - Curragh they once told me. They like the horses when the races come to Leicester once a year. That's about their only pleasure, apart from the grog - always puddled they are,' said Parks.

'If you wanted a gathering locally then, where would they go?' said Shepherd.

'Enderby Hall has gatherings and big parties every weekend, and dinners most nights. Mr Mitchell and has family have house guests most of the time,' said Parks. 'Very posh and some nice people, seemingly.'

'Same could be said of most big country houses, I suppose,' said Shepherd.

'I did come across some funny goings on one night, come to think of it, down at Enderby Mill. The Crowleys were there, and there were some other Irish gentry from the town and one or two strange folk from town too. It was All Hallows' Eve, and they were having a fancy dress party. Caught one or two running backwards and forwards over the fields to Aldeby church - and found a couple tupping on one of the old stones. Bleeding cold it was too; ran off into the dark before I could find out who they were,' said Parks.

'Go on,' said Beddows.

'There were a few orphans there that Crowley said were from the Workhouse; said they were giving them a treat. They were dancing in a circle and singing some silly song about Black Annis. Never forgot the words; haunting...

Black Annis, Black Annis, crawl back to your cave

We children of Leicester want you in your grave

You suckle our blood and you steal our skins

For seven hundred years you've committed your sins

...really creepy, hearing them kids singing like that, dancing round this bloke in the middle dressed up as Black Annis,' said Parks.

'And how long ago was that?' said Beddows.

'About two years ago,' said Parks.

'When did you last know of any burials at Aldeby, Ted?' said Shepherd.

'There's been some down there in the last month. The grounds wet, but you can see where it's been turned over - all outside the consecrated bit of the old church it is now - don't even get Christian burials anymore I expect,' said Parks.

'Who runs the Mill?' said Beddows.

'It's owned by a business in the Borough. The manager who lives there is called Brendon St Clair, another Irishman, from Kilkenny he told me - that's why he keeps friends with the Crowleys. Slick for a miller he is, dresses fancy when he's about, and got his own Growler, better than the Sergeant's here - as well as his working wagon and horses. I'm told he spends a lot of time at 'The Stokers Arms' in the Borough. He does a turn I'm told, a bit of a comedian he is,' said Parks, 'although I would say creepy rather than funny - dead eyes he's got.'

'Right then Constable Parks - time we paid Connor and Mary Crowley a visit,' said Sergeant Marvin, 'as I'm sure our friends here from the Borough have some interesting questions for them.'

The four men set off for The Union Workhouse.

* * * * *

Just approaching four in the afternoon, Connor Crowley occupied himself giving a skinny boy a severe birching, out in the central yard of the two large buildings that made up the Workhouse. Whether intended for the boy's good or for Crowley's sick and sadistic nature was questionable.

Since 1831 the need for places had risen from thirty to over three hundred and sixty in just the nineteen years, and it was not a nice place to be, and probably the nearest thing to a bit of life as it would be in the Borough, this far out of town, as you could find.

Shepherd shivered as the men walked into a small low level annex at the end of one of the buildings, and that housed Crowley's office and private scullery.

Mary Crowley lay asleep in a low chair and a good job too, as when her husband prodded her awake, she fell forward and out of the chair, nearly landing in the open fire grate. Spittle dribbled from her mouth, and over the whiskers of her chin, which Shepherd had noticed and considered far more developed than his own.

'Who the feck have you brought in, now? Thought you were givin' them a good whippin' before tea?' she grumbled, rubbing her eyes and searching through her apron for a pair of old pock-marked spectacles, which were now warming in the embers at the foot of the grate.

'Goodness me,' she spluttered. 'Constable Parks and some of his friends; caught me unawares you did, yer little tinkers yers.'

'They wants to know about some Children that you might know about,' said Connor Crowley.

'And which ones are you interested in? You can take all the little feckers if you want, and do us all a big favour, lazy little feckers they are, one and all,' she growled.

'Where is your ledger of inmates?' said Sergeant Marvin.

'Ledger of inmates? I'm not sure; Connor Crowley have you seen it today?' said Mary Crowley.

'Don't think I have,' said Connor Crowley, 'not for a day or so - probably one of them little shites has hid it'.

'I suspect that you will have access to it when you come to claim your relief from the Union Guardians later this month, and I am sure last month's claim was on time, given Christmas and the New Year to provide for,' said Marvin.

'And where is your register of deaths?' said Constable Parks.

'Prob'ly in the same place,' Connor Crowley laughed, echoed by his wife.

'Then again, it could have been the Guardians took them themselves,' she laughed louder, 'go and ask them.'

'When did your last inmate pass away?' said Beddows.

'Been a few weeks now. Healthier lot than normal; got through the winter they did, although this fog we've been havin' will take a few no doubt.'

'But Connor Crowley, I have seen with my own eyes fresh graves these last few weeks,' said Constable Parks.

'Might have moved one or two older ones and made a bit more room,' Connor Crowley laughed.

'You seem to think this is a matter of some humour?' said Shepherd.

'Nobody is really bothered about the little feckers at all - they're the lowest of the low, the ones who can't feed 'emselves. Nobody wants 'em, nobody loves 'em - they're in the best place, God help 'em,' said Connor Crowley.

'And now they're taking up more space than they deserve, we ain't got that much room, so some are now havin' to share. What's wrong with that?' said Mary Crowley.

'Right then,' said Marvin forcefully, 'enough of this messing us about. Get me the registers now!'

'You can't have them - so there,' said Mary Crowley.

'Right then,' said Marvin, 'we're going to arrest the both of you and lock your sorry fat arses away for a long time - and you won't be in need of the registers, other than in court, to try and save your sorry necks.'

'What are you arrestin' us for then exactly?' said Connor Crowley.

'What about your wife's adverts in the Chronicle to start off with?' said Beddows.

'And that's on top of the deceiving the guardians I suspect,' said Marvin.

'There's nowt wrong with them adverts,' she said. 'Just helpin' the poor get rid of their unwanted runts.'

'But we know you're not doing that, Mary Crowley. We know that's a signal for something more sinister, more depraved - and these are the ones we will find in the graveyard and the ones that will hang you both,' said Beddows.

'You can't hang us for buryin' the dead,' she protested.

'We can, when we can show that you assisted in a murder. And several times we suspect too,' said Shepherd.

 'You can't just go diggin' up bodies,' said Connor Crowley, over-confidently.

'Want to run a wager with me on that?' said Beddows 'You being a betting man, as I understand from good Constable Parks here.'

'Mr Parks,' said Shepherd. 'Where do we find the Chaplain - Reverend Morrison - I'm sure he will know who's been buried here and when?'

'He don't have involvement in *all* the burials,' interrupted Connor Crowley.

'What does that mean?' said Marvin.

'We're going to have to tell them Ma,' said Crowley, looking towards his wife despairingly.

'You'll tell them nothing! Let them do what they have to do. Mr St Clair will be dropping us in a Feckin' hole if we say one word out of turn,' said a very red faced Mary Crowley.

'Parks ; go and find Reverend Morrison,' instructed Marvin, 'and tell him to meet us here at nine o'clock tomorrow morning; and you be here as well. It's getting far too dark to do anything tonight'.

The Crowleys were carted off to the County Police Station, in a very cramped Hansom Cab, arriving there after dark, to be locked away for the night.

Shepherd thought the Crowleys both smelled of piss, and thought that neither of them had probably ever washed, or even washed their grimey rags, and considered them to be rather like a moving outdoor privvie on four legs.

Stopping briefly at the Town Hall, Beddows informed Mr Charters that they had arrested the couple, and that at nine o'clock the following morning, together with Sergeant Marvin, they were meeting the Reverend Morrison at Aldeby cemetery and identifying any new and unexpected graves.

Charters agreed that the Crowleys could have a night sweating, and they would not be interviewed until after they had gone back and been formally challenged at the graves. He personally would join them at The Market Place and they would speak with Mr Goodyer and confirm the extent of the resources they would require for the morning.

* * * * *

About 7 o'clock that evening, Charters visited Coroner Mitchell at Cank Street, as he had finished his duties early for a weekday, and about to sit down for his dinner.

'Twice in one day, Robert, must be important?' said Mitchell.

'Well actually, about our conversation of earlier today, I am going to need either your certificate for exhumation, or that of the Bishop, or possibly both, as it is not clear whether our bodies are in consecrated or non-consecrated ground. But we would like to recover the bodies tomorrow once we have identified the sites,' said Charters. 'Our men are meeting the Chaplain of The Blaby Union Workhouse and he will identify what, or rather who should be there, and more importantly, what or who, shouldn't.'

'So, what time would you like me there? This is one I think I would care to be present at, and I can sort out with The Diocese for you as an alternative, should the need arise,' said Mitchell.

'In that case, can we say Eleven o'clock at Aldeby St John's, near to the old church?' said Charters.

'And so it will be, this should be exciting!' said Mitchell 'Now then, that Sherry you refused earlier? Won't take no for an answer this time.'

*****

Reverend Morrison had been found at St John the Baptist church in Enderby, and brought back to the Union Workhouse by Constable Parks for nine a.m. as agreed.

'Thank you for joining us, Reverend,' said Marvin. 'I think you know these people?' indicating to the Crowleys.

'Indeed I do, Sergeant' said the Reverend.

'Can you explain to us the purpose and status of the old Aldeby St John's church and cemetery?' said Marvin.

'It is now exclusively used for the burial of the poor unfortunates of the Workhouse, who are without any means whatsoever, other than the poor relief,' said the Reverend.

'And how many graves does it contain?' said Beddows.

'Many of them are centuries old and are not recorded,' said the Reverend.

'How many have you buried during your time here?' said Beddows.

'In the last ten years, I suspect about one, most months, occasionally two,' said the Reverend.

'And how many graves will they be in?' said Shepherd.

'The paupers' grave we are currently using was started three years ago, and is mainly one long trench, to which we add bodies, and then fill in. There should be no more than forty bodies in it I would think.'

'And when did you perform your last burial there?' said Beddows.

'That was in late October, I have not officiated since,' the Reverend replied.

'So, there should be no new digging, and no burials since then?' said Marvin.

'No, I can show you where the last one was buried and where the grave should end,' said the Reverend.

'Right, we'll all take a walk down there, including Connor and Mary Crowley, who I am sure are thrilled at the prospect,' said Marvin.

'Can anyone be buried, other than by you?' said Parks.

'Not presently, this is my graveyard, and is unique to the Workhouse,' said The Reverend.

'You don't have the registers for deaths by any chance do you sir?' Shepherd asked the Reverend.

'No, the Crowleys keep those to claim poor law relief,' he replied.

The Crowleys looked like they were already at the gallows, their heads bowed, and with silent icy glances cast to each other and heads shaking. Beddows felt a confession coming, but probably only one, if Mary Connor stood her ground again.

*****

The fields at the old church were saturated from the winter rains and what snow had fallen earlier had melted causing the river to rise. The ground proved boggy, and the party of walkers found it heavy going.

From the Fosse Way, only a couple of fields, with a small track leading across at right angles towards the river, separated them from the graveyard.

Aldeby had been the earliest settled part of the village of Enderby, and this had been the 'Mother Church'.

The place name Enderby, derived from the Old Norse personal name 'Eindrith' and the Old Norse 'Byr' or 'Barrow', meaning farm, or settlement – thus meant *'The settlement of the sole ruler Eindrith'.*

Local legend said the Vikings had sailed up the River Soar when it was navigable and at the rear of the church, a Quay had once existed where their longboats once docked. But now, all but the ruins of the old church remained, and even those were not easily visible. The river had not been navigable for some years.

As they approached the site, it was clear that there had been recent digging, the earth was turned and lighter than the flat and settled patches, unmarked by even the simplest of crosses or memorials to the paupers.

'There is something quite wrong here,' the Reverend Morrison said, 'this is not right. This is the old end of the cemetery that has been dug, and I am not party to that. Also, there appears to be more burials to the end of the current row,' he indicated to the two areas that he said were newly dug over.

'And how can you explain this?' Marvin asked of the Crowleys.

'Must be the gypsies, or someone might have been trying to rob the graves,' said Mary Crowley, looking off across the fields in defiance.

'And you deny having anything to do with it? Be warned - this is a capital investigation,' said Beddows, hoping for the same response he had from Salt a few days earlier.

'How could we be implicated?' said Mary Crowley, hardly daring to make eye contact.

'When our expert Physicians examine the bodies that we may find, particularly those of the children, we will be scrutinising the adverts you posted and going back to find the parents who gave them up to you. And of course you will have recorded them in your registers to claim poor law relief. So, if one of those children has been murdered, and it is one of those in your registers, you will swing with the sickening men or women who actually murdered them,' said Beddows.

'I tell you woman, I would rather take my chances with the jury, than with St Clair and his cronies. It is time we told them what they want to know,' said Connor Crowley.

'I'm saying nothin' about anything; if you've done something, then you reconcile yerself with God. I plan to spend a few more years on this earth yet, yer feckin' idiot yer,' bellowed Mary Crowley, spitting venomously at her husband.

'I only bury them gents, honest, we don't have anything to do with any killing. Mrs Crowley gets the kids from the newspaper, and Mr St Clair moves them straight on to the highest bidders, so he says - If any come back dead, we don't even see them, they're normally wrapped in an old sheet or something, and he tells us to bury them. I never killed anyone in my life, honest, as God is my witness,' said Connor Crowley.

'So how many bodies are we going to find in these two new graves?' said Marvin.

'Four,' he said. 'Three young boys and some Irishman that stepped out of line. He was a bugger to bury; real heavy he was, not like the boys.'

'I think we need our reinforcements Gentlemen,' said Marvin 'From both Borough and County I suspect to sort out this horrible mess, together with Mr Mitchell who is Coroner for both.'

Even though there were no obvious structures nearby, the wind howled, as it blew across the meadows. With the density of the fog, which rolled up from the river, it was an eerie place, sending a chill through the bones of the assembled party.

'Hope that's not Annis herself, blowing across us, coming back for more skins for her aprons?' laughed Beddows.

He noticed Connor Crowley shiver, presumably at that same thought!

*****

By eleven o'clock that morning, the group at Aldeby had grown considerably.

It now consisted of Head Constable Charters; Chief Constable Goodyer; Detective Sergeant Kettle; Sergeant Marvin; Constable Parks; Constables Beddows and Shepherd, and some gravediggers that the Reverend Morrison had arranged.

Reverend Morrison stood with Mr Mitchell, who had also attended, and who possessed both a Coroner's exhumation order, and a Diocesan Faculty, with conditional authority to be used only if so required. Doctors Buck and Hamilton had also arrived, together with their impressive array of instruments.

The party also had procured a large four wheeled hay-rick and six rather hastily crafted Parish coffins that Reverend Morrison had sourced.

'I hope he has not got them off old man Pawley' Beddows joked 'as they will have fallen apart by the time they have half crossed the field'.

'An interesting one this,' said Mitchell. 'It is and yet it is not, in the same sense of the word, an *'exhumation'*. We are recovering bodies that have never been officially buried, but rather disposed of. But we may need to exhume some bodies, in the course of, and in order to recover those *so* disposed.'

'So can we begin to dig?' said Charters, looking to both Goodyer and Coroner Mitchell to make a start.

'You two,' said Beddows, 'can tell us who each of these poor wretches are, and where you, Mary Crowley, got them from. Hope you've got strong stomachs.'

And, in keeping with the previous month's inclemency, the rain began to pour, and the sky turned dark. A long rumble of thunder rolled across Enderby.

Shepherd could still not reconcile the fact that it could rain so heavily, of the same materials as the fog, yet not disperse the fog down in the process - that raindrops could pass through the fog.

'Feckin' told you this would happen. Black Annis is really pissed now; he's turning his wrath upon us,' Mary Crowley barked at her husband.

'Black Annis is a myth, a story,' said Beddows. 'I was only joking about her howling.'

'*He* feckin isn't,' said Connor Crowley. 'He's behind all this, and he's letting us know our time is short.'

'Don't talk such rubbish man,' said Goodyer. 'Can't be the drink - as I know where you've been since last night; must be some *malady of the brain,*' he laughed.

'You'll believe us when you catch him, and he'll give you a run for your money; evil he is, and a hard bastard,' said Connor Crowley.

'These people really do think Black Annis is human,' said Goodyer.

'That's what they said yesterday at the Workhouse; and Parks said it too. The party at the Mill, the children dancing around *Black Annis*; and singing - perhaps HE is a HE - and not just a story?' said Shepherd.

'At last, somebody's listening. Catch him quick, and you save us all a load of trouble,' said Connor Crowley.

'Yers a stupid old Fecker. Think he can't get to yers in Gaol? Yers a dead man Connor Crowley; a dead man - and I'm as good as dead now myself,' said Mary Crowley, starting to cry.

Shepherd looked across through the swirling fog, towards Fosse Way, just in time to observe a shiny black growler, with darkened windows or curtains, with fine chestnut horses, galloping fast, towards the Borough. The driver, dark and stooped over, obscured from view. Shepherd had seen the cab before - as the occupants of the cab had seen both he and Beddows.

'Look, Beddows; the growler from the other night in Eastgates.'

'Bet that's got someone on board we know, or we want to know. And from what they said yesterday, probably Mr St Clair, off to see his backers,' said Beddows.

The Crowleys gave each other a knowing look.

*****

The first body came into view fairly quickly, and was washed of its mud and soil by the strength of the rain, which came down in torrents.

A boy, about the same age as the boy in the river on New Year's Day; his skin an iridescent blend of deathly greys, greens, yellows and blues, and where the skin had broken, a devilish crimson, blackened by decay.

As with the boy in the river, this boy appeared emaciated, and his face gave signs of battering and bruising that would have occurred in life.

Buck and Hamilton measured the boy's height and made notes of the body.

The throat bore similar damage to the boy in the river, thought both Beddows and Shepherd.

'He has only been dead for about two weeks, probably at about the same time as your original body, perhaps a day or two before,' said Buck.

'I don't think there is any doubt that this boy is murder victim one from this dig. Box him up and he will be examined further back at the Infirmary,' said Buck, tying a small paper label on string around his ankle and securing it.

'Who is this one?' Kettle asked the Crowleys.

'The last one we buried. Picked him up from down at the Mill House. St Clair told us he had died digging sand, and had been suffocated. Don't pay to ask Mr St Clair more questions,' said Connor Crowley.

'And where did this one appear from?' Kettle asked Mary Crowley.

'A poor young thing brought him along. All skin and bones he was. She had seven others and this one might have some value. I gave her five shillings for him,' Crowley said.

'Five shillings?' said Mitchell. 'Is that all his life was worth?'

'Little Fecker has got to earn his keep to pay off the five shillings first. Then he's worth more, depending on how much work he does for who has him; and this one was for Mr St Clair - he would have had his money's worth out of him. Hard man he is,' said Crowley.

Beddows looked at her, and spat on her muddy skirt and feet 'Callous bitch, hope you swing for this somehow,' he growled. 'Pick your own preferred spot for later, whilst we are here!'

*****

The second body had been buried about a foot below the first, and looked in a poorer state of decay. The Church's view that a body was just food for the worms was pretty accurate, with large members of the species wriggling in and out of ears, eyes, and nose, and the flesh falling off; other hungry insects had also infested the remains.

The smell was dreadful, even through the rain and cold.

Even so, Hamilton and Buck detected that this to be the body of a small boy, probably younger, and rather better build at time of death, probably a month ago.

Again, obvious evidence that a significant throat wound had occurred, which would be a possible cause of death.

Hamilton tied on a tag, marked 'Number two' which he secured to the ankle.

The grave-diggers had to slide a wooden panel from one coffin lid under the body to recover it, before sliding it into another, and tapping on the lid. 'Slimy little bugger, this one' said one of them.

'And who is that boy?' Kettle asked the Crowleys.

'I buried him December twentieth, my birthday, that's why I remember,' said Connor Crowley.

'He got brought to us first off, by a chimney sweep from Wharf Street. Said he wouldn't climb, so he had to get rid of him. He gave him me for free. The boy went back to the town, to some posh house, a Physician I was told. Wanted a boy to look after house for him and cheaper than a maid suppose. Mr Pawley brought him back dead; told me not to ask any questions,' said Mary Crowley.

'You said you buried them in sheets. I haven't seen one on the first two bodies we have uncovered,' said Shepherd.

'Sheets is money, valuable, why throw them away when I need them for the little feckers back at the Workhouse - a good boil and they were fine,' chuckled Mary Crowley.

'So you can't try and tell us that you didn't know how they'd died, because you took them out of their sheets to bury them,' said Shepherd.

'You silly, greedy old bitch,' growled Connor Crowley. 'It'll be you who'll get us both necked.'

*****

Body three was that of a full grown adult male; buried about eighteen inches below the surface, in part of the grave that had been more saturated, causing the body to bloat, even under soil, and almost implode as it decayed, flesh lying in small chunks or sections that were falling loose.

'Looks like the cheaper stewing meat that is to be found on the butchers counters, well off the High Street, but slightly more gamey and off than normal,' suggested Beddows, trying to find a little dark humour to lighten proceedings.

'Are you trying to put me off meat completely, Beddows?' said a shocked Shepherd, gagging at the mere thought.

'Got any gravy with you?' laughed Beddows.

The body could be seen to have curly red hair, and a full beard, and on the hands, where the flesh had been eaten away, Buck identified old knuckle and finger fractures, suggesting a fighter or street fighter.

On the man's skull, a large indentation that appeared to be very much like that on the fighter O'Riordan could be seen.

'Seen that shaped injury before, Shepherd?' said Hamilton. 'Your body count is growing by each foot they dig.'

A tag with 'Number three' was secured to the leg, or what was left of one of them.

'And this one?' said Kettle.

'This one was brought here by Mr Pawley and some big Irish fella, giant he was. They said he was a Fancy, and had got his head smashed in a fight and he'd died the next day. Funny thing was there weren't any blood other than around his head, and he didn't look like he'd had a fight for years,' said Connor Crowley.

*****

The next body came from the end of the one that reverend Morrison called the *current grave.* Buried about three feet below the surface and clearly the earliest of the four exhumed so far.

The body was of an older boy, again, with no evidence of sheet or clothes. The flesh nearly all decayed, but Hamilton noted a clear fracture in the neck bones, and a gouge on the front of one of the vertebrae, which indicated it too had been caused by a knife or other sharp blade, which had penetrated deep, and with some obvious and deliberately applied force.

'This one has been dead for several weeks, perhaps months, and may even have been re-buried if it has been laid here only since October. That would be my best suggestion,' said Buck.

'Probably been moved - and no doubt to conceal it like the others,' confirmed Hamilton.

A label 'Body four' was attached to a leg bone, before the grave diggers scooped the remains with their improvised coffin lid cradle, and slid the remains into another of the coffins.

'That's all four that you have suggested to us,' said Charters to the Crowleys. 'How many more will we find if we carry on digging?'

'Honest to God,' said Connor Crowley 'There's only been the four since it all started - all the other bodies are just poor souls who died of their maladies or hard work.'

'Hard work?' questioned Coroner Mitchell. 'Sheer brutality more like. The sooner our Politicians put a stop to this abuse and give people rights the better. In my view most of these will have died prematurely because of the lack of state support, or condoned slavery and brutality. Immoral it is!'

'Can I suggest that we stop at this point? Reverend Morrison confirms that this appears to be the only ground that he can confirm as dug without his knowledge. We have enough bodies to keep us busy for a while, and enough no doubt to prove capital offences,' said Goodyer.

'And leave these other wretched souls in peace for a while,' said Mitchell. 'I concur!'

'Gentlemen - we will take our leave, if these kind gentlemen with their cart and our bodies, will convey them with us to the Infirmary, where Hamilton and I shall be busy for a day or so, no doubt,' said Buck.

'And we, Gentlemen,' said Charters, 'have these two prisoners to interview, and more villains to locate,' indicating to the Officers of the Borough.

'Mr Charters, you can have exclusive use of Sergeant Marvin and Constable Parks until further notice. If you are happy to centralize the enquiry from within the Borough, my County is rather stretched as it is,' offered Goodyer.

As the party made its way into separate groups, the Thunder intensified, and the rain washed over the newly exhumed trenches, filling them with a new odorous slimy mud, that would not heal for some days to come.

Whilst Shepherd and the exhumation party had been busy at Aldeby St John's, other darker forces were also at work.

Shepherd had been correct in recognising the shiny black growler as being the same cab that had passed by him and Beddows in Silver Street, nights earlier.

The cab drove along Fosse Way and in toward the Borough, before turning right around St Nicholas Place, through Applegate Street, Southgates Street and onto Oxford Street. The coach then turned into Mill Lane and left into Grange Lane, coming to rest in the shadows of the new factory under construction, just before Twizzle and Twine passage.

The driver of the cab wore a shortened top hat, a dark cape, which was earning its keep today in the torrents of rain and the Thunder storm, and dark trousers and full riding boots. His face was partly obscured by a scarf, which revealed only his eyes, which were dark and menacing.

From the cab stepped the occupant, Brendan St Clair, dressed in a grey woolen three-piece suit, shirt and tie, and matching Derby hat. He had dark red curly hair, and his nose reflected a fighting past, as did the scars around his eyes. He carried a long walking cane with an ornate brass hilt. He looked similar in style and apparel to the good Sergeant Roberts.

The two men walked towards Shepherd's aunt's house on the corner of the Passage, looking around them furtively.

There were few people in the street, one or two coming or going from the Infirmary, and a similar number to or from the Bridewell, which was seen clearly from the Aunt's front door.

'Time for a little retribution,' grinned St Clair, 'and to put Constable Shepherd off the trail once and for all, a lesson he will never forget.'

The driver nodded, stood alongside him, holding a large folded sack.

St Clair struck the front door with the hilt of his cane; *tap...tap...tap...*slow, menacing knocks.

Sally had been making the bed and tidying round when she heard the door, and ran to it quickly. As she did, the door flung open in her face, knocking her backwards and onto the floor, splitting her bottom lip, which started to bleed profusely.

The two men walked in, and before she could react, St Clair brought down the hilt of his cane across the top of her head, and she immediately fell unconscious.

The driver bundled the seemingly lifeless Sally into the sack, and slung her onto his shoulder.

'The life of the Constable has just taken a major turn for the worse,' gloated St Clair, looking outside to make sure that there could be nobody to challenge them, between the door and the cab.

As they confidently stepped off, leaving the front door ajar, St Clair took no undue notice of the old man limping towards him, holding his weight up on a simple wooden crutch, seemingly bound for the Infirmary.

As they stepped nearer, another man stepped out from Twizzle and Twine passage, taller with jet black hair, and wearing a cowman's apron and old boots, cattle prod in hand.

Neither seemed out of place, as St Clair swaggered along, protecting his driver and precious bundle.

Without warning, the man with the crutch swung the wooden accompaniment with great force and struck St Clair across his midriff, causing him to double up in pain, before the crutch came down across the back of his head - and *St Clair* now experienced the darkness.

The driver halted, and stood confused, precious cargo in the sack over his shoulder, and hand reaching under his cape, produced a well worn cut-throat razor.

'Don't go fecking wit' us you bastards,' he shouted, swaying the blade backwards and forwards at the limping man. 'Yers don't know who yers are fecking with - so back off!'

'And don't you go fecking with our friends,' came another voice, as a large brown boot caught him square in the crown jewels, putting him onto his knees, before a hefty cattle prod came down across the bridge of his nose, and he joined his master in that same dark, place.

The two men still standing looked at each other, and the older looking man with the crutch said 'And definitely don't try fecking about with Tanky Smith and Black Tommy!'

Haynes quickly reached and pulled apart the opening of the sack, in which he found the limp body of Sally Brown, now starting to stir.

'Sorry, Miss Sally, we're friends, Sergeants Smith and Haynes, you're safe now.'

Sally smiled briefly, and then threw up all down the front of Black Tommy's apron.

'Always pays to wear an apron when dealing with sickly women,' said Haynes.

'And animals,' laughed Tanky, looking down at their prisoners.

The two assailants were placed into their own cab, their hands bound tightly with rope that both Smith and Haynes routinely carried for such eventualities.

Smith sat inside on the opposite side, next to Sally, who by now had started to recover her senses, but felt decidedly groggy, whilst Haynes took the reins and drove the cab to Town Hall Lane, and the safety of the Borough cells.

'Nice cab this, would be a shame to waste it, as these gentlemen won't be in need of it for a while, if at all,' thought Haynes.

*****

'What have we got here then?' said Sergeant Sheffield, as Smith and Haynes threw their prisoners, brusquely, through the front door to the station, and onto the Charge Room floor.

'These rather nasty gentlemen, are charged with attempting to kidnap young Miss Sally Brown here, the friend of one Constable Shepherd, assaulting two Constables, and threatening to kill the same two Constables - for starters,' said Smith.

*****

By the time the exhumation party had arrived back at Town Hall Lane, it was four o'clock in the afternoon.

Shepherd looked visibly shocked to see Sally, sat in the corner of the muster room, with Tanky Smith and Tommy Haynes, and drinking tea. She looked dishevelled and had blood down the front of her blouse.

'What in hell's name has been going on?' said Shepherd. 'Have you sent for a Physician?'

'Whilst you lot were out digging, your good lady answered the door to two rather nasty Irishmen, who clearly had intentions to cause you and Miss Sally some serious distress. But fortunately, the attentive and reliable Sergeants Smith and Haynes had anticipated some skullduggery, and the two said gentlemen were *subdued* and arrested,' said Smith.

Sally rushed to Shepherd and threw her arms around his neck, and promptly broke into tears.

'Sam Shepherd, what would you have done without me?' she laughed through her tears, 'and look at my nice blouse - after all the trouble I went to, to keep it clean the other night.'

'And who are these gentlemen?' said Shepherd.

'As yet we aren't on speaking terms - but they turned up in a rather swanky growler, which we have parked outside, and which the good Mr Keetley is going to put in his stables for the time being, across the road,' said Haynes.

'And where are these gentlemen?' said Shepherd.

'The posh one is in the far cell, as he obviously prefers more room. His driver is in this cell, here next to me,' said Sergeant Sheffield. 'Mind the posh one, though, I just picked up his walking stick and lo and behold, it is a sword stick, and rather well used by the look of it! Nasty piece of work, so it would seem.'

'Might I go and say hello?' said Shepherd.

'Be careful,' said Charters. 'Don't want any trouble do we?' nodding his agreement.

Sheffield opened the cell door and allowed Shepherd in to see the prisoner St Clair.

'Why Mr St Clair, we haven't officially met, but I take it you know who I am?' said Shepherd, holding out his left hand in front of him.

St Clair looked confused, and had never thought of having to shake hands with a Copper, let alone a left handed one. He held out his hand, but sadly missed the right fist, steaming towards him, knocking him onto the floor and breaking his nose.

'Glad you've settled in,' said Shepherd. 'I'll be back shortly, to finish this conversation,' at which point Shepherd backed away and slammed shut the cell door again behind him.

'That didn't take long?' said Sheffield, drawing deeply on his pipe, displaying a broad, knowing, smile.

'Didn't have that much to say' said Shepherd. 'He was having a nose bleed and it clearly wasn't the right time,' rubbing his hand lovingly.

'All right lad?' asked the cluster of Detectives who were talking with Mr Charters and Beddows.

'Much better thank you gents - don't think he is one of 'The Fancy' though.'

Mr Charters briefly shook his head, remembering his youthful days, and the satisfaction that came from a well deserved occasional slap.

*****

Detective Sergeant Kettle had now been sent by Mr Charters to the Infirmary, where he had drawn the short straw of liaising with Doctors Buck and Hamilton, during the Post-mortem examinations that were to be carried out.

There still remained the urgent matter of convening, and opening Coroners Inquests on the bodies they had recovered, and Charters was off to see Mr Mitchell to take advice on how many there would need to be, or whether one for Physician Wilson and one combined inquest for the four bodies in the Aldeby graves would suffice.

Mitchell and Charters established that midday tomorrow, Friday the 11th January 1850, would be suitable. There were to be two inquests, one for Wilson, and one combined inquest for the unidentified bodies. A venue needed to be sourced and an Inn with a suitable area for viewing the bodies, and then to hold the Inquest processes that would ensue.

Charters suggested that as the bodies were already in situ at the Infirmary, it might be agreeable to hold the viewing of the bodies there, and then adjourn to 'The Turks Head' which stood between the Borough Gaol and the Infirmary, the Inn ironically being the favoured grand-stand at hangings which took place outside the gates of the Borough Gaol, and for which Leicester's finest paid a guinea for the best vantage point on the upper floors.

Mitchell indicated that he would need two juries, one for each inquest, and agreed with the venue. 'The Landlord does a nice haunch of venison every now and again, and very agreeable Port. Good choice Robert.'

Charters tasked the late shift to select and summons the required jurymen to be at 'The Turks Head' as required before midday on the 11th.

*****

Detective Sergeant Kettle had by now had his fill of Post-mortems. Four in one day; more than any man should have to stomach.

The two doctors, working in their best suit trousers, pale and close-fitting and with only aprons to protect them, were now covered from chest to toe in a vile mixture of blood, brains, decaying flesh and the various contents of guts, bladders and various other glands that they had pierced during the course of the examinations.

The butchers block table they worked on, had become slick with the same materials, as had the sawdust they had placed across the floor of the operating room, to soak it all up.

Even the doctors had had to open the outside door to the elements, to let out the foul stench of death and decay, and to let in Leicester's best air, clawing and smoky though it undoubtedly would be.

The examinations took the two men several hours to complete, and in between each, they stopped, wrote up their notes of the examination, before turning to the next. Their note books were also matted in the same debris as the rest of the room.

Kettle looked at his boots and trousers, and even though he stood several feet back throughout each examination, he was soiled as well.

His wife would not be wishing to get too close to him for days, if ever again, and his boots and trousers would be boiled or confined to the yard - or more probably the back of the privvie.

The results of the four Post-mortems were recorded as;-

Body 1. Unidentified male; - Age approximately 7 or 8 years. Poorly nourished; partially (early stage) Decomposed. Dark lanky hair; 4 feet eight tall; Significant cut to throat tissues and larynx. Cut suggests left handed killer. Sodomised prior to death; Time of death around 3rd week of December.

Body 2. Unidentified male;- 5 to 6 years. 4 feet 4 tall; short blond hair; later stage decomposition; Evidence of throat injury consistent with body 1. Probable evidence of sodomy; Time of death around 2nd week December.

Body 3. Unidentified adult male;- 5'9 tall. Stocky build; Advanced decomposition; Fractures to knuckles both hands; Massive fracture to skull; Injury size, shape and measurements consistent with man O'Riordan. Time of death around second week December as body 2.

Body 4. Unidentified white male child;- 11 to 12 years; Short dark spiky hair; Advanced decomposition; Fractured neck.;

Evidence of sharp object on interior of fractured vertebrae.
Time of death- as early as September last. Unable to determine
any sexual interference due to decay.

*****

As the St Martin's clock struck six, Sergeants Smith and Haynes
began their interviews of the two men that they had earlier
detained.

To start off with, they had decided to interview the driver,
Michael Maloney.

'Tell us what you were doing earlier today, in Grange Lane,' said
Smith.

'Doing as I was told,' said Maloney.

'And told by whom?' said Haynes.

'Mr St Clair,' said Maloney. 'No point in denying it, is there?
Fecking obvious I should think!'

'And what had he told you to do?' said Smith.

'He said he and his friends had been seriously threatened by a
number of Constables, including your Constable Shepherd, as he
called him.'

'Go on,' said Haynes.

'And that we were going to fetch Shepherd's little girlfriend and
teach the man a lesson he would never forget.'

'And what would that be?' said Haynes.

'Mr St Clair provides entertainment for a lot of rich, wealthy,
powerful people, and she was to be entertainment, so he said.'

'What sort of entertainment might that be?' said Smith.

'Probably ridden her, shagged her, and then cut the bitch's throat,' he coldly grinned.

'Who would have done that?' said Smith.

'Whoever paid the highest price of course - perverted lot these feckers are, so I'm told.'

'And you have seen this happen before?' said Smith.

'Several times - but mainly in Ireland. Not been at it long over here; been waiting for The Ole Witch to come back over.'

'The ole witch?' said Haynes.

'Black Annis; he's the killer, he's the one we should all be frightened of.'

'You don't seem frightened now?' said Smith.

'Cos I reckon if I tell you everything from the start, you'll cut me a deal. And I ain't done enough to hang. I got nothin else here, but I hear the Colonies are a bit warmer, so I'll take what's comin' to me like a man, provided you give me some protection.' Maloney grinned, like a cat about to get the cream.

'Might be able to, and then again might not. Might be your Mr St Clair will stitch you up, and you'll go to the gallows together,' said Smith.

'Mr St Clair is an honorable man. I give you him, he gives you Black Annis and he walks away with a deal as well; and then poor ole Black Annis can get what he deserves - and all his rich fecking friends,' Maloney sneered.

'You seem rather confident?' said Haynes.

'We talked about this so many times before. What we would do if we got caught; I know what he'll do, and he knows what I am doing right now.'

'Carry on then; let's hear a bit more,' said Smith.

'Mr St Clair is a fixer. He fixes anything that Annis wants, because Black Annis pays handsomely. He wants a boy, St Clair taps up old mother Crowley. He wants a lady, he taps up Manky Lil. He wants in on a big money deal; he has people in his pocket like your sniveling Mr Salt or Sergeant Roberts.'

'Go on,' said Haynes.

'He fixes, he delivers, I drives him and give a bit of muscle here and there, he gets paid, I get paid - life in balance!' he grinned.

'And where was Miss Brown to be delivered?' said Haynes.

'She was special. There was to be a special guest night tonight, at the Ole Stokers.'

'And would you and St Clair remain there, whilst all this goes on?' said Smith.

Maloney nodded.

'And you wait until after she's killed before you get paid?' said Smith.

'Yes; Annis pays St Clair, St Clair pays me, and we feck off and leave it to them.'

'And the bodies?' said Haynes.

'We get our pet Mr Pawley, and the late lamented O'Riordan, to lose them for us, with the help of Connor Crowley.'

'Why did O'Riordan get murdered?' said Smith.

'Murdered? He got feckin slaughtered; there was blood and brains everywhere and it made a load of them toffs sick to watch.'

'He was slaughtered in front of an audience?' said Haynes.

217

'It's like a knackers' yard they've got set up, down in the Bower, under the back room. O'Riordan fecked up and dumped that kid in the river instead of taking him to Crowley, and opened up this fecking can o worms. So Annis tied him to a beam, nearly took his brains out pole-axing the big Fecker - and then cuts his feckin throat! Evil bastard is that Black Annis!'

'O'Riordan had been sodomised,' said Haynes.

'O'Riordan was always getting sodomised. He was Mistress Salt's Molly - Salt's reward for all his help, and Salt's Bruiser for when things got rough, til he fecked up. Salt cried like a baby when he got topped.'

'And today we have dug up three young boys and one red headed, bearded male, from Aldeby graveyard, who Crowley has buried recently. What do you know about them?' said Smith.

'The boys were all entertainment. They were all taken to The Stokers, and after Annis and his friends had their fun, Pawley and O'Riordan took them to Crowley as usual.'

'Who was the red-haired bloke?' said Haynes.

'He was Mr Pawley's first helper, like O'Riordan. But when he done the first job he got a bit gobby and didn't like the coin he was given, said he would tell someone what was going on unless he got more - silly Fecker. So Annis tapped him with his pole again, and finished him off with his usual signature.'

'What do you mean by that?' said Haynes.

'Cut his throat. Learned his trade as a slaughterer, back in the Ole Country - wasn't a bull or a horse didn't go down first time with ole Annis, so they don't have a chance.'

'And why is he called Black Annis? The legend is of a woman, a hag, a witch,' said Smith.

'He likes dressing up as her, and he makes kids disappear.' Maloney laughed loudly, tears rolling down his face.

'And you are not going to tell us who Black Annis is?' said Smith.

'Cos I don't feckin know, that's why; he only dealt with St Clair.'

'You say that the killing was done in the Bower, why call it that?' said Smith.

'Cos that's what Black Annis lives in - most of the time - so the legend goes.'

'So, Mr Maloney, what sort of a deal do you think we can get for you?' said Smith.

'I want to go to the Colonies; I want a different name; and I don't want to be tried at the same assizes as Mr St Clair, as nor will he with Black Annis, I'm sure.'

'Would you not think, that as an accomplice, kidnapping the victims, taking them to be killed, staying til they've been killed, in order to get paid, that they might want to hang you, as you are as guilty as Black Annis?' said Smith.

'They wouldn't do that in the ole country, not as just accomplices,' said Maloney.

'But yer not in the fecking ole country are you squire?' grinned Smith. 'Think yer deal might be off the table based on what you've told us.'

'In that case I'll deny everything,' sneered Maloney.

'I think you've done more than enough to put a rope round a few necks, including your own, and with no resistance. That was just too easy. Anyway, there's two of us that will testify what you have just told us,' laughed Haynes.

'In that case I may as well also tell you that it was me and St Clair that gave wee Shepherd his kicking - clears up everything then, I think.'

*****

About an hour later, Smith and Haynes took Brendan St Clair into the office at the rear of the Muster Room, and sat him in the same chair that had accommodated Maloney.

'So then Mr St Clair, I understand that you are a man likely to be looking for a deal, just like your friend Mr Maloney?' said Smith.

'Might be, if the terms are right,' he smiled.

'How's the bonce?' said Smith. 'Forget how hard a crutch can be at times; must be a bleeder to walk with all the time?'

'It was a rather unnecessary bit of violence,' said St Clair.

'And if I hadn't, I don't suppose you would have considered reverting to your little sword-stick?' laughed Smith.

'Why, I never gave it a thought,' laughed St Clair.

'You seem to like jumping people from behind. Shepherd too big to take on face to face?' said Smith.

'Only a frightener - a wee kicking is good for the soul, or is it the sole?' he laughed.

'Anyways, that's the pleasantries over. Now then, this deal?' said Haynes.

'I take it Mr Maloney has done the honorable thing and told you about me and only about me, hierarchically speaking?' said St Clair.

'If you mean placing you at the top of Mr Maloney's *direct* food chain; that would be right,' said Smith.

'Then you must expect me to tell you about Black Annis?' said St Clair.

'That would be rather nice, if you would,' said Haynes. 'Mr Maloney was most helpful.'

'Have you ever heard of a man called Dubh O'Donnell?' said St Clair.

'I have heard the name once before, his name came up in relation to possibly being behind running 'The Stokers Arms',' said Smith.

'The Stokers Arms'; 'The Fox and Grapes'; 'The Horse Breakers'. He's the man with the money that runs the Rookeries and what money there is left down there to be made,' said St Clair.

'He sounds a bit bigger than that to me, if he mixes with Toffs and our hoi-polloi,' said Smith.

'If you think Irish, think big! Look at England now. Who's building all the new Industry, the Railways, the Canals. What do they all need? Navvies! Who runs the market in Navvies? Dubh does. Money is power and power is Money, and Dubh has access to the fecking lot,' said St Clair.

'And how many *business ventures* does he have his hands in the Borough and County at the moment?' said Haynes.

'Just look at Leicester railway station, and now they want to take the railway all the way through to London, through Market Harborough, as well as Rugby. That will be worth thousands to him, if he can get a piece of the action. That's where he makes his name, and meets his hoi-polloi.'

'So, what do you want to tell us about the killings?' said Smith.

'I want to make it quite clear that I am just a middle man; a fixer; on a different level to Maloney. But it's Dubh that pulls my strings - and I dance like a puppet, except this time, I don't want to dance like a puppet on Jack Ketch's strings, if you know what I mean?'

'How many has Dubh murdered?' said Haynes.

'You know why they call him Black Annis?' laughed St Clair.

'Because he likes to dress up, and he can make people disappear?' said Smith, 'or so your friend Maloney says.'

'Dubh means Black, and he is a black hearted bastard. Then again, don't think he has a heart, and he kills for fun, and he's a dirty bastard! Has a taste for little boys, and sodomises them. The dressing up is just for parties and some of his special events; keeps him anonymous with them that don't know him. But you're right; he makes people disappear, just like Black Annis, and thus that's the name he earned in Ireland,' said St Clair.

'So, how many?' said Haynes again.

'If you want to go digging up railway embankments and cuttings, or empty the odd canal; you'll find dozens probably, here and back in Ireland. Anyone who crosses him he murders, or should I say, slaughters. That's his favourite.'

So, let's talk about the last three or four months, let's say from last September?' said Smith.

'There's four lads I know of, and two big fellas who were both bruisers for him, but let him down,' he replied.

How did he kill the boys?' said Haynes.

'They were all play things. He would look after them for a few days, treat them nice, and give them a good seeing to. Loves young arses he does. Then, when he's bored, he takes them to the Stokers, sometimes on special nights, and shares them with his perverted associates. And when it's all over, he cuts their poor little throats and we have to get rid for him, or rather we fix it,' explained St Clair.

'Who are these associates, these hoi-polloi?' said Haynes.

'Gents and Ladies they call themselves - what a fecking joke. At least one MP; a Recorder from out of the Borough, two or three Borough men, including that little faggot Salt; a Sheriff, from somewhere - all debauched and in a wild frenzy. But I'll tell you no names. I'm sure if you take a look at the cabs around the side streets you'll find out who they are,' said St Clair.

'And what about our Detective Roberts?' said Haynes.

'Ah, Dubh's lap-dog,' laughed St Clair. 'What a man won't stoop to when he's driven by greed - and your Mr Roberts is a greedy wee man.'

'Where is he?' said Smith, 'as I would like to get my hands on him myself.'

'Probably sitting on Dubh's lap, or licking his balls, waiting to be fed another wad of cash,' said St Clair.

'Who killed Wilson, The Physician?' said Haynes.

'Roberts did it himself. His own fecking brother-in-law; just to stop him turning evidence against him about the boy in the river,' said St Clair.

'Why was that?' said Smith.

'O'Riordan panicked the first time and dumped the boy in the river, then he fecked up completely and tried to burn it all. Wilson was there when the boy was killed, joined in he did. He had brought him from his own house down to the Bower. When he saw the body in your boat he shitted himself, and Roberts knew he was getting nervous. Dubh told Roberts to sort out the mess and get rid of Wilson, or Dubh would get rid of them both,' said St Clair.

'So, where can we find your Dubh O'Donnell now?' said Smith.

'What time is it now?' said St Clair.

'About half eight,' said Smith.

'Well at about half past ten, no later, you might care to drop by the Bower and gate-crash a little soiree that might just be going on,' grinned St Clair.

'Well, we might just have to do that,' said Smith.

'Now, that deal you might offer me?' said St Clair.

'I don't offer deals. Anyway, I like the thought of you as a puppet - Jack Ketch's puppet - just like you said,' said Smith.

*****

Smith and Haynes quickly locked up St Clair, in the largest cell in the station. Tonight, any other prisoners would be bailed or summonsed quickly. More room would be needed later, and most likely, room at the County Cells as well.

Charters listened attentively to the briefing, before sending a runner to Mr Goodyer at the County Office.

'Sergeant Wright, keep the day shift on until I say so - I want the night shift ready in the Muster room by half past nine!' said Charters.

At half past nine, Charters and his counterpart Goodyer had assembled Thirty Officers from the Borough night shift and the County 'Reserve'.

In Town Hall Lane, a row of cabs, some belonging to Goodyer's Force, some 'arranged' through a helpful Removals company, in which up to ten men could be concealed under a canvas shell, and a couple of cabs that were in trust with the Borough - including St Clair's own - were lined up and the men briefed.

The main arrest party would be Head Constables Charters and Goodyer, Sergeants Smith, Haynes, Kettle - now back from the Infirmary, Sergeant Wright from the night shift, Beddows and Shepherd, Sergeant Marvin, and Constables from the two forces.

The orders were simple. Fifteen Constables were to secure the perimeter of 'The Stokers Arms', with Sergeant Wright in charge. Fifteen Constables to secure entry to the variety hall, and the 'Bower' that St Clair had described as the event location.

The arrest team would then deal with those in attendance. The arrest team was issued with short cutlasses owing to the likelihood of extreme resistance, as well as having their truncheons.

Speed and secrecy were imperative, and once briefed there could be no delay. Men were checked onto their cabs, and everyone was accounted for.

The convoy of cabs set off at twenty minutes to ten. The perimeter team separated and covered Belgrave Gate, Wilton Street, Bedford Street - at the back of the block and Gower

Street. The arrest team and enforced entry team went straight to the front of the pub.

There were several bruisers on the door, and they were not going to give way without a fight. Fists and weapons flew, and Constables and bruisers fell about fighting, but the sound of Police truncheons seemed to have the edge.

The main team went straight through the bar, took down two further bruisers at a rear door to the variety room, and gained entry.

The room was full, and a woman singer was in full voice, surrounded by well healed punters, and a fare share of Fancy. More fights started, which the uniform Constables were ordered to subdue.

Charters and Goodyer, with the arrest team went through a small wooden door and down a flight of short wooden stairs, into what appeared to be a large underground cave, from which cheering and yelping could be heard.

The 'Bower', lit with small theatrical arc lamps, which gave a fierce bright white light, gave the overall impression was of a damp, dingy cave or cavern, which smelled of a slaughter house, complete with tightly stretched skins - hopefully of animal origin.

The floor was covered in saw dust, and around the area in the centre, strewn with old barrels, upon which about fifteen 'customers' sat. This was the source of the shouting and cheering.

Each customer, dressed as if attending a masquerade, with unique and hideous costumes, had their face hidden behind one of a variety of macabre masks and wigs.

In the centre of the floor, a naked man, kneeling. The man had what appeared to be a pig's face pulled over his head, and the man had been tethered with a short length of rope, to a strong beam, which stood upright in the floor, the rope then tethered through a large wrought iron ring, bolted to the beam.

On the floor, and immediately behind the naked man, crouched a figure; dressed in a dark black gown, with a blue face mask which bore a crooked nose, and a long grey hairpiece, and wearing an apron of skins, similar to those stretched around the walls, as in the legend of Black Annis.

The figure - half-knelt, half-crouched behind the naked man, who in turn was knelt over a bale of straw. The man in the gown simulating sodomy with the other man; in his left hand, he held a short riding crop, which he continued to bring down across the man's back, and the man in the pig's mask screamed with each blow.

The crowd was chanting 'Annis...Annis...Annis...' in a frenzied manner.

The gowned and masked figure suddenly became aware of the interlopers, and reached for a pistol, which lay on a barrel to his side, dropping his whip and grabbing the pistol simultaneously.

As he did so, a well worn wooden truncheon smashed into his left arm, a distinct 'Tank' and then crack of bone could be heard over the chanting, as the gun dropped to the floor.

Smith grabbed the broken arm, whilst Haynes took hold of the other arm, and the two detectives drove the figure, hard, into the sawdust on the floor, with a loud crunch and exhalation of breath from the figure, struggling beneath them.

Next to the barrel, a large butcher's knife; and stood against the post, to which the first man was tethered, a slaughter-man's pole-axe, still stained from previous killings.

Detective Sergeant Kettle secured the knife and pole-axe.

Beddows walked up to the figure bent over the bale, and took hold of the pigs face, which had been freshly cut and stank of newly cut raw pork flesh, which had been draped over the man, covering his own face in blood and gore.

'Good god,' exclaimed Charters, 'If it isn't Sergeant Roberts. Looks like we got here in the nick of time, else you were Black Annis' next victim.'

Roberts cried; great heaving sobs, as huge red wealds began to show from the whipping he had been receiving.

'Thank god, sir, indeed you have saved me; he was going to slaughter me, just for the sick pleasure of these, these - degenerate bastards,' cried Roberts, looking around at the gathered guests.

'Bit of a waste of time though, me old duck,' said Beddows, 'cos where you're going, you're for the gallows anyways. Damned if you do, damned if you don't; life's a bitch, and then you marry one, and then you die!'

Charters walked up to the man that Smith and Haynes were pinning to the floor, still screaming as a result of a little *gratuitously applied crepitus* from where the two ends of his broken arm were grinding together, as he strained to break free.

'It's only the pain that hurts,' smiled Smith. 'Not as bad as the pain you'll experience on the drop, so I'm led to believe.'

Charters pulled off the mask and wig - to reveal Black Annis' true identity.

'Mr Dhub O'Donnell, I presume, at last?' enquired Charters. 'That seems to be all the main offenders, now, safely in custody'.

'Go Feck yerself. Yers got nothin' to gloat about. Yous'll never get me to the rope - watch and see,' the man snarled.

228

'Now then, Mr Goodyer, let's have a look at the other fine people we have gathered around us. Should be an eye-opening experience,' said Charters.

'If you would all be so kind as to remove your masks and wigs,' shouted Beddows.

'Good evening, Your Grace,' said Mr Goodyer, nodding in acquaintance, 'nice to see you again; how is the Duchess?'

'And good evening to you Alderman, sorry *Aldermen*. How are the plans for the railway expansion coming along? And Manky Lil - see you've come to check on the interests of some of your toffs, eh? Or looking for some new Toffs as well? Learned anything have you? Lots of beams to choose from at Number 12, hey?' said Goodyer.

Of the assorted deviants who had been watching the assault on Roberts, many were well known, and many, public faces. Many were known to the ordinary Constables who looked on, shaking their heads in disbelief.

'Could have had a lodge meeting while you waited?' smiled Charters. 'Shame Mr Thompson couldn't come along; would have made for some entertaining press, next edition. Mind, we shall probably read of one or two public notices and resignations shortly, isn't that right?' continued Charters, scanning the faces in the 'Bower'.

'Right now, I want Mr Roberts and Mr O'Donnell back to the Station. They have some talking to do, or is it squealing Mr Roberts?' said Charters.

'And you other fine people, you have been seen, you have been recognized, you have been shamed; and now we shall be seeking your assistance, as no doubt you will wish to give us a statement?' laughed Charters.

'Will raise a few eyebrows at the Assizes!' smiled Goodyer.

The two prisoners were escorted back to the Borough Police Cells, by Sergeants Smith and Haynes, Beddows, Shepherd, Charters, and a guard each, of four officers.

Above the 'Bower', Sergeant Wright and his other uniformed Constables had been joined by Chief Constable Goodyer. Goodyer would take the statements from the deviant hoi-polloi himself, assisted by his own Sergeant Marvin, in the comfort of the County Station, where they - the deviants- were to assemble.

The other Constables were still restraining assorted Bruisers, and both groups were showing signs of the violence that had been initiated, with cuts, bruises, the odd broken nose and lost teeth; but 'The Fancy' who had been there when the raid started had fled for fear of incrimination.

The vast majority of paying guests stood in shock at the events of the previous few minutes. They were shown out by Constables who were able, and were told in no uncertain terms, that they should avoid the Stokers like the plague, for the foreseeable future – 'the Gipsy's warning!'

*****

By midnight, 'The Stokers Arms' lay in complete darkness, secured for a proper examination the following morning. But, all around the Rookeries lights burned later than usual, and in the other pubs, 'The Fox and Grapes 'and 'The Horse Breakers', word spread rapidly that Black Annis had been taken, and things would never be the same again.

In 'The Fox and Grapes', Clodagh Murphy, called for a moment's silence, and raised glass of stout, the froth already clinging to the old woman's moustache that grew wild over her top lip.

'To Black Annis - a hero to some - a bad Fecker to many - a greedy, nasty bastard, love him or loathe him! God help yer for what yers got coming to yers.'

230

'Black Annis,' came the unconvincing response.

Old man Delaney, whose yard had been the site of O'Riordan's disposal and who Dhub O'Donnell had skimmed for cash from every job he had ever pulled, sank his pint with relish and slammed his empty glass down on the counter. 'Give me another pint of yer best, Clodagh me lass, as I think I can finally wash the taste of Black Annis away for good!'

'Yers a brave man, Delaney; there's a lot in here who will think yers bad mouthing him - and what will yers do if he comes back?'

'From what I hear he'll be wishing he really was the old hag herself, and riding off in the night. Cos' unless he's dead clever, he's a dead man already,' said Delaney.

'The Fancy' were abnormally quiet, as were the Bruisers. In all the Irish pubs, and throughout the Borough, similar conversations were taking place, and already the talk of swung to who would now fill the top seat and run the empire O'Donnell had left behind.

Left behind - as there now seemed to be no hope for the man.

Back at the Borough cells, the two men were unceremoniously bundled into separate cells.

By this time, Maloney and St Clair had been moved to the cell in the yard at the entrance to the Great Hall, ready to put them back for interview again if Roberts or O'Donnell changed the level of their involvement.

Neither could shout to O'Donnell, and neither *wanted* to shout to Roberts.

*****

Charters pulled his Sergeants and Constables together in the Muster Room.

231

'Well lads; a good night's work. We are going to let these two gentlemen have the night to think about their situation. And in the morning we will be interviewing Sergeant Roberts first, and that is a job for Detective Sergeant Beddows and Constable Shepherd.'

'Detective Sergeant Beddows, you just said, sir. Do you mean Constable Beddows or Detective Sergeant Kettle?' queried Beddows.

'No, *Detective Sergeant Beddows* - as of now - and I shall be advising the Watch Committee of the restoration of your rank tomorrow, and of your new status; and well earned I must say! And we are short of one Detective Sergeant, now, anyway,' said Charters.

Shepherd shook Beddows' hand, and Beddows was almost knocked over with the pats that rained on him from Smith, Haynes and Kettle. 'Well done, Beddows!' came the response.

'And once Mr Roberts tells us the sordid details, and only then, will we talk to Mr Dubh O'Donnell - and when we have so much black on him, he won't need to confess!' said Charters.

'The interviewing Officers will be Sergeants Smith and Haynes.'

'What about me, sir?' said Kettle.

'Ah, the small matter of two inquests to supervise and the Coroner to entertain. I want you at the Infirmary for midday, then with the juries and Mr Mitchell to The Turks Head. You will be assisted by Sergeant Marvin and Constable Parks from the County Force, courtesy of Mr Goodyer.'

Kettle sulked; the short straw again. 'Certainly, sir. Twelve it is.'

'Tonight though I want four armed officers, two on each side of O'Donnell's cell, inside and out, as I don't want any of our Irish brethren to try and spring him. Night Sergeant to lock up the

Station, and entry only once recognized. I want everyone back here for eight o'clock in the morning.'

*****

It was just after one in the morning when Shepherd walked through the door of his Aunt's house, in Grange Lane. A candle had been lit in the front Parlour, and Shepherd could see Sally, curled up on a cushion on the seat by the small grate, a simple blanket held tightly around her.

Shepherd kissed her gently on her forehead, and Sally stirred, opening her eyes and smiling broadly. 'Oh young master Sam, you're home safe at last, I was worried when you didn't get back earlier.'

'Sorry, sweet Sally, but we have had a most eventful day, and we have now got all of the main suspects locked up; but tomorrow will be even busier, and I must be back by eight.'

Sally looked at Sam coyly, and took his hand. 'Don't let me be alone tonight. I didn't think I would see you again earlier, and I am so afraid. Don't leave me again tonight,' kissing Shepherd softly, wincing, as her own cut lip reminded them of her earlier ordeal.

Sally set off up the short staircase to Sam's room. The glow from the candles she and Shepherd carried gave off enough light for Shepherd to see the shape of her fine slim legs through the cotton nightdress, and her slender ankles and perfect toes. Sam felt a familiar stirring.

Sally sat on the bed, as Sam began to undress, still sore from his beating.

'You have a fine, strong body Sam Shepherd, even when it is bruised and battered; and tonight I want to hold it so close to me that I may never let it go again!' and she eased her night gown over her shoulders and head, before letting it fall to the floor.

Even in the candle-light, Sam could fully admire the perfect breasts, small and pert, and the slim waist and narrow hips, that he had studied so intensely when painting or sketching her - and now they were there for him alone - Her eyes were innocent but twinkled, tantalizingly, pleading for his response.

She loosened her hair, which fell across her shoulders and brushed her nipples, as it had done previously, causing them to react and harden, reaching out temptingly for the caress of his lips.

Sam stepped out of his breeches, and stood admiring Sal's beauty from the foot of the bed, aware that his manhood was responding independently, and was now beyond his control.

Sally lay back and for the first time, her slim legs separated, and her moist warmth revealed, just as he had imagined, pale and delicate, and Sam gently climbed above her, slowly lowering himself, and feeling her hips rise in response, until they were coupled and as one, gently stretching, swaying and writhing, as he had so many times desired as he had dreamed.

'Why, Mr Shepherd, whatever would your Aunt say?' Sally giggled.

'I love you, Sally Brown, and I will make you Mrs Shepherd one day soon, if you will permit,' whispered Shepherd. 'But for now, shush, I have other things in mind,' as he lost himself in the moment.

*****

At Eight o'clock sharp, Detective Sergeant Beddows and Constable Shepherd assembled their papers and spoke briefly with Head Constable Charters, who had also woken early.

234

Charters again offered the two men the use of the Office next to the Muster Room, for the interview of Detective Sergeant Roberts.

Roberts appeared, brought from the cell by the two Constables who were tasked with guarding him overnight.

'I thought they would have given me to Smith and Haynes, rather than a disgraced old slop, and a 'puppy' that's still wet behind the ears?' mumbled Roberts.

'Thinks he's still something important, does our Mr Roberts,' said Beddows.

'It's Sergeant Roberts to you, Beddows,' he growled.

'No, and that's where you're wrong. As of about half an hour ago, you are now Mr Roberts, or even ex-Detective, ex-Sergeant bleeding Roberts, dismissed as having been a bad apple of the Borough. And the Watch Committee has also just appointed me Detective Sergeant, as it happens, Mr Roberts!' grinned Beddows.

'Fuck you,' grunted Roberts.

'That's a fine thing to say given what you were involved in last night; this little piggy went to... no we'll come back to that later,' Beddows grinned.

'So, Mr Roberts. I think you are well and truly scuppered; and we really don't even have to talk to you other than to confirm a point or two, as most of your fine compatriots have done most of your talking for you,' said Beddows.

'Don't think so; And may I say, I am surprised to see Mr Shepherd here today; thought he would be out looking for Miss Brown,' Roberts laughed.

'Ah, the kidnapping,' said Shepherd.

'Was she kidnapped? How horrible - where might she be?' laughed Roberts.

'She's well, and the last time I saw her she had just made me breakfast, and packed my sandwich; about an hour ago, actually,' smiled Shepherd.

'Perhaps you were thinking she was still in the pleasure of the company of Mr St Clair and Mr Maloney?' said Shepherd.

'Sadly, the two gentlemen bumped in to Sergeants Smith and Haynes yesterday afternoon, or should I say, were bumped by them - or Tanked as it may be, and are now in the yard cell themselves,' said Beddows.

Roberts suddenly looked rather ill.

'And most helpful they were too. They both seemed to think that we were civilized over here. A bit like in the 'ole country' as they thought, so they told us everything straight off in order to broker a deal. Honest, didn't try and hide a thing - cos they thought accomplices couldn't be hung,' laughed Beddows.

'Told us all about you and your Brother-in-law, from down by the river, right through to how you shot him, and why? And about you and Mistress Salt; and you and Dubh O'Donnell himself,' said Beddows.

'Treacherous Irish bastards,' grunted Roberts. 'If I'm hanging, I'll make sure that they will too - not as clean hands as they might have made out.'

'We sort of thought that might be more the case,' said Shepherd.

'Let's go back to the boy in the River then, and start there,' said Beddows.

'I heard there was a body down the Ship - that bit was right. But when I saw what you'd got, nearly shit me pants I did; Very expensive ones, which Shepherd still owes me for,' said Roberts.

'Don't think it will be worth buying another pair where you're going,' said Shepherd.

'Smug little fucker already aren't we? Working too much with Beddows!' said Roberts.

'Last time I had seen that boy, he was on the floor of The Stokers Arms having just been buggered by Mr O'Donnell and had his pretty little throat sliced; and I thought he had been took to Mr Crowley to be hidden away,' he continued.

'And who sliced his pretty little throat?' said Beddows.

'Looked like Black Annis to me. But he didn't skin the little sod like Annis did in the song,' said Roberts.

'And what was your part?' said Shepherd.

'I was just the arranger; kept the punters in check that had paid to watch, and then sought the services of our friends to tidy up afterwards,' said Roberts.

'Friends?' said Shepherd.

'Pawley and Caffrey to start off with, before Caffrey got tapped. Then Pawley and O'Riordan.'

'Who was Caffrey?' said Shepherd.

'Ginger fella with a big bushy, ginger beard; used to 'Bruise' for Dubh, but got greedy. You don't piss off Dubh O'Donnell and come away lightly,' said Roberts.

'Okay, so let's go back to the boy in the river - who was he?' said Beddows.

'He was just a little bum boy. Wilson had him first as a house-boy, but he got bored and took him to O'Donnell. O'Donnell played with and got bored with him too. Probably getting a bit sloppy being passed around; and Dubh probably wanted change, so he topped him - right in front of Wilson – threw up everywhere he did!'

'And how did Wilson happen to come by at the river, as I had sent for a Physician?'

'Saw one of the other little river finders who owed me. So I gave him a penny and told him where to go, and slipped him a note so Wilson would know,' said Roberts.

'Know what?' said Shepherd.

'That the body was the kid he used to sodomise, and he might get recognized,' said Roberts.

'So, you briefed him first?' said Shepherd.

'Too right; if it came back to him, it would come back to me. And how right I was?' smiled Roberts, in an ironic sort of way.

'And what about the way he described the wounds?' said Beddows.

'He'd covered for O'Donnell before, down in London when Dubh went to stay down there a year or so ago. Dubh got drunk and ripped a Toffer, so Wilson tried to change the killer's M.O.'

'By making out we were looking for a right handed killer?'

'Spot on. Worked then, should have worked now! Can't think why it didn't,' said Roberts.

'Couple of clever and observant pairs of eyes worked out that the killer was left handed, Mr Roberts, that's what happened,' said Beddows.

'So O'Donnell murdered the prostitute, in London?' said Shepherd.

'Sure did. Didn't fancy paying, and she was going to scream, so he saved himself a few bob,' grinned Roberts.

'So when the boy in the river was recovered by us, what did you do?' said Shepherd.

'While Wilson was tidying things up, I went down the Market Place and found Salt. He is the man who puts right with people like Pawley. Told him to make sure that the body was secured and gotten rid of properly this time. Gave him ten guineas; two for him for his trouble, and eight for Pawley, four up front and four when he finished; and a warning if he fucked it up again it would be him in a box.'

'But he messed it up again?' said Beddows.

'Useless little runt. Instead of taking it straight back to Crowley, they took it back to Pawley's yard after you lot had been crawling over it; and O'Riordan fucked up trying to burn it down. So Dubh topped him as a punishment and as a message to Pawley and Salt. O'Riordan was Salt's Molly - rode him for years he did,' said Roberts.

'And what was your relationship with Salt?' said Shepherd.

'You don't think I'm a Molly do you? Salt should have gone down for backhanders over the New Union Workhouse on the High Fields, but I saved his bacon. He is in with the Aldermen and high-rollers that are looking to do business in the Borough, and a lot of it there is. He gets my Mr O'Donnell new leads; Mr O'Donnell makes a very nice living. I get a percentage of Mr O'Donnell's coin, and Mr Salt gets a percentage of my coin from O'Donnell - and we all live rather nicer than we would, or I would, on a Copper's wages,' Roberts grinned.

'So Dubh kills O'Riordan?' said Shepherd.

'Tied him up and prepared him, just like he was getting ready to do to me last night. Dresses himself up and then slaughters the big bastard, just like he would a beast. The smack on the head sounded like thunder, and we all got covered in brains and blood and snot.'

'Who was there, then?' said Beddows.

'Normal *Special* guests; sick bastards they are. Some are there every special night - must just like to see killings; wouldn't think rich folk would pay for such a thing,' said Roberts.

'Probably the same folk who will pay the most for a seat at the Turks Head to see you swing,' laughed Beddows.

'So why kill Wilson, your own Brother-in-law?' said Shepherd.

'He was becoming a danger. He kept going on about how you would work out who had killed the boy, and that we should turn in Dubh, and walk away from it as unwilling witnesses; bottle had gone completely it had,' he replied.

'So, what did you do?' said Shepherd.

'Easy it was. Told him I needed to get him to sign another statement for Mr Mitchell. He sat down at his desk, and as he sat down, I shot him, straight through his head. Bit of a surprise it was, went everywhere, just like O'Riordan's,' he replied.

'What then?' said Shepherd.

'Thought he should turn left-handed; with a left -handed suicide and a confession, thought it would stop you all in your tracks,' grinned Roberts.

'But you forgot that it was I who took his statement, and shook hands with him not two weeks prior,' said Beddows.

'Clever bastard; see why you got my old job,' sneered Roberts.

'So what else do you want to tell us about Dubh O'Donnell?' said Beddows.

'He's been a fair man to me and paid handsome. But he's diced with death for such a long time, he told me recent he thought his time was coming, and probably is,' said Roberts.

'We have just exhumed more bodies from the old Aldeby Church in Enderby. How many bodies has your Dubh O'Donnell buried there, or you for that matter?' said Beddows.

'Don't know exact, from his doing. There have been a few boys since September, and he did a favour for Sooty Palmer down Wharf Street, took a boy who got scared going up chimneys; toyed with him before he cut him well. He should be down there,' said Roberts.

'Where else does Mr O'Donnell get rid of his bodies?' said Shepherd.

'He used to dump them in the waste pits off the bottom of Belgrave Gate, until the scavengers started ferreting. Had to move one rather quick, got a bit near the top of the pile. Some dog dragged the body out, what was left of it and a Constable was called. Asked some rather pointed questions, but he backed off when we gave him some coin. Wise bloke! Pawley and Caffrey took the remains and buried them again at Aldeby.'

'So there are more bodies in the pits?' said Shepherd.

'So he reckons,' said Roberts, 'but he used to tell folks in the Rookeries that so as to scare them; what with that and then telling them Annis had the kids and they were in her Bower up Dane Hills.'

'What about you? You buried anyone else?' said Beddows.

'You didn't find my wife when you were digging did you?' said Roberts.

'Should we?' said Shepherd.

'She's somewhere down there. That's how O'Donnell got to me first - bit like he would have with Sally Brown if Tanky hadn't intervened. He told me I'd go the same way if I didn't help him out. Anyway, I didn't like her anyway; too much like her bleedin' brother; Trouble she was, and always nagging.'

'So O'Donnell killed her?' said Shepherd.

'No. St Clair and Maloney. They kidnapped her and ran her through with a sword-stick, so I was informed,' said Roberts. 'As I said, their hands aren't as clean as they make out.'

'Anything else you want to get off your chest, before we charge you?' said Beddows.

'I nicked a bag of tea from the scullery last Christmas. Mr Charter's own I do believe. You can ask if I can have that taken into consideration,' Roberts laughed.

*****

As the clock on St Mary de Castro struck Twelve, Detective Sergeant Kettle walked over the first jury, twelve men of true, from 'The Turks Head', together with Sergeant Marvin, Constable Parks, and Coroner Mitchell. They walked over to an obscure door on the ground floor of the Infirmary, overlooking the Bridewell.

There the jury and Coroner Mitchell were there shown the body of Physician Wilson, displayed to them by Doctors Buck and Hamilton. The party examined the body before adjourning back to the Inn.

The second Jury was then employed in similar mode, to observe the four bodies recovered from the Aldeby site.

The reaction of the second jury could only be described as general utter revulsion, and more so when the Doctors moved the remains to demonstrate wounds, and with the abhorrent stench and gut-wrenching sight, many were physically sick.

Once both juries were seated back in the Turks Head, one in a side room, and one in the main bar where the first Inquest convened, Mitchell ordered a bottle of rum to be shared out to both sets of men.

'A tot is fair for everymen for what they have just endured,' said Mitchell, 'and the Crown is paying anyway, so a tot for us all'.

Evidence was given verbally by Doctors Buck and Hamilton, and Detective Sergeant Kettle, and Sergeant Beddows' accepted in statement form.

The first Jury took less than fifteen minutes to agree a verdict of Murder for Physician Wilson.

Chief Constable Goodyer, Head Constable Charters, and the two doctors gave verbal evidence at the second Inquest, and by statements of the Officers who had interviewed St Clair, Maloney, The Crowley's and Roberts.

Again, within fifteen minutes, the second jury came back with verdicts of Murder for the Aldeby victims.

The juries signed their expenses forms, happily accepted a second tot of rum, and duly fulfilled their obligation to the Coroner and the Crown.

*****

At about Two O'clock, Detective Sergeants Smith and Haynes took O'Donnell into the office at the Borough Police Station.

'How would you prefer us to address you?' said Tanky Smith.

'What?' grunted O'Donnell.

'Is it O'Donnell, or Black Annis?' said Smith.

'The names O'Donnell, Dubh O'Donnell, Black O'Donnell in your feckin mother tongue; Black because I have no heart, no compassion and no fear.'

'Dubh it is then,' said Smith, 'short and not so sweet.'

'Your fear seems to have washed away a little since you were locked up,' quipped Haynes. 'Already fighting for top dog down in the Rookeries they are. They don't think you're coming back' said Haynes.

'Feckin losers - deserve what they get,' shrugged O'Donnell.

'And we don't see many of your hoi-polloi knocking on the door trying to free you; no posh Lawyers trying to come in to represent you,' said Smith.

'Well, yers born alone, and yers die alone,' smiled O'Donnell.

'Oh don't worry, you won't die alone,' said Smith. 'There'll be a few of you taking the drop together; only the others can't fly, which will be a big advantage for you.'

'What the feck are yers on about?' said O'Donnell.

'Black Annis, roaming the sky, flying around on her broomstick; forgotten already?' said Smith.

'Funny man,' said O'Donnell. 'Why don't yers ask me about the real deal. That's what I'm here for isn't it?'

'Okay; just thought we'd break the ice a bit,' said Haynes.

'So what do you do in Leicester, Mr O'Donnell?' said Smith.

'I'm a businessman, Mr Smith,' he replied.

'What sort of business?' said Haynes.

'The sort that's made me rich, the sort that makes money that you can only ever dream of,' said O'Donnell.

'The sort that gets your neck rung,' said Smith.

O'Donnell smiled.

'Your trusty followers are not as obedient as you may have thought, Mr O'Donnell,' said Haynes, 'In fact, they have been busy snitching, to try and save their sorry necks.'

'D'yers think I'm surprised? I told that shite Roberts that I saw the end coming when fecking Caffrey and then O'Riordan started trying to hit on me, took me for a mug they did.'

'Sounds like some of your right-hand men got a bit too close?' said Haynes.

'Too close?' said O'Donnell.

'Not in a sodomistic sort of way; well, not all of them, it would seem,' said Smith.

'Very funny! We all have our little idiosyncrasies,' said O'Donnell.

'Too close in the sense that you let them in to your inner sanctum, too close that they knew what you were doing, and so close that they have been able to turn it against you,' said Haynes.

'I should have murdered the feckin' lot! That's the mistake I made; too many mouths still moving,' said O'Donnell.

'So you aren't going to deny that you are a killer?' said Haynes.

'Murderer, please. You really think that any court will give me a fair trial? Once the birds have done their singing, I'm for Jack Ketch - no doubt!' he replied.

'So how many people have you killed?' said Smith.

'Killed or murdered?' said O'Donnell.

'Is there a difference?' said Smith.

'When I murder a man, I do it myself. When I kill a man, I can get someone else to do it for me if I wish. I get them killed, I kill them,' he replied.

'Let's start off with killing then,' said Haynes.

'If you go back to Ireland, there's a lot who crossed me. And there's a fair share; take a trip along the Cork, Bandon and South Coast Railway for example. If you dug it all back up, you might find something of interest every few miles. A disgruntled politician, a greedy landowner, a nasty Navvie - there's a few I had killed along the way; but that was business,' he replied coldly.

'And what about Murder?' said Smith.

'Ah, now that's personal, and relates to matters of the heart,' said O'Donnell.

'How many?' said Smith.

'A good few, but mainly my play things, when they stop giving me love' said O'Donnell. 'Or people who should love me but stop, like O'Riordan and Caffrey. I let them into my family, and they betrayed me, broke my heart they did,' he laughed coldly.

'And these *play things*. I take it that you are talking about children?' said Haynes.

'They should be children, poor little feckers. It's 1850 and they are just used and abused, beaten and broken. They shouldn't be picking fluff for eighteen hours a day, or climbing hot chimneys, or having to scavenge in the river or the gutter.' Tears were welling in his eyes.

'I was never a child,' he said. 'I was fecking beaten and kicked and did more hard work than the feckers who made all the money. I swore I would never have to work hard when I grew up, and I swore I would never let children suffer,' said O'Donnell, now crying loudly.

'How can you say that, when you sodomise them and cut their throats?' said Smith.

'Because, Sergeant Smith, even though it is only for a short time, they are loved. They are looked after, they are fed, they are hugged and loved, which most have never experienced,' he replied.

'But sodomy and murder?' said Haynes.

'I was sodomised Mr Haynes; every day for years; and my daddy did it, and my uncles did it, and I was told it was 'cos they feckin loved me. And I loved my daddy and my uncles,' he replied.

'So sodomy to you, is a way of showing your love?' said Smith.

'As, so is Murder. It is a mercy for the poor little feckers,' he replied.

'And how is that so?' said Haynes.

'What have these little boys got to look forward to? Who's going to love them after me? How are they going to scratch out a meaningful existence with no money and no hope? I do them a favour, and it's quick and merciful,' he replied abruptly, tears again in his eyes.

'I think that's a load of old bollocks,' said Smith.

'I think you loathe boys, and probably because of what happened to you as a boy; that you were somebody's Molly or Blind Cupid, and it hurt, and you didn't like it, and now you can get your own back,' growled Smith, thumping the desk with his clenched fist. 'Don't give me all that love bollocks. You love murdering them; that's why you like your Black Annis act. You make them disappear; you are a refuse man, you get rid of what you and nobody else wants.'

'Feck you,' he spat.

'Have I hit a nerve Dubh? Hey? Is this getting your own back for what happened to you? Cos it certainly doesn't sound like love to me,' said Smith.

'My daddy and my fecking uncles took me and half the young boys in the village, and rode us til we bled. I couldn't walk for weeks, sometimes. But they told us they loved us, and I don't have anything else' cried O'Donnell. 'And my mammy wouldn't touch me, told me I was dirty and we would all go to hell - and that no woman would ever want any of us, so I grew up with men, and sodomy is the only comfort I've known.'

'And what about the Toffer at Guys Hospital last year?' said Smith.

'I knew Wilson and Roberts would snitch on me for that,' he replied.

'So how can you try and tell us you can't go with women?' said Haynes.

'Feck you,' replied O'Donnell.

'And we know you tupped her, and that you slit her throat so you didn't have to pay the bill,' said Haynes.

'Dirty fecking whore deserved what she got. Wanted me to pay her!' he growled.

'So all this bollocks about love and sodomy; you have what you want, when you want, and when you've done with it you throw it away,' shouted Smith.

'I am doing what none of your fecking radical reformers can yet do. Every week I read in the papers, John Buck will get this done, William Biggs will get this done, Joseph Dare will get this done, and we're all the same, we all want to get rid of the shit and rubbish that is choking Leicester, and starving it to death; but I get the job done, where they just talk about it.'

'So now you are a social reformer?' said Haynes, tongue in cheek.

'There are far fewer mouths to feed, and far fewer begging, and far more to go round in the poor Irish families left with nothing; because I take away and get rid of what they no longer want, or what is a nuisance to them; I am a reformer - yes.'

'You are just a deluded monster, Mr O'Donnell, and Black Annis probably reflects your appetite, far better than anything else you have offered us as yet,' said Haynes.

'Black Annis is a harmless old hag. It is what is inside her when we meet that is really cold and black - Dubh himself,' laughed O'Donnell.

'The truth is that you have murdered young boys, and have murdered one young woman that we know to at least, and two of your inner circle who betrayed you, at least, and if we had not stopped you, Roberts would have been added to that list.'

'You were a couple of minutes early, you could have saved Jack Ketch a job,' he laughed

'And what was to be his fate?' said Haynes.

'He was becoming a bull. He was pushy, loud, and blew in my face when he bellowed; and you know what happens to bulls?' he replied.

'So it was tethering, pole-axe and the trusty slaughterer's knife, just like Caffrey and O'Riordan?' said Smith.

'Caffrey didn't last long enough for the knife, I must have took all his brains out in one swipe, would have been an unnecessary final touch. But, it's my signature and the audience were waiting for it,' he replied, grinning.

'And what about Robert's wife?' said Haynes.

'You are mistaken there if you have been told that was me. I told St Clair and Maloney to kill her. I did not murder her, they killed her for me,' he replied smugly.

'Thank you for confirming that, Mr O'Donnell,' said Haynes.

'And Roberts will hang, for his brother-in-law?' said O'Donnell.

'Roberts will hang for Physician Wilson, to be sure,' replied Smith.

'Shame really, the boy went out of his way to help me in London. But a shocking Physician; wouldn't let him bathe a cut,' O'Donnell laughed.

'What about Mr Salt?' said Smith.

'Loves the feel of a woman's clothing, but a clever wee man he is; made me some good contacts and lots of money. Felt really bad when I brained his fella O'Riordan; world must have fell out of his bottom. Hasn't spoke to me since.'

'Hardly surprising as he is locked up at our pleasure too,' said Haynes, 'together with his man Pawley, the Undertaker.'

'Undertaker me arse - he couldn't get rid of a body to save his life - a weakness I should have eliminated a long time ago,' O'Donnell replied.

'Eliminated,' said Smith. 'That's a new word?'

'You haven't asked me about the ones I've eliminated yet, they're a whole different bunch altogether,' he grinned.

'You're joking, aren't you?' said Haynes.

'Sort of. They're in amongst the ones I killed, but not the ones I murdered; they're the pitiful useless ones,' he replied.

'You say St Clair and Maloney killed Roberts' wife for you; that they murdered her themselves?' said Smith.

'That's right, as I said,' he replied.

'How many others have they killed for you?' said Smith.

'You'd better start digging down near Enderby and then you might get the answer to that one,' O'Donnell replied. 'Probably all tucked up and cozy with Mrs Roberts, they'll be.'

'And the Crowleys?' said Haynes.

'They're nice folk; got me some lovely play things. Won't have a bad word said about them,' he looked seriously at both men. 'Not a bad word. And they look after them when they get them back - well Mr Crowley does given half a chance, if you know what I mean,' he winked.

'And the hoi-polloi at The Stokers Arms; your posh friends?' said Haynes.

'They're just paying punters; just like the ones upstairs who like a sing-song and a comedian, except these like a bit of rumpy-pumpy or sodomy, and as a special treat, a wee slaughter to round off the evening. Pay me a lot of money they do; murder and killing don't come cheap!'

'Mr O'Donnell, you have some depraved associates,' said Haynes.

'What more would you expect, from Black Annis?' he grinned.

'To fly away in the night and never be seen again perhaps?' said Beddows.

'You never know,' laughed O'Donnell, 'but then again you've got my broomstick.'

The Leicester Borough Assizes were held quarterly, and were calendered for the first whole week after the 28th of December, 31st of March, 24th of June and 11th of October annually. This always proved inconvenient when arrests and remands fell mid-period, and meant a long time could pass between arrest, interview and trial.

The earliest Assizes would be during the week commencing Monday 25th of March 1850, and the Trial, which had already received much attention within the local newspapers, therefore listed to commence of the Monday, given the number of prisoners, the array of charges, and the nature of the events.

Charters and Goodyer had sought the best Prosecution Barristers from the Midland circuit, and Messrs James Mawby and Francis Coleman, were appointed.

A Defence Barrister had been chosen and funded by Mr O'Donnell himself, *for himself only*, and known to be one Henry Horrobin, who had an appetite to defend dubious causes.

Messrs Carlton and Morris had been appointed by the Crown to represent the other defendants.

By nine o'clock, a large crowd had gathered around the Great Hall and buildings of the Town Hall, and many had come early, and found vantage points along the route from the Borough Gaol, to the Great Hall, where the Assizes were sitting, and the trial held.

The appointed presiding Judge would be Lord Chief Justice McGregor, a hard and seasoned justice, given the capital nature of many of the offences that were being tried.

Lord Chief Justice McGregor sat in the centre of a raised dais at the opposite end of the Great Hall to the Police Station, amidst clerks, clergy and legal advisors.

To one side of his bench sat the jury, 12 good men of true. No women were allowed to be selected or sit on a jury.

On the other side of the judge, was assembled the prosecution and defence counsel.

Beyond the counsel stood a small witness box; beyond the witness box, directly opposite, an area, separated from the Judge, jury and counsel by a wooden beam, mounted on two posts, behind which sat the defendants *'at the bar'*.

Only trials for Murder and Manslaughter which had originated from Coroner's inquest had an automatic right of trial, but in this instance, it had been agreed by Grand Jury, who had sat previously, that the lesser charges should also be tried at the same Assize, owing to the relativity to Capital offences.

Thus, at the bar stood Dubh O'Donnell; Brendan St Clair; Michael Maloney; William Roberts; Daniel Salt; Edward Pawley; Connor Crowley and Mary Crowley.

O'Donnell continually stared across at the co-defendants, glaring at them. Brendan St Clair, not an easy man to scare, felt an increasing urge to inch away from O'Donnell and only the man's shackles gave him a sense of some security.

Maloney looked toward St Clair, seeking some reassuring glance or nod to the effect that they would stick together.

Daniel Salt sat with his head bowed, and shook visibly, fear pulsating through his veins.

Edward Pawley sat looking towards the ceiling, content that he faced a term of imprisonment, but that he would unlikely to suffer the same fate as the men to his left.

The Crowleys sat looking around the courtroom, as if seeking somebody out in the gallery, but remaining ignorant of the severity of their complicity in the horrendous and odious offences, and contemptuous of the guardians of Blaby Workhouse for prosecuting them for fraud, *after all they had done for the Parish.*

William Roberts felt grossly out of place. He had occasionally stood in the witness box, when it had previously suited him to get involved in some case or other as a Police Sergeant, and now, more aware of his downfall, than of the fear he would have to face on the Gallows that would probably see him meet his maker.

By half-past nine, the indictments had been read to the defendants.

When asked how he pleaded to his Indictments, O'Donnell replied.

'Not guilty. In fact, I am not just *not guilty*, I am criminally and madly insane, and I offer my insanity as my defence to all of these absurd charges, and urge you that I should have been charged under the name of Black Annis who more often than not I become, and she takes over my mind and renders me, Dubh O'Donnell incapable of rational and willful thought,' he ranted, foaming at the mouth and shaking in his shackles.

The public area broke into loud and unprompted laughter, shrieks, and roars, at the outburst.

'Order, order,' called Justice McGregor.

O'Donnell suddenly sat bolt upright and went silent, looking straight at the judge and jury.

'She took me over again, didn't she? I have no control; she is terrible evil,' cried O'Donnell.

St Clair and Maloney looked at each other, and St Clair whispered 'He's going to try and wriggle out of all this, and you and me are going to take the fall for him.'

St Clair and Maloney then both entered 'Not guilty' pleas to the charges of murder and conspiracy to murder.

'You have only the word of a deranged and evil man to hang us by; you have nothing else. Just because we offered to turn Queen's evidence,' protested St Clair.

'When young Sean comes to get me, I'm leaving you feckers behind to swing,' O'Donnell whispered across to St Clair and Maloney.

A short time thereafter, the trial of the remaining defendants Dubh O'Donnell, Brendan St Clair and Michael Maloney, moved forward to opening addresses.

James Mawby spent the remainder of the morning, and well into the afternoon session, before he completed the summary of the depositions obtained from Prosecution witnesses.

Later in the afternoon, William Henry Horrobin stood before the jury and opened his defence.

'My Lord, Gentlemen of the Jury; I represent the defendant Dubh O'Donnell, who has advised me that he is also, on occasion, called Black Annis, who is an evil witch, and who takes over his mind and causes him to commit such heinous and repulsive crimes. I am advised that Mr O'Donnell, aware of this 'occupation' of his mind, is therefore not of sound mind when these offences with which he is indicted, have taken place. It is therefore my intention to prove that he is Insane, and as such cannot be held guilty of *any willful act*.'

Sebastian Carlton, representing St Clair and Maloney then stood and faced the Jury.

'I represent my clients, the defendants Brendan St Clair and Michael Maloney. They have both indicated a plea of Not Guilty to murdering Louisa Roberts, a plea that they have been compelled to offer, as they have been refused the right to turn Queen's evidence against their co-defendants. I will demonstrate that the evidence that the Prosecution will bring of their guilt is weak and flawed, and that the evidence of an insane man which incriminates them is invalid and therefore cannot be used to convict them.'

Lord Chief Justice McGregor adjourned the first day of the hearing at five o'clock in the afternoon, and advised the court that it should resume at nine o'clock the following morning.

*****

On Tuesday, shortly after the court reconvened, Lord Chief Justice McGregor met with both prosecution and defence counsel, in the Jury chamber provided above the Mayor's Parlour.

'Why did we not have some idea of the insanity plea, before the trial?' said McGregor?

'It was never discussed by Mr O'Donnell until the pleas were entered today, My Lord,' said Horrobin, with some amusement.

'That in itself worries me, Mr Horrobin, it sounds rather contrived, by someone who has had time to think or read up on a defence,' said McGregor.

'Mr Mawby, do you have access to expert witnesses who you may call to refute the plea?' said McGregor.

'Yes, My Lord; we have two expert witnesses, either of whom we would wish to call. One is James Buck, General Practitioner and attending Physician at Leicester Lunatic Asylum, who is already familiar with the defendant and his behaviour, and the second is one Doctor Hopkins, the visiting psychiatrist from the same institution,' said Mawby.

'That of course will be in addition to our key witnesses, who will look to demonstrate that O'Donnell's actions and thoughts are those of a sane, cold and callous killer,' Mawby added.

'And, Mr Horrobin, do you have an expert witness?' said McGregor.

'I had understood, My Lord, that we were to be availed of Doctor Hopkins ourselves,' said Horrobin.

'In that case, if Mr Buck represents the Prosecution and Mr Hopkins the defence, it should make for an interesting contest,' said McGregor.

'I propose to hear the evidence as we would do in normal trial, and then we will call the special witnesses for Mr O'Donnell's defence. I think it will be hard enough for the jury to comprehend without complicating it with legal and medico-legal arguments thrown in as well,' said McGregor. 'By segregating the issue of insanity to the very end, it will give them more opportunity to make their deliberations.'

* * * * *

In 1843 a set of rules, subsequently known as the McNaughton rules, had established five criteria for future insanity defence pleas, following the acquittal of a man – Daniel McNaughton, who had murdered Edward Drummond, who an *allegedly* deluded McNaughton had mistaken for the Prime Minister, Robert Peel.

The rules defined the defense as 'at the time of committing the act the party accused was labouring under such a defect of reason, from disease of the mind, as not to know the nature and quality of the act he was doing, or as not to know that what he was doing was wrong and that the defendant could not appreciate the nature of his actions during the commission of the crime'.

Five rules were proposed;-

1. Every man is to be presumed to be sane and to possess a sufficient degree of reason to be responsible for his crimes, until the contrary be proved.
2. An insane person is punishable 'if he knows' at the time of crime.
3. To establish a defense on insanity, the accused, by defect of reason or disease of mind, is not in a position to know the nature and consequences.
4. The insane person must be considered in the same situation as to responsibility as if the facts with respect to which the delusion exists were real.
5. It was the jury's role to decide whether the defendant was insane.

*****

'I want each of the Medical specialists to have an opportunity of spending time with O'Donnell. I propose we adjourn the court until Nine o'clock On Thursday morning, and that during tomorrow, each be allowed to interview O'Donnell at the Borough Gaol,' said McGregor.

'My Lord, I have taken instruction from my client, and he does not wish to be prodded and poked by medics, and has threatened to devour them and leave their skinned corpses at his Bower in Dane Hills,' explained Horrobin, holding back an obvious smile. 'He is of the opinion that if he is called to the witness stand, and cross-examined before the court, that the jury will be in no doubt that he is indeed insane,' added Horrobin.

'He can be called and cross-examined on Thursday. My direction is that he will be medically examined; and if the good doctors are still alive and well on Thursday they may be called to give their evidence of Mr O'Donnell. I am not risking an acquittal on technicalities. McNaughton is quite clear, and I intend to test it, with expert witnesses,' said McGregor.

*****

Wednesday the 27th of March started cold and bright, the early spring Sun trying to warm up the stagnant and acidic Leicester air, and almost coloured enough to touch.

As it slipped through the fingers of the passing public, it crept up their noses and into their lungs, and the town echoed to the sound of rasping coughing throughout virtually every street and through-fare.

John Buck had the first appointment with O'Donnell at nine o'clock, and would have the pleasure of his company to no later than one o'clock.

Dr Algernon Hopkins, visiting Psychiatrist, who would have been summoned from the Bedlam Asylum in London, had he not been on his monthly visit to the Borough, had the second appointment with O'Donnell at Two o'clock and had until Six O'clock.

Both had a maximum of four hours, and would have far less if eaten or skinned as O'Donnell has indicated to Horrobin.

'Mr O'Donnell, we have not had the pleasure,' said Buck.

'It is no pleasure to me, sir, as I had told the feckin' lawyers I wasn't going to be prodded and probed,' said O'Donnell.

'And why should I prod and probe you, sir, as I am here to get a better view of your mind, not your body,' said Buck.

'Cause that's what doctors do, isn't it?' said O'Donnell.

'You sound like a man who does not make use of the medical profession,' said Buck.

'Fit and healthy, that's what comes from hard graft and good living,' Said O'Donnell.

'And what about Black Annis?' said Buck.

'What do you mean?' said O'Donnell.

'She is fit and well?' said Buck.

'She is a spirit, a dark spirit, that permeates men's minds when they are ill prepared, and takes them to dark places; she is in no need of medical attention,' said O'Donnell.

'So when does she permeate you, Mr O'Donnell?' said Buck.

'When I'm in a black mood, when I want to seek retribution, when I have been badly done to, sir,' said O'Donnell.

'And when she arrives?' said Buck.

'She and I take that retribution, and the bad fellas and the lost souls receive their dues.'

'And you and Black Annis kill them,' said Buck.

'No, sir, we murder them. I have other associates who kill people,' replied O'Donnell.

'So Murder and killing is not the same act?' said Buck.

'Murder requires you to be close and it is personal, and you have control of that final passing,' said O'Donnell.

'Whereas killing is just?' said Buck.

'Killing is getting rid of unwanted or unwarranted nuisance, it is not personal, it is business,' said O'Donnell.

'So when you kill the boys?'

O'Donnell interrupted. 'Them boys don't get killed, they get murdered, they're personal and I make it quick and send them on their way mercifully.'

'And what is Black Annis doing when this is going on?' said Buck.

'She whispers in my ears, and watches my back; we are as one, we are as two,' he replied.

'You speak as if you are similar spirits, lost and black, and taking out your retribution in your own special way,' said Buck.

'She likes to skin them, and I like to cut their throats, my way is far more humane, and hers is torturous,' he replied.

'So why doesn't she control you and you do her bidding in her way?' said Buck.

'I am my own man, and she respects me for that,' said O'Donnell.

'So even though she permeates you, you do not let her dominate you?' said Buck.

'I don't do domineering women; fecking bitches like me ma, and that whore in London; no fecking bitch dominates Dubh O'Donnell – nobody,' shouted O'Donnell.

'You have a problem with women Mr O'Donnell?' said Buck.

'Doesn't every man?' said O'Donnell. 'I took it for so long, but not anymore, so now I become Black Annis, and I am in charge, and I have the fear she brings, but it is me who they should really be afeared of; me, Dubh O'Donnell.'

'And why kill the young boys?' said Buck, 'or O'Riordan, or Caffrey?'

'I fecking told yers. I don't kill people like that; I murders them, me and Black Annis.'

'Would you like me to do some prodding and probing next, so that I can tell the Judge I have done so?' said Buck.

'Now you are getting personal Mr Buck, and you are on borrowed time if you even try,' said O'Donnell.

'Borrowed time?' said Buck.

'I'll fecking skin yer alive, let alone Black Annis; just you fecking try; see if I don't!' said O'Donnell.

'Perhaps I shall not then,' said Buck 'I Think I'd best leave you for Mr Hopkins after lunch. Guards, let me out please.'

*****

Doctor Hopkins arrived at the Gaol, at Two o'clock prompt.

The Gaol, on appearance alone, a daunting place, but compared to Bedlam, palatial.

Bedlam had become quite run down, although in its present position in St Georges Fields since 1815, it remained far better than the older buildings it once occupied. However 'The Unfortunates', the name given to its inmates had not changed, as nor had their disposition.

A prison seemed a far friendlier and hospitable place, even to Leicester's asylum, which in comparison to Bedlam, came across to Hopkins as small and well funded for the numbers it catered for.

The noise struck Hopkins first; shouting, and the sound of the crank, and hard labour, but there were no screams. The screams he did not miss.

'Good afternoon, Mr O'Donnell,' said Hopkins.

'Oh Goody, two fecking doctors in the same day,' he replied.

'And how was Mr Buck?' said Hopkins.

'You mean you haven't spoken to him? Then again, perhaps I've eaten him, have a good look around first and make sure you don't fall over any bones,' he laughed. 'Only joking!'

'And who are you today?' said Hopkins.

'Who the feck do you think I am?' he replied.

'Who would you prefer to be?' said Hopkins.

'How about the fecking Pope; clean clothes, three square meals a day, and loaded; now there's a business that works; loaded he is,' laughed O'Donnell.

'I need to be able to argue the case for your insanity, so I need to know what takes over you - when you kill,' said Hopkins.

'I keep telling you all, it's not killing, and it's murder! Not killing, not eliminating, fecking murder,' he shouted.

'And it is Black Annis that possesses you to do the murders?' said Hopkins.

'No, I take her with me, she comes along to watch,' replied O'Donnell. 'Anyway, enough of this rubbish, are you representing Mr Horrobin?'

'I am the Psychiatrist who will represent the defence and try and get you off the scaffold,' said Hopkins.

'Then you have all the answers, wee man?' said O'Donnell.

'What do you mean?' said Hopkins.

'You are the man who knows what to say to get me off; to prove me insane?' said O'Donnell.

'No, I am a doctor, a psychiatrist; an expert,' said Hopkins.

'So how much do yer want to get me off?' said O'Donnell.

'Sir, you offend me,' said Hopkins.

'Sir, everyman has a price, and I have a pot of gold to make you a *very* wealthy man. Now where do we start the bidding?' said O'Donnell.

*****

Thursday the 28th of March dawned as had the Wednesday, but the sun seemingly even warmer still.

Spring, definitely now in the air, the frost melting, and a vibrant sparkle masked the normal dullness of the Borough, lifting the spirits after the long, cold, foggy winter's day previous.

At Nine o'clock the court was back in session, and Lord Chief Justice McGregor presiding.

Mr Mawby stood and called *Dr Hopkins* as his first witness.

Horrobin stood and interjected. 'My Lord, Dr Hopkins is my witness; Dr Buck is his.'

Mr Mawby interrupted and said, 'My Lord, I believe it is your best interest to allow me to call Dr Hopkins as a *Prosecution witness*, as Mr Horrobin may shortly wish to prepare a new defence. '

Lord Chief Justice McGregor said, 'Call Mr Hopkins - as a Prosecution witness. Mr Horrobin, you will have the right to cross examine, but this is somewhat unusual.'

'Dr Hopkins, please tell the court how you found the defendant O'Donnell yesterday,' said Mawby.

'My Lord, I am not in the habit of being procured to conduct such an examination for a Capital offence, only to find that the subject of the Capital offence is so clear of mind to believe that I am open to Bribery, as was the proposition yesterday. As much as I may appear on behalf of the defence, my reputation rests on my expertise, and to be told that there is a pot of gold provided that I construct evidence of Insanity, lends me to believe that the man O'Donnell is NOT insane, but is a cold and ruthless Murderer, as would be supported by Dr Buck's evidence,' said Hopkins.

Every person in the Courtroom must have gasped simultaneously.

'My Lord, may I ask for a short recess, whilst I take guidance?' said a clearly embarrassed Defence Counsel.

'You'll fecking die for that you weasel! Nobody fecks with me; you could have been a rich man,' bellowed O'Donnell from the bar, causing Prison guards to physically restrain him and pull him back onto his bench.

'Order, order,' called Lord Chief Justice McGregor. 'I think Mr O'Donnell has just confirmed what the good doctor has said.'

'Mr Horrobin, do you still wish to call Mr O'Donnell as a witness?' said McGregor.

'I fear, sir, it may not do any benefit to the case, so no My Lord,' said Horrobin.

'You bastard O'Donnell,' hissed St Clair, 'you've fecking probably hanged me and Maloney as well as yers own sorry neck now. Should have topped yers me self, years ago!'

'Yers a brave man now, with me in shackles, St Clair,' howled O'Donnell, 'a fecking brave man, to be sure. I'll see how brave yers really are when yers're dancing for Jack Ketch.'

'I think they're all done for now though,' whispered Shepherd.

'O'Donnell's up to something,' whispered Beddows. 'He really thinks he's not going to hang!'

*****

By Ten Thirty in the fourth morning of the trial, Lord Chief Justice McGregor had sent for the remaining defendants who had been remanded pending sentence, and he began his summing up.

Renowned for being a lengthy orator, today would be no exception, with his closing summary taking over one hour, and which ended thus;-

'That is, Gentlemen of the Jury, the end of my speech. You have listened intently to a tale of such depravity and greed, brutality and slaughter, to turn most men's stomachs. You have before you a small but miserable group of wretches who have committed every devilish crime known to man. Theft, Fraud, Burglary by those at the bottom end of the food chain; Fraud, Conspiracy to the greedier elements in the middle; Fraud, Sodomy, Conspiracy and Murder by those at the top of the food chain. And sadly they have all colluded to build this disgusting empire that has taken from the weakest, poorest and humblest sections of our Community. I must now task you, to make your way to the Jury room, above us, and to consider your verdicts.'

*****

At 12 Midday, all eight defendants sat on the bench behind the bar; the jury in their upper room, deliberating; the Judge and his clerks and advisors were in the Mayor's parlour awaiting the Jury.

Shepherd stood at the back of the Great Hall, with Beddows, Smith, Haynes and Charters, speaking with Coroner Mitchell, who had left his chambers, and made his way to the Great Hall for the conclusion of the trial.

The clerk who had been advising the jury, came back into the hall, and went into the Mayor's Parlour. A few minutes later, the jury returned and Lord Chief Justice McGregor re-entered the courtroom, as everybody seated rose.

O'Donnell sat defiantly, before being hauled to his feet by his guards.

'You will stand, Mr O'Donnell, as you are before not just me, but before our Sovereign Victoria, and our Lord God,' said McGregor.

'Feck you all, there's no God where I'm going, and I for one won't be sad that it will be hot and sulphurous and full of deviants, rather than boring and full of chubby half naked harpists,' bellowed O'Donnell.

'Gentlemen of the jury, have you reached verdicts for each of the defendants O'Donnell, St Clair and Maloney who have pleaded not guilty or insanity for their crimes?' said McGregor.

'Yes, My Lord,' said the Jury spokesman, fearing to make eye contact with any of the three main defendants.

'In the case of Dubh O'Donnell and the charge of Murder of James O'Riordan, do you find the defendant guilty or not guilty as a result of his Insanity?

'Guilty, My Lord, but *not insane,*' said the spokesman.

'You fecking bastards; Black Annis will seek you all out and skin the fecking lot of you,' shouted O'Donnell at the jurymen.

The remaining verdicts were declared 'guilty' for each and every defendant.

*****

'Gentlemen of the jury, you have served your Queen and the realm with great honesty, wisdom and not a little courage, given the circumstances of the trial, and having delivered your verdicts, you may stand down,' said Lord Chief Justice McGregor, discharging the men. 'It is now my duty to pass sentence on you depraved and pitiful souls, and I shall start off with the little fishes, so to speak.'

'Connor Crowley and Mary Crowley, you have been found guilty of defrauding your employers, The Guardians of Blaby Poor Law Union Workhouse. I sentence you each to five years imprisonment, with hard labour, in order that you get a taste of what you have caused others to suffer.'

'Edward Pawley, you have been found guilty of Conspiracy and Burglary, and theft of a tarpaulin and a cadaver. I think that you have displayed utter contempt for the dead, and denied them a lawful and Christian burial, and I wish I could sentence you to more, but you will serve seven years imprisonment, with hard labour.'

'Daniel Salt, you have been found guilty of conspiracy to commit Burglary, and have been recognized as a significant accomplice in the more serious offences that may never now be put before this court. You have used your position of trust within this Borough to further the wealth of these evil and greedy men that stand alongside you. I sentence you to ten years transportation to the Colonies, where you will be as far away from the Borough as I can allow by law.'

'William Roberts, you have pleaded guilty to murder, and to conspiracy. You have abused your former position as a Police Sergeant, and possibly tarnished their reputation in doing so, in the eyes of some, for your own greed.'

Lord Chief Justice McGregor picked up the black cloth from his desk, and placed it upon his head.

'The court doth order you to be taken from hence to the place from whence you came, and thence to the place of execution, and that you be hanged by the neck until you are dead, and that your body be afterward buried within the precincts of the prison in which you shall be confined after your conviction. And may the Lord have mercy upon your soul.'

The same then individually announced to St Clair and Maloney.

'And now, last but not least. Dubh O'Donnell. You have been found guilty of seven murders, conspiracy to murder, conspiracy to kidnap, conspiracy to assault, and procuring another to murder for you. You are without doubt, the head of a vile, depraved, and corrupt empire, to which many of those sentenced with you belong. Yours is a wicked and evil world, and the world will be all the better knowing that you will no longer be a threat to it.'

'The court doth order you to be taken from hence to the place from whence you came, and thence to the place of execution, and that you be hanged by the neck until you are dead, and that your body be afterward buried within the precincts of the prison in which you shall be confined after your conviction. And may the Lord have mercy upon your soul.'

'Go Feck you all,' spat O'Donnell. 'Sean Crowley will see that this travesty is avenged - believe me - and one day soon.'

'Sean Crowley?' Beddows and Shepherd exchanged puzzled looks.

Whilst the prisoners began the rest of their lives, or in the case of just four, what little remained of them, a telegram had been sent to London, seeking the attendance, post-haste, of the Executioner of All England, the legendary William Calcraft.

William Calcraft, seen by many, as the most famous English hangman, so far, of the 19th century, had been a cobbler by trade. Calcraft learned his trade from the City of London's hangman, John Foxton, who he had met, while selling meat pies in the streets around the prison. Originally Foxton used Calcraft to conduct his floggings, for a few coins.

Following Foxton's death, Calcraft had been appointed as the official Executioner for the City of London and for Middlesex. As an executioner he was also in great demand *throughout* England.

Sadly, he had become of great interest to the public, as he favoured a short drop method of hanging, often neither quick, nor effective, and he had resorted to some ingenious *tricks of the trade* to complete his morbid task.

There had not been an execution in Leicester, since 1846, when William Hubbard hung for the brutal murder of his wife.

The Gallows that were to be used were retained in Harrison's Wood Yard in East Street, opposite the Leicester Railway Station, and were erected there, as was the norm, before being transported down to the area at the front of the County Gaol on Welford Road by Horse and Carriage.

The sentences, although passed at the Borough assizes, had determined confinement and execution of each of the prisoners at the County Gaol, which was now better suited to such events.

*****

By eight a.m. on the morning of Monday the first of April 1850, April fool's day, a large crowd of about twenty-five thousand people, including men, women and children had assembled on the large open area between Welford Road Gaol and The Bridewell.

As Shepherd had been told earlier in the investigation, a disturbance broke out at the front of 'The Turk's Head', where many of Leicester's wealthier population were trying to outbid each other for the best seats in the house, on the upper floor parlour facing over the Gallows.

During the course of the morning, about thirty members of the crowd had approached a number of the one hundred Constables on duty, many of whom had been drafted in from adjoining County and Borough Forces, as pre-arranged, to report thefts, supposedly by pick-pockets.

So much for the Death Penalty serving as a final deterrent!

So many officers had been drafted in, as there remained some concern of somebody trying to release O'Donnell at the last minute, resulting from his comments about one Sean Crowley after sentence, and upon which he would not elaborate.

Head Constable Charters, Detective Sergeants Smith, Haynes, Kettle and Beddows, together with Constable Shepherd, stood at the side of the Gallows, awaiting the prisoners, who were running late, as was their prerogative.

As the gates to the Gaol opened, the four condemned men, flanked by a large number of prison officers, and led by the Chaplain of the Gaol, marched slowly towards the scaffold, and the care of William Calcraft.

Shepherd noticed that there was a lot of movement in the crowd, and that some extremely large and hard looking men were moving towards a position at the front of the gallows.

'Beddows; look at this lot - Bruisers by the look of it,' he warned.

Beddows eyed up the group that formed and made Mr Charters aware of the potential for a possible escape attempt.

Charters had not only seen what was happening, but had made a pre-arranged signal upon which a large number of uniformed Constables also closed in on the group.

Shepherd noted that O'Donnell had a gleam in his eye, which worried him, given what was about to happen, and Shepherd's hackles began to rise, and his hand found itself winding the strap of his concealed truncheon into a secure grip.

O'Donnell appeared to nod at a man at the front of the bruisers.

The man stood large, well over six feet tall and heavily built; dressed in a expensive brown woolen three piece suit, and a brown Derby hat, and had the scars and flat nose of a Fancy. He reminded Shepherd of Roberts – perhaps Roberts and St Clair shared the same tailor?

The man nodded towards O'Donnell and smiled.

*****

The scaffold had been constructed with a main beam, reinforced at intervals with uprights, from which Nooses dangled over a common trap-door, which extended the length of the floor, apart from a few feet either end, on which the Chaplain and Calcraft could stand.

The most obvious detail was that not a great deal of drop existed below the floor of the device, unlike long drop devices that had been employed by previous hangmen. Too many souls had lost their heads, literally, decapitated by the long drop.

The four men, shackled; hands behind their backs; were walked onto the scaffold, and stood apart, each beneath their own, personal noose that had been placed around their neck on the trap. Each man's legs were then strapped.

Noticeably, the floor of the gallows creaked loudly, audible to the crowd and the whole scaffold appeared to be quite generally unstable.

At one end of the device was a large wooden handle, which when pulled backwards released a beam holding the floor in place, from which the condemned would drop.

Beneath the gallows, was a large void, where access could be gained by the executioner and staff.

As the men walked on to their positions, Calcraft walked up before them.

'Gentlemen, I have some good news and some bad news.'

O'Donnell scowled and said 'Get on with it man, I have a hot date waiting,' looking anxiously towards the group of men who had forged to the front of the gallows.

Maloney said, 'What is the good news?' looking weak and tearful.

Calcraft said, 'the execution has been called off,' and laughed.

'And the bad news?' said Roberts.

'It's April Fools' Day, and I was only joking really,' Calcraft laughed out loud, tears rolling down his cheeks. 'What a wonderful, funny, morning to go!'

O'Donnell looked at the man at the front of the group, fear now taking over his previous confidence.

'Sean; what the feck?' shouted O'Donnell.

The man in the suit and Derby hat smiled, and then called back to O'Donnell, 'I love April fool's day, as do my boys; can't beat a good laugh.'

Shepherd sensed that this had not been what O'Donnell had expected.

The Chaplain looked hard at Calcraft, who apologised, and then without waiting, Calcraft leaned on the lever, and the four men were sent crashing through the floor of the device, to meet their maker.

Although Roberts and Maloney appeared to have instantly snapped their necks, St Clair and O'Donnell clearly were physically much stronger, and the drop had not killed them outright.

As the prisoners themselves had related several times, they gave the appearance of dancing puppets – Jack Ketch's puppets!

'Not again! He has a habit of this apparently; done it several times in London I am told,' said Charters, grimacing.

Calcraft firstly crouched under the scaffold, and came up under St Clair's legs, and began swinging off them and bouncing, desperately trying to finish him off.

Shortly, his dancing stopped, and St Clair was at last lifeless. He had pissed his pants in the process and a dark stain now visible, much to the amusement of the gathered crowd.

Whilst this played out, O'Donnell, instinctively and desperately tried to save his own life, bucking and swinging his legs to and fro.

Calcraft jumped up onto the floor of the device and jumped onto O'Donnell's back, again trying to add his weight to snap O'Donnell's neck or strangle the man.

'God, this is most barbaric,' said Shepherd, not impressed with Calcraft's bungling.

'Can you hear what Calcraft is singing?' Beddows grinned.

As the men strained their ears over the noise of the crowd, faintly could be heard;-

'Black Annis, Black Annis, crawl back to your cave

For the children of Leicester want you in your grave

You suckle their blood and you steal their skins

For seven hundred years you've committed your sins'

A dull crack could then be heard by the men assembled close by the scaffold, and at long last O'Donnell hung still, forever; and nobody had tried to spring him.

*****

Shepherd and Beddows walked up to the man In the Derby hat, who had just finished applauding the errant executioner.

'Sean Crowley, I presume?' said Shepherd.

'Mr Shepherd and Mr Beddows I presume?' he replied.

'I don't think Mr O'Donnell was expecting that?' said Beddows.

'You know,' said a smug Crowley, 'I don't think he was either. I'll be off then, as will my boys. We have a wake to attend.'

'Be seeing you again?' said Beddows.

'I might pop back from time to time; keep an eye on my business interests,' Crowley replied, 'and check in my old ma and pa!'

*****

At eleven o'clock, most reasonable members of the crowd had dispersed, and only the few ghoulish hangers-on remained, all trying to touch the bodies before they were cut down, still believed to be by many, a remedy for many ailments.

Charters gathered his small team of men in the same room at 'The Turk's Head', that had recently been occupied for the Inquests of the four boys and the man Casey, together with that of Physician Wilson, and earlier as a grandstand for the executions.

Head Constable Charters rose to his feet, and glass in hand announced, 'Gentlemen, courtesy of the good Mr Mitchell here, I have the pleasure of being able to offer you a small but well earned tipple and as a toast to you all...

...The Borough Boys - Your good health and continued success!'

26079910R00156

Made in the USA
Charleston, SC
24 January 2014